The Cure for Grief

A Novel

Nellie Hermann

Scribner

New York London Toronto Sydney

SCRIBNER
A Division of Simon & Schuster, Inc.
1230 Avenue of the Americas
New York, NY 10020

First Scribner hardcover edition August 2008

SCRIBNER and design are registered trademarks of The Gale Group, Inc.,
used under license by Simon & Schuster, Inc., the publisher
of this work.

For information about special discounts for bulk purchases,
please contact Simon & Schuster Special Sales: 1-800-456-6798
or business@simonandschuster.com.

Book design by Ellen R. Sasahara
Text set in Fournier MT

Manufactured in the United States of America

10 9 8 7 6 5 4 3 2 1

Library of Congress Control Number: 2007039761

ISBN-13: 978-1-4165-6823-0
ISBN-10:   1-4165-6823-9

FOR MY FAMILY

Choose life, that thou mayest live . . .

—Deuteronomy 30:19

The Cure for Grief

Prologue

Let's begin with the moment of contact; the moment of violence and release. After it all, before it all, despite it all, it becomes as simple as this. In the summer of 1998, on a stretch of boulders along a curve of beach in Bass Harbor, Maine, I push my brother Aaron and he falls. Look: here are my hands, my arms moving forward quick as trains, my palms, the fingers flexed and tense, coming against Aaron's shoulders, fitting into the pockets of flesh just below his shoulder bones. Here is my face, wet with tears, my forehead wet with sweat, my eyes shut tight, my mouth twisted with fury.

This stretch of beach is where our family used to spend vacations when my brothers and I were young, though it is just the three of us—Aaron, my mother, and I—here today. Beyond us down the beach is the site of the house that our family used to own. The sun is high and hot, oppressive. The water, a few feet from where we stand, is a deep blue, an oasis of cool that we do not touch.

This is what happens, a simple moment with a simple consequence. Aaron, eight years older than I at twenty-eight, comes toward me over the rocks. He reaches for me, but I put my hands out; I use all my strength, I push him, and he falls. Our mother, standing a few feet away on a different boulder, tears streaking her face, gasps.

I push Aaron, and he stumbles—his foot comes behind him and almost catches him, his right Adidas sneaker with his golf-socked ankle reaching blindly for the boulder behind him, just barely touching it; his arms go out to the sides like wings, strained in a quick, awkward flap; his eyes widen, his thick eyebrows rise in fear, his head turns. There is the possibility for one split second that he isn't going to fall, that he will catch himself, his arms flapping, his body wobbling like a perilously placed piece of driftwood, like some precarious thing, a leaf subject even to the gentlest wind. We are all three of us forced to witness a grown man's strong body as unsteady as a twig.

Then, the inevitable fall, the unpreventable fall, Aaron's body crumpling between the boulders like a puppet released from its strings, his head coming back quickly, hitting the corner of a rock like a discarded piece of fruit. I watch, I see the look on Aaron's face in the moment that his head hits the stone, his eyes clenched tight, bracing for a hit. The lines by the sides of his eyes, his smile lines, the feature of his face that makes him most resemble our father, are outlined in clear definition. A thought is present in the back of my mind: how interesting, that smile lines would be as pronounced in fear as in laughter.

I stand where I am and watch my brother fall; I watch the consequence of my action unfold. Watching my brother fall is like watching time move—unstoppable time, unrelenting and inescapable time, time so utterly, so infuriatingly neutral. Here is time in effect; here is the personification of time: my brother's falling body.

Then it is over, and Aaron is crumpled between the boulders, and there is blood on the back of his head. I have heard many times about lives flashing before people's eyes in moments of grave danger or imminent death; for me, it is now, it is right now that I see it all, and that I feel the full weight of life's terrible fear. Loss! Regret! Change!

It is always just one movement away. I have expressed myself; I have released my anger, just this once, but it can never be enough. I stand there, before my brother's fallen body, my hands still raised before my waist, fingers still flexed, my eyebrows, my father's eyebrows, pointed upward in surprise. And now I know—this is helplessness, this is guilt, this is fear. This is the true impetus for change.

Time. What time was all that? How slowly the days passed then! And who was that strange child, walking home, tired, with a tiny blue and white jay's feather in her hand?

W. G. Sebald, *The Emigrants*

1987

The Family Galaxy

Ruby Bronstein was nine years old the winter she found a gun. It was a Tuesday in December; she and her family were on vacation in Maine.

That morning, after breakfast, Ruby stood by the window of the closed-in side porch, watching her brothers. They were far out on the beach, moving across the expanse in front of the house and then stopping: a cluster of dark, stop-and-go bodies like raised, mobile moles on the pure flat of low tide.

It was always strange, she thought, to watch people moving outdoors when you were in. A window of cold, you saw faces huddled into collars and hands in pockets, and you understood it, you believed it, and sometimes, you became unaware of the warmth of your own body and more present in the sight you were witnessing, so that an exposed patch of skin was alarming, dry and bitterly frigid. She watched her three brothers move: she saw them laugh, Aaron throwing back his head, and with a gloved fist, reaching out to punch Nathan on the arm; she saw Abe point out to the distant mouth of the inlet, where the few boats moored in the harbor were just white dots on the dark water. Despite how far they were, she felt as if she were watching them from a few feet away.

Behind her, in the kitchen, her mother was washing the dishes. "Rube, why don't you go join them?"

The sound of her mother's voice made Ruby aware of how intently she was watching her brothers. Her mother's voice cut through the air and, like a lasso, pulled Ruby back from the beach. She was warm; she was standing at the window.

And she did want to join them, she did, despite having earlier given in to the feeling of being left out. When her brothers had moved to go out to the beach, when Aaron had said, "Let's go outside," and the three of them had gone into the closet by the porch, rummaging underneath the coatrack for hats and rubber boots, Ruby had sat at the table pretending to read *Bridge to Terabithia*.

But now, with a decisive movement, she turned from the window and moved from the porch, past her mother in the kitchen, past her father, reading a Hebrew book in the living room—their dog, Wally, lying awkwardly in his lap—and up the stairs to her bedroom to dress. In the closet off the porch she slipped her feet into a pair of too-big rubber boots; grabbed a coat, hat, and mittens; and moved to the back door. She stepped into the swirl of cold air outside as into the darkness of the house at night when, after getting up to pee, she had to make her way, blind, back up to her room, holding her arms out to feel for walls.

Ruby's brothers often moved as a unit when they were in Maine, with nowhere else for them to go, no other friends for them to escape to, and no way for them to distinguish their three separate worlds. At home in Massachusetts they were wildly different boys. Abe, nineteen and a college freshman, was tall and serious, with thick eyebrows that nearly touched at the bridge of his nose. He was the one with the "brains," as their parents put it, a virtuoso violinist by the age of six, the favorite of all his teachers, the one who excelled at everything he tried without much effort. He used to be obsessed with his appearance, taking multiple showers a day (prompting the nickname Mr. Clean from Nathan), but in the past few years he had developed terrible acne and grown his hair long. Aaron was skinny and precocious and covered in freckles; he was the most active of the three; already, at seventeen, he'd been to the emergency room four times for stitches and once to remove a fishing hook from his earlobe. Nathan was fourteen, with a thick body and a head of blondish curls. He was a cellist and guitarist, a lover of music, completely uninterested in school. Constantly calm, rarely angry or tense, he found humor in the subtlest details—words, facial inflections, body language. He created all the family nicknames and was the one Ruby felt closest to; her eldest brothers were present but much more distant stars, Nathan the telescope she could hold and look through at the whole family galaxy.

At home, it was easier to ignore, but in Maine, the division between Ruby and her brothers was more pronounced. The boys came together as if they were not three stars but a planet, and when Ruby was with them, she was a satellite moving in their gravitational pull. She could never completely be with them as they were with one another—she was the girl, the little one, the one they used as a prop in their games (a favorite a few years ago was "Blintz," where they'd roll her up in a thick blanket and then push her down the stairs). Yet to be with them was intoxicating, no matter what it entailed (tears, Indian sunburns, bruises); to be with them made her part of an undefeatable team.

Ruby's brothers, after all, were most of the reason she was who she was. They were the reason she raced all the boys at school during recess, letting her curls puff up wildly with the dust of the playground while the other girls stood around and watched; they were the reason she liked the Grateful Dead more than she liked the New Kids on the Block. They were the reason she loved video games, and basketball, and playing the violin, which Abe had played before her; they were the reason her best friend, Oscar, was a boy, and why she never got that into Cabbage Patch Kids.

Outside, she stood on the wooden landing and looked around her. Her brothers seemed farther away now than they had when she was inside. The smaller house next to theirs sat still, the window boxes filled with dried and cracking dirt coated with a layer of frost. The curtains in all the windows were drawn.

Ruby's parents rented the smaller house to a mother and son, the Kanes, whom the Bronsteins hardly ever saw. A few times, Ruby and Nathan had tried to spy under the curtains—crawling on hands and knees around the Kane house, the grass prickling their skin, creeping up the sides of the house to the windowsills. These missions always ended in fits of giggles, or with Nathan saying "Run!" in a hoarse whisper, the two of them diving frantically across the lawn and into the safety of their own house. Ruby imagined now that she was being watched, tried to see movement in the curtains, a glimpse of eyes or hands. She saw nothing, but raised her hand to her forehead anyway in a salute the way Abe's friend Dan, who had joined the navy, had taught her.

In front of Ruby, on the Kanes' lawn, was a wooden dinghy, resting just where the land began to slope toward the beach. The boat looked out of place, she thought, on the frosted winter grass, like something from another planet. She imagined, briefly, the boat falling from the sky and landing there—*whooomp!*—intact on the lawn. The earth was so still it was hard to imagine that anyone would be disturbed by things, even boats, falling from the sky.

. . .

Ruby moved carefully down the wooden steps—the boots awkward on her feet—and across the lawn to where the beach began. This was always a place for careful footing; at the edge of the grass the ground grew deceptive, promising solidity where there was none, small peninsulas of earth flopping over the mud boundary at the top of the beach. She moved off the grass onto the slope of tiny rocks that began the beach, willing herself not to look for skipping stones, and with one tentative boot she stepped off the rocks onto the low-tide flat, testing the mud as she would test the temperature of a swimming pool.

The land the Bronsteins' houses sat on was private; the only other houses within sight were along the bank across the water maybe two hundred yards away. In front of the houses was a wide inlet, like a lake with mouths on either end, one mouth leading out to the ocean and the harbor—they could see boats moored there in all seasons—and the other leading around McKhekan and Hutches, the lumber company, to a less familiar area where the water rushed under a bridge and out to a marsh. The beach out beyond the lumberyard was where they once found a giant jellyfish that Ruby's brothers made her poke with a long piece of driftwood. She braced herself for the shock, vaguely proud to be the one to take the hit, but when she poked the stick into the jelly, nothing happened.

The open water in front of the property was wide, and when the tide was out, the inlet drained, the edge of the ocean moving back, back, exposing the water's muddy undersides—its secret rocks, its pockets and pools and vulnerabilities—to the world. The ocean drained like a bathtub and showed its insides, its seaweed and mussels and clams and creatures, exposing all the subtle movement and life of its body beneath its skin, inviting exploration of even its most private places. Ruby thought of their frequent exploration of the muddy low-tide flat as a violation of the ocean's privacy; she thought of the harshness of their booted feet sinking into its mud like hands plunging into an open wound, and when they pulled their boots out, when they sometimes had to reach down to hold on to their boots as they yanked so they didn't pull their feet clean out of them, Ruby felt the violence in this pulling, the fight between mud and human, and how humans always won. They pulled their feet and the mud made a farting sound as it tried to hold on but had to let go, and then they plunged them in again.

This was how she made her way then, across the flat toward her brothers, who had split their cluster and were walking at small distances from one another. She kept her head buried in the collar of her coat, her hands in her pockets, concentrating on each step. The mud was not sucking now, perhaps because it was too cold. She didn't understand why the water didn't freeze; she thought the temperature must be way below freezing. Was it because there was so much of it, or did it have something to do with the salt? Did salt water ever freeze? She thought she should remember to ask someone: maybe Abe knew.

Her brothers had their backs to her and their heads down, Abe and Aaron in thick dark coats, Nathan's an army green, ripped in two places, she knew, and then sewn. Suddenly, looking up at them, she felt a swoop, as if she had become for an instant a large bird, gliding over the expanse, looking down at her brothers and herself. How tiny she was, down there, bundled inside that puffy red coat! In a flash she felt the inlet as small, she saw the water pouring into the ocean just beyond the far mouth, she swooped out to the ocean that went on and on, and there were whales out there and whole islands and boats that were lost and would never be found, and that ocean didn't even know about this part of it, this part wasn't even a fingernail of that ocean's body, not even a fingernail. Then she swooped back and there she was, standing in the tiny inlet in front of her family's house, behind her brothers, who were themselves small. For an instant she was dizzy with it, and then it passed.

At her feet, wedged in the mud, she saw the intact carcass of a crab, legs and all, which she did not bend to pick up. Then she heard Abe's voice through the wind: "Hey Rube!"

She looked up at him. There was a strip of his face visible between his hat and the zipped-up collar of his coat. Aaron and Nathan raised their heads and turned, stiff like mummies, scanning the landscape until they found her, and she waved to them, a little wave with her hand at her side. Her arrival did not disturb or surprise them. Abe waved back to her.

It was then, just as Ruby began to cross the remaining distance to her brothers, who were now, she felt sure, beginning to be bored and therefore close to heading back to the house, that she caught sight of something sticking up from the ground: a small, roundish shape, a stark reddish orange against the dark brown of the mud. She bent to get a closer look; whatever it was, it was heavily rusted, and the shape of it protruding from the mud made her think of the round rubber triangle that Dr. Robb used to check her reflexes, hitting the pointiest edge against the soft pocket beneath her kneecap. She used her foot to try to dislodge the thing, digging her boot into the mud and lifting, and the top of it moved; she saw that the body of it was longer than Dr. Robb's triangle, it was attached to something that wouldn't pull free.

She took off her mittens and bent, taking hold of the triangle with her fingers and wiggling it. As soon as her fingers were exposed to the air they were painfully cold, cramped against the metal; she thought they might crack off if she didn't get the thing loose. She put her left hand in the pocket of her coat and felt it warming as she used her right one to pull. The mud was loosening, loosening, slowly letting go of its hold, she could see the thing emerging in a clump of mud, and she switched hands, using her left one to work on it. She was crouching now, all of her concentration focused, she wiggled it and pulled, and then with a sucking sound the mud offered it up in a big clump and it was free.

She felt a quickening in her chest as she looked down at it. For a moment she put both hands into her pockets, warming them. Her breath came out in a white cloud. She puckered her lips and blew it out like smoke.

"What you got, Rube?" she heard Abe call from a short distance away, his voice slightly muffled beneath his coat.

She didn't want her brothers to come over, not yet, not until she was sure what she had found. "Not sure yet," she called back.

Swiftly, then, she moved her fingers into the cold mud, which dropped away in wet clumps. There could be no more doubt as to what she had, but still she couldn't quite believe it, even as it was there, in her nearly frozen hands: a gun. A gun, rusted over and defeated but unmistakable. She held it; she forgot, for a moment, her freezing fingers, the ache in her knees, the cloud of her breath, the itch of her wool hat against her forehead. The gun sat in the bowl of her palms. It was hefty and real and she was holding it.

She thought of her father, whose aversion to guns was intense. He reacted to them on television shows, in movies, and in any way they appeared in their home—the cap guns her brothers had been obsessed with a few years back, the BB gun they'd kept hidden from him until he caught them with it outdoors shooting squirrels (grounded for two weeks). He told them over and over again never to point guns at each other, even fake guns, even in jest, even if it was just their fingers in the shape of a gun. He always looked so serious when he said it, he always looked at them each so sternly when he said "never," and when they asked him why, what was the big deal, he always said "Guns are not a joke" and "Don't ask me why, just don't do it."

Now, with her brothers coming toward her, Ruby knew her find would be discovered, and she raised the gun with a rush of energy and pride and defiance. Still covered with mud, it was barely recognizable, but its shape was clear. With both hands, she pointed it in the direction of her brothers. "Get 'em up!" she squealed, standing.

They stopped, feet from her; Ruby saw the surprise in their bodies, the hesitation, as if a guard dog had leapt at them. It was just an instant, but the control thrilled her, and sent a warm shiver through her body. Then they relaxed, and Abe stepped in front of her.

"Jesus, Ruby," he said.

"What is that?" Nathan asked. He reached out to take it from her, and she gave it to him. Though she had forgotten how cold her hands were, when the gun left them they came back to her in searing pain. She put her hands into her mittens, mud and all, and shoved them into her pockets to thaw.

"Holy shit." Nathan put his face down into his scarf while he moved his gloved fingers over the gun, cleaning more of the mud off the rusted metal.

"Is that a *gun?*" said Aaron, next to them now, speaking through his cinched hood. His voice was muffled but insistent. "No way! Is that *real?*"

"It's real," said Ruby. "I just found it! It was just sticking up in the mud!" She was happy, now, to be sharing it with them.

"Oh, my God." Abe reached out his hand. "Nate, let me see that."

Nathan paused, then shrugged one shoulder and passed the gun across to Abe's waiting hand. Abe held it, bobbled it to feel its weight, and turned it over. He had exposed his face, his collar under his chin. The scars from his acne looked raw, red mounds on the landscape of his face.

"Wow," he said. "This thing must have been buried here for *years.* Look"—he held the gun up to Aaron's eye level—"it has barnacles on it."

"Yeah." Aaron peered closely at it, the front half of his body angled over toward Abe. He was hungry for the gun, Ruby could tell. "Can I see it?"

Abe pulled the gun back and turned it over again. Aaron held out his hands. "Come on, man, let me *see* it." Abe passed him the gun, looking at it as he let it go.

Aaron held it up close to his face and peered at it. *Eagle Eye,* Ruby thought, which was the nickname their father gave Aaron for his gift of observation. His eyes were quick and always focused—he could spot a crab in a tide pool from fifteen feet away. Whenever their family stayed in a hotel, their father enlisted Aaron to sweep the room before they left to make sure they didn't forget anything. "Eagle Eye," he would say, "inspect, please."

Aaron inspected the gun as if he had created it, as if it was one of his sculptures from the class he used to take at the art school near their house. He held it up in front of his eyes and turned it over. "Wow. I can't believe this. Right here in the freaking *mud*." He grinned, his hood showing a round oval of his face. "Good find, Ruby! How did I *miss* this?"

Ruby shrugged, grinning too.

"How do you think it got here?" asked Nathan, his hands back in his pockets.

"Someone was trying to get rid of the evidence," said Aaron. "That's the only explanation."

They were silent for a minute, imagining this. Ruby saw a man in a rowboat, holding the gun in his lap and then dropping it into the water, peering over the side of the boat as it sank. What did it look like, the metal falling through the murky water, like a fish? A few summers ago Aaron had caught a shark off the side of their father's boat—it was a little one, but still about half Ruby's size at the time. She was leaning over the side of the boat when he reeled it in, and she saw it slowly materialize from the depths, at first just a vague flash of color, then a strange twisting shape, and then slowly, a fish, growing larger and larger, rising headfirst toward the surface. Nathan, leaning over the side with Ruby, yelled, "It's a shark! It's a shark!" and Abe, who was lying back in the rubber dinghy, tied to the boat and trailing behind it, shot up immediately and yelled, "Pull me in! Pull me in!" When the shark came up from the water, and Aaron was holding the line high so the slick body flopped helplessly, their father laughed at Abe, saying, "Look, he's just a little baby shark." But Ruby had agreed with Abe, there was danger about the shark, even after Aaron laid it out on the deck and took the line from its mouth. She never took her eyes off of it, and when Aaron leaned over the side to release it, Ruby leaned out too. As she watched the shark disappear into the depths, becoming once more just a wave of color and then nothing, she felt a sense of relief and of sadness.

Now, each of them was looking at the gun in Aaron's hands.

"Oh, this is so cool," said Aaron. He raised it toward the opposite shore, aiming it as if he might be able to spot a target, a tin can to shoot at all the way from here. "Wow"—he wriggled his face free from the hood—"it's so heavy when you hold it up like this."

"Let me try," Nathan demanded, but Aaron said, "Hold on." Ruby could see his face forming into its concentration pose.

Ruby heard her father's words, *not even in jest*. "Aaron!" she said, and the sound of her voice surprised her, high-pitched and whiny, a tone she hated.

"What?" He lowered the gun and passed it to Nathan.

Nathan raised his arm to aim, and it made Ruby even more uneasy: gentle Nathan pointing a gun. This was wrong, she felt suddenly with certainty; she should not have pried this thing from the ground. Nathan was smiling. "Cool."

She tried to make her voice low and strong. "Come *on,* you guys, just . . . just give it *back.*"

"What are *you* going to do with it?" said Aaron.

"I found it," she said, and then couldn't stop the next words from rushing out. "It's mine."

They all looked at her. Nathan lowered the gun. Aaron shook his head, then reached out and took it back from him. He raised it again and aimed at the horizon as he spoke, his back to her. "Sorry, Rube, you're just too little to have a gun."

He gave a quick glance back to the house, swiveling the top half of his body. "I hope Mom and Dad aren't watching."

At this, Abe stiffened. He turned back to the house. "Yeah, maybe we should just bring it in."

Just before Abe had graduated from high school, almost a year earlier, he had been picked up in a police car because he was walking out on the main road by their house holding a cap gun. With his long hair and denim trench coat, the cops said, they didn't know, how should they have known the gun was fake? Abe was shaken. The cops had pulled up, and one of them had pointed his own gun at Abe over the door of the car. "He just said 'Drop it,'" Abe recounted at the kitchen table after the cops had gone, "like I was some kind of murderer or something." Their parents agreed, he shouldn't have been carrying the gun, but the policeman's reaction was exaggerated. It was because it was such a busy street, they said, the police couldn't take chances, and anyway why was he walking on that street carrying that gun? Their father was particularly upset—at the policemen ("treating a young person like that") and at Abe as well ("what would possess you to do such a thing?"). He had stayed up late talking to their mother about it, but then, as far as Ruby could tell, had let it go.

Ruby wondered if Abe was remembering this too. He turned back to them and pulled his hands from his pockets. "Come on, guys, let's bring it in."

"To Mom and Dad?" Aaron said. "Why?"

"I think we should. I think we have to."

Aaron shook his head. "No way. They'll *never* let us have it."

"Probably not," said Abe. "But what do you want with it, anyway? It's a gun, Aaron."

"I *know* it's a gun, Abe," Aaron said slowly, holding the gun. He gazed at it, almost lovingly, as if it were a pet. "I don't know, we could at least fix it up or something."

"Do you think it still works?" said Nathan. He pulled his gloved hands to his mouth, cupping one inside the other, and breathed on them.

"No way," said Abe.

"I think we should tell Mom and Dad," said Ruby.

Aaron looked at her. "Of course you do."

"Come on, Aaron, don't be mean. She found it," Abe said.

"I know, but what does she know?"

Abe turned to Nathan. "What do you think, Nate?"

Nathan looked at the gun. "I think we should keep it. At least for a few days, clean it up, see if we can find anything out about it. Then we'll decide."

Abe nodded. "Fine. But if either of them asks about it, I'm not lying."

They made their way back toward the house, waiting for them on the edge of the land. From this distance, their house looked as small as it was—an old farmhouse with weathered shingles, the second story really an attic, the cottage next door barely more than what would be a garage at home in Massachusetts. Abe carried the gun and led the way, making a determined line through the mud and toward the lawn. Nathan and Aaron traded scenarios, lifting their voices from beneath their pulled-down hats and cinched hoods. Ruby's hands, though now warm inside her pockets, felt as if they were burning. She clenched her fingers together and held them still.

"Maybe it was the Kanes!" offered Nathan. "There's no dad, right?"

"That's true . . ." said Aaron.

"Maybe that's why he went away. Maybe he killed someone, stashed the gun, and took off."

"Yeah, maybe that's why they never go outside. The mom is hiding the kid so he won't tell anyone what happened."

"Right." Nathan gestured with his gloved hands. "Maybe it was a friend of theirs, someone they knew, and he killed him right in the house in front of them!"

They laughed, and Abe whipped around to face them. "Cut it *out*, you guys," he said, his voice elevated above the wind. He was holding the gun delicately across his two gloved palms like it was a bird's nest. "We have no way of knowing who it was, so quit making stuff up! It could have fallen off a boat and never even been used for all we know." He paused, collecting himself, then added in a gentler voice, looking at Ruby, "Anyway, you're going to give Ruby nightmares."

He turned around and started walking again. Aaron and Nathan looked at each other, and Aaron pursed his lips together, raising his eyebrows as if to say, *What's with him?* Nathan shrugged.

As they approached the house, Ruby wondered how it would go and felt a subtle resentment that it was beyond her control. There was never any possibility that she would hold on to the gun, despite the fact that it was she who had removed it from its hiding place, despite the burning of her hands. Still, there was this mystery that they were bringing into the house together (the door made its swishing sound, and Abe was inside). She tried not to feel ownership over the gun; it was not hers, she didn't even want it, and this was one of the rare times that they were all equal and united. On the other hand, this was what always happened: little Ruby at the back of the line, little Ruby so little and so without claim.

She was in, and she shut the door behind her. The boys were taking off their coats and bending to remove their boots, and they were exclaiming at the warmth, and Ruby felt it too, the warmth was a shock, the warmth sent shivers through her body. They heard piano music from the other room but no voices.

Abe stood by the kitchen door, waiting for the rest of them to finish taking off their boots and coats. "Kids?" their mother called. "You back?"

"Yeah!" Abe called toward the living room. He handed the gun to Aaron. "Here, you take it," he said.

Aaron took the gun and looked down at himself for a place to hide it.

They could hear movement in the other room. "Quick!" said Nathan in a strained whisper. Aaron looked around frantically, then tucked the gun under his sweater. It bulged beneath the wool.

"How was it?" their mother said, appearing in the doorway, an expectant look on her face.

They were doomed. As soon as she saw her mother, Ruby knew it. This was the woman who could detect lies as if they were curls of smoke; there was no way they could get something like this by her. Aaron tried. "Fine," he said, his hand curled under his sweater hem, his freckled cheeks flushed. "Really cold though." He tried to move his hand farther back, pulling the gun along the inside of his sweater.

"What's that you've got there, Aaron?" their mother asked, nodding her head toward the bulge, one hand on her hip.

As soon as her mother discovered the gun, Ruby knew they had lost it. In the hallway, as Aaron slowly pulled the gun from beneath his sweater and reluctantly held it up, she could already feel the loss of it;

it was in this very gesture, this offering up, and she saw the way that Nathan, Abe, and Aaron all watched the gun as it passed from Aaron's hands to her mother's, as if they were watching coins roll irreparably down a drain.

In the living room, her father received the gun calmly in the chair where he was still sitting with his book, massaging his gums with his massager, the tiny golden handle so small in his big hand. Wally was lying now on the floor by the woodstove; her chain jangled as she looked up at them with curious eyes. Their father immediately set about the gun's removal from the house—getting up, stepping into his slippers, and facing his children before he went into his bedroom to get ready to go out with it into the sunlight.

Only Aaron really fought. Abe and Nathan, their exuberance gone, were more resigned. After a few minutes, Abe sat down on the couch and barely looked up again.

"What are you going to do with it, Dad?" Aaron asked, facing him, his chest squared. He was as tall as their father now, though far narrower.

"I'm going to take it to the authorities," their father said. He was calm, but it was clear that if tested he wouldn't stay that way.

"Why?"

"Because that's where it belongs."

From just behind Aaron, Nathan piped up. "But we *just* found it! Can't we just keep it for a little while?"

"Who found it?" said their father, his voice raising slightly. "Who?"

"I did," said Ruby. She was crouched on the floor by the stove next to Wally, holding her hands toward the warmth. Wally's nose was reaching out, sniffing at the air by her hands.

"Ruby!" her father said, raising his free hand toward the ceiling, as if this detail alone provided evidence for his response. He was holding the gun in his other hand. The look of it, her rusty, barnacled discovery in her father's familiar hand, his irregular pointer finger (the tip of which he'd sliced off when he was young, on the kibbutz, trying to fix a tractor) resting near the end of it, was unreal. "Ruby found it!"

He raised his eyes to the ceiling, sighing. He looked at the boys one after another. "Do you want your sister to have a gun for a toy? Do you, really?"

All of the boys looked at the floor. Ruby could see Aaron's fists clenched at his sides, his jaw set in a frustrated lock. "I know you don't," their father said. Ruby was the only one who met his eyes, but she knew he wasn't really speaking to her. She smoothed down Wally's ears, which popped back up after her hand passed over them.

"I'm sorry," he said, as a final punctuation mark on the topic, "but a rule is a rule. There will be no guns in this house. When you live in your own houses you can do what you want, but as long as you live under my roof I make the rules."

"As long as you live under my roof" was one of their father's favorite catchphrases, one of a series that came out when there was no use in arguing. There was "Do what you're told" and "You'll do as I say," all as definitive as the click at the end of a phone call—when they heard these, they knew they wouldn't get their way. He also used "Honor thy father and thy mother," his favorite of the Ten Commandments, and "Children should be seen and not heard," one that Ruby was particularly sensitive to.

He was often an unmovable man, wanting what he wanted and believing what he believed without compromise. It was because of how he was raised, Ruby knew—essentially without parents, in a concentration camp in Czechoslovakia and then in Israel, in a world far harder than and very different from hers—but no matter how she felt she understood it, it didn't make his determination, when it came, easier to take. He was often warm, lighthearted, and fun, and could be lenient at the most unpredictable times, but when he was sure of something, it was as if he never even heard anyone else. This was the most difficult part: the way he dismissed, the way he would not discuss.

He went into his bedroom to change his clothes, and the rest of them sat in the living room. Aaron said, "But it doesn't even work!" loud enough that their father could hear. Their mother regarded him with a pursed mouth but said nothing; it was not her fight.

Without another word their father was gone, and so was the gun. It was as if a window had been opened briefly and then violently closed; this new object had come into their lives, had briefly united them in discovery and then, just as suddenly, it was gone, never to be explained, never to be seen again. It was unfair; it was confusing; it was beyond their control. Who was there to be angry with?

They sat with their mother in the living room. They heard the car turn on and disappear down the driveway, the tires crunching the gravel, and then nothing. It was as if their father had taken their energy out with him and driven away with it.

Their mother, sitting at the table, crossed her legs and angled her head toward the window behind her, one half of her hair, a dark gray thinly streaked with the remaining black, hanging over her shoulder. The room was warm, the flame in the stove glowing through its small dirty window. Ruby, still sitting on the floor by the stove, held her hands together; they had returned to their regular temperature. Next to her, Wally's eyes were closed, her head resting between her paws.

"Kids," their mother said finally, "you know your father has real reasons for not liking guns."

Aaron nodded his head, like he was waiting for her to say this. "Right," he said, "the war."

She looked at him severely; he met her eyes and didn't look away.

"Yes, Aaron, the war," she said. "And Israel, and the army. He was around soldiers and guns when he was very young and it profoundly affected him."

"Did he tell you that?" asked Nathan gently.

She shook her head. "No, but to me it's pretty clear. He doesn't have to tell me. He has a strong reaction to guns and that's all I need to know."

"But why doesn't he ever tell us that?" Nathan asked. He seemed genuinely curious. "He's never once told us about that."

She nodded. "I don't think he thinks you need to know why. I think in his mind it is enough to tell you not to play with guns, and he's your father so you should just do as he says."

"But, Mom," said Aaron, "it's not like we're going to shoot anyone! There's no way that gun even works!"

"I know, Aaron." She spoke slowly and carefully. Ruby could see she was trying very hard not to get angry. "But that's not the point. It's the principle of guns that your father is against—all guns, and what they represent in the world." She uncrossed her legs and crossed them the other way, resting her hands on her thighs.

"Do you remember, Aaron," she said, "that time we were here and you were out fishing in the marsh by the school and that kid took a shot at you?"

Aaron nodded, and Nathan looked surprised. Abe kept his eyes on the carpet. "What happened?" Nathan asked.

"This kid who lived in that house across from the school took a shot at Aaron," she said. "He missed, of course, and who knows why he did it, but it was scary, wasn't it Aaron?"

He nodded reluctantly. Ruby thought he looked younger than he really was.

"With a real gun?" said Abe. His eyes were wide, still focused on the floor.

"Yes. And Aaron came home and told your father, and he immediately turned around and marched him right over to that house and rang the doorbell."

"And what happened?"

"Well, the kid's older brother answered the door, and Dad told him what happened, and I guess the brother gave the kid hell because it never happened again." She paused. "You didn't think guns were so great that day, I remember," she said to Aaron, with a slight smile.

"I just hate the way we all have to tiptoe around Dad sometimes," Aaron said, quieter now. "Like we all just sit in here talking about his 'past' like it's this big secret, but he doesn't even remember enough to even tell us anything for sure!" His voice rose and he threw his arm out. "I mean, we were out there on the beach talking about how there was no way he'd let us keep it—we knew!"

"Aaron," their mother said, her voice more impatient, "there's nothing you need to know beyond what you see. You know your father doesn't remember much about what happened to him. He hates guns, and he doesn't want any in his house—that's it. If you choose to interpret why this is, that's fine, but he doesn't owe you any explanations. The gun is gone. That's the end of it."

With a quick grunt, Aaron rose from the couch and disappeared up the stairs. Their mother gave them all a weak smile. "I'm sorry, kids," she said then, "really. Do you want to tell me about how you found it?"

———

For all of Ruby's life her father's past was like an envelope, tightly sealed, that she carried but could not open. Every year, in Hebrew school, when Holocaust Week rolled around, she'd hear herself say the words: "My father is a survivor," but when her teacher and the other students looked to her for the next sentence, their eyebrows raised (in what she sometimes thought of as impressed surprise, sometimes pity), she would close off like a faucet. She felt a great swell inside her when the word *survivor* was mentioned, a balloon filling with air. She wanted the five words *my father is a survivor* to be enough, because they were all she had.

Her father was one of the lucky few, she told herself, as her mother had told her, who had blocked out the memories; it was the only way he could be at peace. Her teachers would ask her if he wanted to come in and speak, maybe share some stories with the class. "I'm sure he would," she'd say, "but he doesn't remember very much. He was just a child, he blocked it all out." She'd say this, and then her teachers would nod, very slowly, with their eyes closed.

He was a stocky man, a couple of inches shorter than her mother but so commanding that for years into their marriage she had believed he was what he told her: one inch taller than she. He had gone with Ruby once to Hebrew school, on a bright Sunday morning last April, and she was proud walking into school with him— proud of his accent, proud of the secrets that he held inside him, horrible, sad secrets, survival turned into success, proud of his hand that released hers at the classroom door. He had insisted on dressing nicely, and wore suit pants and a button-down shirt, and was clean-shaven and soft, to Ruby, even his hand was soft. That morning, before they left, Ruby had performed the job for which he sometimes paid her fifty cents: pairing up his mountain of dark socks, fresh from the laundry, picking one from the top and then searching through the pile for its mate. It was a task that he couldn't stand but that she loved—standing by the side of the bed before the pile, searching for the sock with the blue line across the toe, the one with the thick elastic at the top, the thin one that was wearing out. Slowly, the pairs came together and the mountain shrank. That morning, she had laid aside a pair for him to wear before stuffing the rest into his dresser drawer.

Ruby's teacher shook his hand with respect and sat him on a

white chair in front of the class, where he answered the most basic of everyone's questions, just as he had always answered hers. The hands shot up, and her father nodded at her classmates and said "Yes?" and Ruby felt an excitement that this enigma was a man who shared her home, that this was the man who would take her hand after class and drive her home in his car. They were questions she had memorized. *How old were you?* Seven. *What camp were you in?* Terezin. *How long were you there for?* Four years. But when it came to the details—*Did you go by train? What did you eat?*—his answers were always the same. "I don't remember," he'd say, and the questions fell like sandbags.

Her father was a mystery Ruby sometimes felt she could solve, as a cloud can seem just close enough to touch. When she was very young, he taught her to eat the whole apple, even the core. After the war, he explained, he and the other children were sent to a Red Cross camp to be *fattened up.* The nurses rationed their food so they wouldn't get sick, even though they were so hungry they wanted to eat everything they saw. An apple, he said, holding hers up half-eaten before him, was the most delicious delicacy they could imagine. Ruby almost never left the core of an apple uneaten again.

She tried to trace the journey that had led her father—first a boy, then a man—over continents, to her mother, and then to her. But much as she tried, she could not transport herself back in time to his childhood; she could not make herself *be* her father—or for that matter her mother, who had her own fascinating past, educated by nuns in a poor Irish neighborhood in the Bronx—although that was the only way, Ruby was convinced, that she could ever understand either of them. Last winter, she'd found a photograph in the back of a drawer in his study—unmistakably her father, young, with his arm around a woman she did not recognize. When she asked him about it, holding it up to where he sat at his desk, he told her he had been married before. It was after the war, after Israel, after the army, when he went to Australia to work in his uncle David's camera store. She was also a survivor, and he was young and confused. They had no children, and they had divorced soon after they came to America; a long time had passed before he met Ruby's mother.

And it wasn't surprising. Among all the unaccounted-for years that were Ruby's understanding of her father's past, the addition of another woman was no less shocking than if he had declared he had spent a brief period of time under the tutelage of a priest. He sat at his desk in his cable-knit sweater and his soft, pale jeans, looking down at her, explaining this piece of his past in a calm, even tone. He looked the same, but somehow the explanation only made him seem more distant, as if he were drifting from her, slowly, like a retreating train.

After dinner that evening, Nathan washed the dishes while Ruby dried. At the sink, in the dim light of the narrow kitchen, Nathan drowned the plates in the soapy water and called out "Help! Help me!" in a high-pitched, whining voice, gasping for air, and then he swooped in the blue glasses as if they were eagles, saying, "Don't worry, we'll save you," in a calm, steady voice. He narrated, "It's a dark day for the silverware, oh, what a dark day, there is just no hope for them, no hope," while he searched in the soapy water for the knives and forks, his sleeves rolled up and his hands plunged in to his elbows. Their mother, circling, cleaning the table and giving them the remainder of the dishes, said, "Nate, can you just do the job please?" and Nathan picked up a pot and stood it at attention on the edge of the sink. "Certainly, ma'am, I'll do the job right away, right away, I'll rescue them all, right away ma'am."

Drying the dishes while Nathan washed was a routine that Ruby loved, a time when she got to be with him alone and had his undivided attention. Whenever it was his turn to wash, she volunteered to dry. Slowly they made their way through the dishes—behind them in the rest of the house there were voices, but they were not listening—and when they were through, Nathan felt around in the water, now full of floating bits of food, scrunching up his nose and saying "Eeeuwww," and then he said, "I think that's it." He turned to Ruby with his hand on the side of the bin—"Ready?"—and then he tipped the bin up and poured the water over the side, and they both watched a wave of rushing water roll up and over the lip and disappear down the drain. Nathan held his hand to his ear and bent toward the sink, and there was the deep gurgling sound that he had once told her was a giant fish creature with legs that lived under the sink and swallowed all the water. She knew it wasn't true, but she imagined it anyway, standing down there in the dark with its giant fish mouth open, all the water pouring into it, and the scaly Adam's apple in the middle of its exposed throat moving up and down with each glug.

When they were done, they went upstairs, and Ruby went to her room to put on lighter clothes. She could hear Aaron's and Nathan's voices through the permanent crack in her latched door. Dressed, she crossed to their room. Her brothers looked up at her and stopped talking. The round fluorescent light in the center of the ceiling was on, casting a bluish glow through the evening light. She stopped just inside the door. "What's up?" she asked shyly.

They didn't respond, but she didn't want to go downstairs alone, so she went and sat next to Nathan on his bed.

"We were talking about staging a rescue mission for the gun," said Aaron, with a wild grin. "Maybe going to the police station to try and get it back."

Ruby looked at him, and then to Nathan. She was amazed; her brothers had an endless capacity for surprising her. "Seriously?"

"Well, not really. I don't know. Nate's not into the plan."

Nathan smiled. "I like your enthusiasm, though."

Aaron turned and looked out the window. Ruby imagined the three of them in black, wearing ski masks that pulled down over their faces, crawling through the police station on their hands and knees.

"Yeah." He sighed finally, nodding. "Man, it sucks, though. I bet we could have gotten a lot of money for that thing."

Aaron's baseball card collection, on a shelf in his closet at home, was four shoe boxes full of cards he had spent years cultivating and cataloging, using little index cards on which he wrote in tiny, careful handwriting. He had of course forbidden Ruby to touch them, but sometimes when he wasn't home she went into his closet and ran her fingers over the tops of them, pulling some out at random like cards in the card catalog drawers at the library. Once she had sat on the floor with him while he was looking through the book that told him how much each card was worth, sliding the valuable ones carefully in and out of their plastic sheaths, and he had explained them to her with his voice full of pride. She always wanted them to fill her with more awe when she snuck looks at them, but they never seemed more to her than pictures of men holding bats and balls.

When their father had come home from the police station, a few hours before dinner, he'd slipped back into the house and disappeared into his bedroom without saying a word. Wally had trotted out just before he shut the door and come to Ruby in the living room. There had been no more words about the gun.

Now, Ruby thought of the gun sitting on someone's desk, so far from where it had grown comfortable, in the mud, beneath the water. She thought of the police station that they passed every time they went anywhere while in Maine, the building that she had always vaguely noticed but had never truly thought about as a real place with people inside and with desks on which to lay rusted, old guns. Now, she knew, every time they passed it would be different for her, a place that was somehow connected to them, a place that had a new role to play in her life. That police station could never again be anonymous, could never again be the same; she would think of it from now on as the gun's new home.

1988

Liberty, Yes

The day Abe came home from college crazy, Ruby, who had just turned ten, won a spelling bee. The entire fifth-grade class gathered in the auditorium that morning, and Ruby stayed onstage the whole time, as one by one her classmates misspelled words and Mrs. Henderson, the school secretary, rang the tiny, hand-held bell to signal that they were eliminated from the competition. Ruby's final word, the one that won her the trophy she held as she made her way out to the waiting school bus that afternoon, just before her father walked up the long drive toward her, had been *profligate*, a word she had never heard before but somehow managed to spell. *Prof-li-gate*. The word came apart nicely, Ruby's favorite kind of word. It divided itself in front of her, so she could see the letters as she spelled them out.

Everything went smoothly that morning, the words floating before her, cooperating, dividing themselves into neat little sections she could easily read. Mrs. Butterworth, her teacher, sitting at the front table next to Mrs. Henderson, had a smile on her face whenever Ruby stood before the microphone. Mrs. Butterworth would say the word, and Ruby would repeat it back, and she would look at Mrs. Butterworth and Mrs. Butterworth would smile, and nod, and the word would float up before Ruby and divide itself. It was almost effortless.

After the spelling bee, the day was a blur, the trophy burning a hole in the floor next to Ruby's backpack. Avi Meltrin, who Ruby's mother insisted had a crush on her, passed her a note during math class that said, *Hey Champ, how do you spell nerd?* and for a second she was embarrassed, but then she remembered the last time Avi had made fun of her, when she had worn her brand-new brown loafers with the white soles to school and he'd hissed that they were "boy shoes," and then how he'd called her up a few days after making her cry to ask her to go with him to a dance at school, and she touched the trophy with her foot and crumpled the note up and pushed it back to him. She couldn't wait to surprise her parents with the trophy; she kept imagining their faces, their mouths like O's, her dad saying "My buttons are popping," her mother making Swedish meatballs for dinner to celebrate. They were the ones who would understand. When she thought of the spelling bee, it felt like a dream, and she couldn't quite believe it had been her up there, conquering those words as if she were on horseback, swatting them out of the air with a long sword.

But when the day was over, and Ruby was finally making her way to the school bus, walking in the line of kids down the sidewalk outside the front doors of the school, cradling the trophy in her arm like she did her favorite stuffed animal, Bear, whom she had won at a fair, her father was coming up the walk toward her, and the expression on his face was not curious or proud but grave, and he barely looked at the trophy as he took her hand and led her away. Her friends called out to her—"Bye Ruby!"—and she was walking away from them with her father in his suit, but this wasn't the way she had pictured it, not at all, and she couldn't remember the last time her father had picked her up from school. Had he ever? No, she was pretty sure he never had, and yet here he was, the back of his suit jacket a bit rumpled. And it was disorienting, having her father there on a Thursday afternoon; it made her somehow feel it was a Sunday, and she was leaving Hebrew school, and there would be bagels in the car and chive cream cheese, her favorite—but no, it was a Thursday, and so why was her father here? She walked with him toward the car.

They reached the car, and she got in the passenger side. The trophy sat on her lap and came up to her chin, and she looked at it while her father settled into his seat, and she remembered the word—*profligate*—and wondered what it meant, and she wondered why her father hadn't mentioned the trophy yet, how could he not notice the trophy?

Her father had his hands on the wheel and he put the keys in the ignition but he didn't start the car. He said, "Honey, I'm picking you up from school today because something's happened."

He looked at her, and she saw his eyes dart to the trophy, but then he looked back at her face and kept his eyes there. "I just wanted you to know about it before you got home, I just wanted to warn you," he said. "Abe's home, he just came home, his friends drove him here. He's not feeling very well. In . . . his head. He's not feeling well in his head."

He paused, and Ruby looked at his suit collar, the skin bulging loosely over it—the skin there so smooth and hairless, unlike the skin on his cheeks, which he would rub against Ruby's face to make her squeal. His face was very serious, there was no trace of laughter, but he wasn't angry, and this combination was rare. His bushy eyebrows shadowed his eyes.

"He's okay," her father said, "he's all right, but he's . . . sick. He might act strange, you might notice that he's different, but you don't have to be afraid. I just wanted you to know."

Her father stopped talking and looked at Ruby; she didn't know what to say. Whatever was going on, it was serious, that much was clear. She remembered the last time she'd seen Abraham, a few weeks ago, when he was home for his spring break, crying at the dining room table. She remembered hearing him say "I don't want to go back," the words drifting up the stairs as she made her way down, she remembered his shoulders slumped, she remembered her mother standing behind him and rubbing his back, she remembered him wiping his eyes when he saw Ruby come in the room, trying to smile at her. She had never seen any of her brothers cry like that; she had only seen them cry in anger, usually at their father, but never like that, at the dining room table, shoulders heaving, head in hands. Was this related to what was wrong with him now?

Her father gestured at the trophy. "What's that for?"

"I won the spelling bee." But this wasn't how she'd pictured telling him, in his car with him in his suit, his face so serious, not at all. The spelling bee seemed far away now, the trophy heavy on her legs. Abe was home from college, he was sick in his head, and she shouldn't be afraid, but then why was her father there, sitting with her in the car without turning the key? She looked at her father, and he took her hand.

"Oh, Ruby," he said, "that's so great. I'm so proud of you."

He gave her hand a squeeze, then reached for the key and started the car. No music began when the car turned on, no Book on Tape voice in midsentence. Just the two of them and the sound of the car's engine. Her father took a deep breath and let it out before they moved.

When they pulled in to the driveway, Abraham was standing in front of the house. There he was, sick in his head, just standing there, the blue shaker shingles of the wide colonial house behind him. "He cut his hair," Ruby's father said as they drove toward him. "I forgot to tell you."

Abe didn't move as the car rolled toward him. He was grinning, and he waved. Ruby couldn't remember the last time she had seen him with short hair. She thought of the cover to the album he and his friend Jeff had made their senior year of high school, two years ago now. In it, Abe was standing with his arms crossed over his chest, wearing an acid-washed denim coat that fell to his ankles, his hair in short curls on the top and then flowing just past his shoulders. She saw this image of him clearly, down to his skull earring, the expression on his face a tough pout with a tightly controlled smile just threatening to come through. But there he was in front of her, through the windshield of the slowly moving car, and he was wearing jeans with a hole in the knee and a red Hawaiian shirt she had never seen before, and his hair was cut so close to his head that there were no curls anymore. Her father had warned her—she shouldn't be afraid, but what would she be afraid of? Abe was standing in front of the house waving.

He came around to her side of the car as her father turned it off. His grin was wide, wildly wide, he couldn't wait for her to open the door, it was as if they hadn't seen each other in years. "Hey sis!" he cried as she opened the door. She thought she saw something different in his eyes, like they were focused on something far away even as they looked at her. She got out of the car and said "Hi," aware of her shyness. This was Abe, this was someone she knew, why did he suddenly feel like a stranger to her? He took her in his arms and lifted her off the ground. The trophy hung down behind his back. "I missed you," he said softly, as if he didn't want their father to hear.

Their father came around the side of the car just as Abe was releasing her, gently, back to the ground. "How are you, Abe?" he asked, and Ruby noticed the formality to his voice, it was as if Abe was someone from his office.

Abe nodded, still with that grin, as if he was just so happy to be standing in the driveway by the car, so happy. He stiffened a bit in their father's presence, and barely looked at him—he kept his eyes on

Ruby. "Pretty good, Dad." He put his hand on Ruby's shoulder. "Even happier now that I see my sis." He grinned at her.

She tried to smile back, but she was still shy. Abe was looking at her as if she was the only person in the world.

The three of them went into the house.

Later, Abe sat with Ruby at the kitchen table. Their parents had disappeared upstairs, Nathan was not home yet from school, and Aaron was away at college. They were alone. The trophy sat on the end of the table, by the door.

The kitchen was bright and clean, and the late-afternoon sun came in from the window over the sink. Their father's briefcase was sitting on one of the kitchen chairs, where it never sat. Abe, his grin now just a vague smile, was drawing a frog on a manila envelope that had been lying on the table. The frog squatted with wide legs, and held up a peace sign with two long, bulbous fingers. When he was through, he pushed the envelope over to Ruby, who sat next to him, watching. He was grinning again. "Peace frog, see?"

Ruby nodded and smiled down at the cartoon. "His fingers are like E.T."

"You're right." Abe looked carefully at the drawing. Then he pushed the pen over to her. "You try."

Ruby took the pen and drew another frog on the envelope next to Abe's. She tried to follow his lines. In a drawing class one summer at camp, she had practiced following the lines of another drawing without picking up her pen, and she tried to do that now, following the lines of Abraham's frog, the wide legs, the two bulbous fingers in a V, the mouth full of teeth. When she was finished, her frog was smaller, the lines lighter, shakier, the fingers a bit more out of proportion, but there were two frogs and their knees were touching. She pushed the envelope over the table to him.

Abe laughed. "Awesome." He nodded. "Awesome." He took the pen from her. Over his frog, in capital letters, he wrote *Ruby,* and over her frog *Abraham.* He pushed the envelope back to her. "Right?" he said, and she looked at him, her brother with his close-cropped hair, and she thought maybe it was just the hair that was so different, maybe he was all right after all. She smiled back. "Right." But she didn't know what she was agreeing to—even if she thought she did, even if she thought she understood something about her frog being shakier and having Abraham's name, something was wrong with Abe now, and no matter what she thought he meant she couldn't be sure.

———

The next morning, in her nightgown, Ruby was cutting a grapefruit at the island in the center of the kitchen. Her parents were in their bathrobes at the table, eating and reading the newspaper. The three of them always had their breakfast together at this time. Nathan never came downstairs until two minutes before his car pool arrived; he ate bananas for breakfast, grabbing them on his way out the door.

Ruby's parents were quiet this morning, but she told herself they were just tired; she had woken up in what she thought was the middle of the night, and though she didn't hear any voices, their light was still on, the rectangle of it reaching diagonally down the hall and onto the floor of her room. There were doors on either side of her bedroom, and she usually slept with both of them open; her parents slept with theirs open as well. Her brothers, by contrast, all kept theirs closed.

She was cutting the grapefruit sections with a knife, sliding the blade around the sides of a triangle, then lifting it, sliding it into the next triangle, and slicing again. It was a task her mother normally performed for her, but this morning Ruby had told her she wanted to do it. It made her feel good, to do this for herself, her parents seated at the table. It was as if she was cutting the grapefruit not for herself but for them.

Then, it happened in slow motion. She heard footsteps on the back stairs, someone was coming down toward the kitchen, and she looked up. Slowly, the door swung open, and there was a naked man standing there, just standing there, at the bottom of the stairs, and she looked at the man's face and saw that it was Abraham. It was her brother Abraham, and his eyes were empty and he was looking at her, he was just standing there, naked, on the bottom stair, the door swung wide open, looking at her, standing by the island in her nightgown. And just as she realized that it was Abraham, this naked man, his torso a triangle pointing down toward a black clump of hair, his penis, Abraham's penis hanging, Abraham's blank eyes, she heard her mother gasp, and her father leapt up from the table and cried "Abraham!" and he was rushing toward the door and Abe was just standing there, and then her father was blocking Abe's body, and she heard her father say, "Go back upstairs!" his voice frantic, and they were moving back up the stairs, and then they were gone, and Ruby was still standing by the island with the knife in her hand, held straight, the blade facing down toward the grapefruit.

Her mother sat at the table for a moment with her back to Ruby, her shoulders round and her head turned down toward her plate so Ruby could see the roots of her hair in a straight gray line leading from back to front. She took a deep breath and let it out, and then she stood and came to Ruby and said, "Oh, Ruby," and took her into her arms as if she were a stuffed animal. She was hugging Ruby close to her terry-cloth robe, saying, "I'm sorry, I'm sorry," but Ruby wasn't sure what she was sorry for. The image of Abe in the doorway was in her mind as a square of light lingered after she looked at a lamp; her face was pressed against her mother's stomach; her mother was holding her tightly and rocking her. She said, "It's okay, Mom, I'm okay," and she squirmed; she didn't want to be hugged like this, she didn't need it, it made her feel like she ought to be crying, but she wasn't crying, and she didn't fully understand why she should be. But her mother did not stop rocking her, and finally Ruby closed her eyes against the terry cloth and allowed herself to be rocked. There were footsteps moving above them. Abraham, naked, with an empty face. "Oh, Ruby," her mother sighed, her voice hushed and muffled above her head, "what's happening to us?"

Ruby didn't know what was happening, but something was. She got ready for school as usual; she wore her favorite ballerina sweater, it was probably too warm to wear but it was what she wanted to wear, and she put it on, with her favorite blue cotton pants, elastic waist, and it was just like any other day, she was dressing in her room and putting her books in her backpack. The trophy from the spelling bee was on her dresser—she saw it on her way out and thought briefly of the night before, when she had shown it to her mother, who took her into her arms and said she was so proud, she was so proud, she was so proud, just like that, three times, and for some reason Ruby didn't want to look at that trophy anymore, that trophy seemed too big and ugly to her now, she wanted to hide it somewhere, she wanted to throw it out the window, she wanted it to disappear.

She made her way downstairs with her backpack. The house was a foreign space, familiar but unknown, unpredictable, as it sometimes was in her dreams: hers but not hers. Her father was upstairs, down the hall in Abe's room, speaking to Abe in hushed tones, and when Ruby went down into the kitchen Nathan was there, sitting across from their mother, who was wiping her eyes.

"Ruby, you're going to be late," said her mother, getting up and checking the clock on the stove. "Oh, the bus will be here any minute. I'm sorry, honey, but I didn't have time to make you a lunch." She stood, helpless. "Hopefully there will be something good at school today. I'll give you some little things for a snack." She gathered up an apple, some cookies, and a fruit punch box, and dropped them in a bag, which she handed to Ruby by the door, saying, "Have a good day, honey," and kissing her cheek. "Bye, Rube," said Nathan, still sitting at the table.

Ruby walked out to the end of the driveway. There was a time when Nathan used to wait with her, here, for the bus; she could remember the days when they went to the same school, before he started going to Featherton, the private school where both Abe and Aaron had gone before him, and where she would go too, next year. She remembered when they used to wait together, and board the bus together, and Nathan played that game where he tucked his lips over his teeth and pretended he was an old man, or he did the silly dumb voice that he picked up from cartoons, the voice that made him sound like he was talking underwater. A different game for every ride, a new personality every morning, and the Callin quadruplets from down the hill used to scream with laughter, and Ruby would feel proud, he was her brother and so she was closer to him, she got to act like his jokes were as familiar to her as the sun.

She missed him now. It had been a long time since Nathan had waited with her but she often missed him, waiting for the yellow minibus to pull around the corner, kicking against the big rock with their house number painted on it, scuffing her feet into leaves or snow, humming to herself, talking to herself, making up songs and stories and games, and this morning she missed him especially. She couldn't help but see Abe's naked body, framed by the door of the back stair-case, Abe with his hair cropped so the shape of his scalp could be seen, his eyes wide and not-seeing; she couldn't help but hear the horror in her father's voice as he rushed toward Abe. What would Nathan say about it? What had happened to Abe; who had brought him home from school; how had he arrived; when was he going back; what was he trying to show all of them by standing at the bottom of the stairs and looking into the kitchen as if there was something there to see?

There was the bus, rounding the corner. It slowed to a stop before her, and she got on. They rolled down the hill to the cul-de-sac at the bottom to pick up Ruby's best girlfriend, Beth Callin, and her four older siblings, the quadruplets: Sadie, Joe, Michael, and Drew. They climbed aboard, the whole group of them; Beth sat next to Ruby and her siblings sat around them—two in front, one to the left, and one behind.

All of the Callins were small people, and Ruby had never been able to understand how Beth's mother had carried four babies inside of her—it was impossible but somehow true. Drew had a deformed leg from the way that he'd been positioned in the womb. His limp was a constant reminder, to Ruby, of this strange occurrence in the world, the four Callin children cramped together inside tiny Mrs. Callin.

Next to her, Beth said hi. "Hi," Ruby said, suddenly shy with the friend she had known since kindergarten. There was something new in her life, but she did not know yet what it was.

"Hey, the spelling bee was cool yesterday," said Beth, "I didn't get to tell you. I saw that trophy you got, though, pretty cool."

"Yeah, thanks," Ruby said.

"Too bad I got out in the second round. Stupid Miranda of course got the easy word."

"Of course."

"I was so happy when you beat her I almost peed my pants. Seriously. Did you see the look on her face? She was all . . ." Beth opened her mouth to a perfect O and her eyes as wide as she could. Ruby laughed, perhaps harder than the face deserved; the laughter burst out of her as if it had been waiting.

"Seriously!" said Beth. "She pouted all through Mr. Harding's class afterwards. She had her head down and everything. It was so great." She paused, leaning back fully in her seat, her ponytail pulling her head back.

Ruby let herself relax, the borders of her world closing in around her. It *was* great that she had beat Miranda Chen. She remembered the way she had felt yesterday when Mrs. Butterworth handed her the trophy, the warmth inside of her when the auditorium applauded for her, her hand shaking as she reached out to her teacher. The whole school, clapping for her! She had all but forgotten it.

The bus driver called out "We're here!" and swung open the door. Ruby surrendered to her feet, carrying her off the bus and into school, to her place in a line of children.

That night at dinner, Abe was almost silent. He was already downstairs, sitting at the kitchen table, when Ruby and her mother lit the Shabbat candles, Ruby saying the blessing, her mother striking the match, letting it flare, and then offering the flame to the wicks, the wicks receiving and flaring too. The two of them waved their hands briefly over the flames and then covered their eyes; Ruby's mother had taught her that this time, when her face was covered with her hands, was a chance to send her personal prayers to God. Ruby wasn't sure if she believed it—she always felt a little awkward asking for things in her mind with her hands over her face, her mother standing next to her. Why would her thoughts be heard now if they weren't heard all other times? But she felt committed to the ritual, regardless, on the off chance that it might be real. She asked for generic things—peace in the world, health for her family—and sometimes allowed herself to ask for personal stuff too, like Bobby Newberg, or those patent leather shoes she had seen but her mother wouldn't let her get. She tried to make sure that she felt what she asked for, that when she said the words in her mind she was really desiring the product: when she said "world" she imagined the world, like the globe in Mrs. Simpson's class; when she said "health" she pictured each of her family members in turn, standing up, looking themselves.

Tonight, however, she felt strange talking to God while Abe sat silently behind them at the kitchen table; she could feel his eyes on them, those changed eyes, boring through her chest and into her prayer. She rushed through it, thinking the words but not feeling them. *And health for my family,* she thought, but she saw Abe, as he was right then, sitting behind her at the table, instead of how she usually saw him, and what did this word really even mean? *Health,* she heard the word echo as she lowered her hands, and she saw her mother standing next to her with hers still on her face. *Health.* Abe was the same, technically, physically anyway, and yet somehow now he wasn't healthy. She wondered at the word, which she used every week. Had she been praying somehow for the wrong thing?

Ruby turned from the candles, the flames long and dancing, and looked at the table, where Abe sat. He was staring at a point on the tablecloth, and his eyes were wide. "Shabbat shalom," Ruby's mother said, taking Ruby's head in her hands and leaning over to kiss her cheek. "Shabbat shalom," Ruby said back.

"Shabbat shalom, Abe," said her mother, and Abe looked up at her, but it was as if he didn't quite understand what she had said. His face formed a slight smile.

Ruby's father came in from the front hall, where he had been opening the mail. He had changed from his suit into a cotton sweater and corduroys.

"Call Nathan, will you, Josef?" Ruby's mother said. She was looking into the oven. "Dinner's ready."

The five of them stood by their places at the table. They sang the blessing over the wine, and then each of them raised a cup to drink.

Each family member had a wine cup, moving up in size from Ruby's tiny thimble to her parents' goblets, which had small jewels encrusted in the goldlike metal. The collection of cups had been a gift from Ruby's father's mother, who had found the set at a shop in Tel Aviv and sent them to Ruby's parents soon after they were married. The individualization of these cups, the match between cup and family member—Abraham's the biggest of the kids' cups, tall and narrow with a wide lip; then Aaron's, more bowl-like but shorter; then Nathan's, strangely curved, with a dent on the bottom; and then hers, like a thimble with a wide base—was complete and total, and had happened without official plan. Ruby loved the way the table looked when it was set for Shabbat, a setting for each family member, so that even when they weren't at the table it was as if their personalities occupied the space.

Ruby said the blessing over the bread, her hands hovering over the challah; she felt on display and rushed through it, then removed the cover and allowed her father to reach in to cut the loaf. The family was silent while he distributed pieces of the first chunk for them all to eat. Ruby passed a section from her father to Abe, shyly, as if he were a guest. The presence of his body next to her was a constant sensation, like the feeling of pressure that arrived in the front of your face when you held a finger to the bridge of your nose. She thought of him earlier, without his clothes, his thin body in the stairwell, and wondered if he knew what he was wearing now—the blue sweater, the jeans. She looked to Nathan, who was looking at Abe, and saw that the expression on his face was not fear but curiosity. The air hung heavy in the room. They took the bread, chewed, and then sat. Ruby's mother went back to the stove.

"It's nice to have almost everyone here," said Ruby's father after a minute. "It was getting lonely here with only four of us, wasn't it, Ellen?"

Her mother carried a blue bowl filled with steaming green beans to the table. "Sure was," she said, putting down the bowl in front of her husband.

"I spoke to Aaron this afternoon," he said. "He said he was sorry he couldn't be here for Shabbat." He paused, spooning green beans onto his plate. "If you want, kids, we can call him after dinner, I'm sure he'd love to talk." He passed the green bean bowl to Ruby and helped himself to a piece of chicken off the tray that her mother now held out to him. When he had loaded his plate, he looked down at it.

"What," he said, "is this it?"

"That's it," Ruby's mother said, with a smile, sitting down.

"Does this come with a microscope?" her father asked. It was his standard joke. No dinner was big enough for him, unless it was something he didn't like—pretty much any new recipe her mother tried—in which case he wouldn't say anything at all.

Ruby looked at her father, who was always one to enjoy his own jokes, even if they were the same ones he made every week. Often he would tell them jokes he had heard at work—a prominent accounting firm—and even when they were funny, he was the one who laughed the most, slapping the table and his knees, tears flowing from the sides of his eyes so that he had to wipe them with his napkin. Laughing, in turn, would make him sweat, which he always did when he ate a hot meal—Chinese food, especially, for some reason—so that he would have to use his napkin to wipe his forehead and his bald spot as well. He was the kind of man who could not conceive of a joke going unacknowledged—if no one laughed, he would ask why. And it wasn't just jokes; her father somehow demanded a response to his every move, even if he wasn't asking for one. He was a man you paid attention to.

Now, Ruby caught his eye, and he winked at her. He was smiling, but something about his face felt artificial to her. Was it her response to him that was off, the weak smile she gave back, the knowledge that his joke felt forced, tonight, though it never had before? Or was it something about the gleam in his eyes, the way they tried so hard to reassure her that this was just any other Friday night, with any other helping of chicken and green beans? There was an uneasiness at the table with them as they ate, as if a pipe somewhere in the house had begun to drip, no one knew where, but they all knew there'd be a flood.

————

Late the next night, Ruby was brought to the surface of a deep sleep with the distinct feeling of rising, against her will, to consciousness. Slowly, slowly, she became aware of noise: raised voices, crashes and bangs, footsteps. In her half-dream state, she thought it was her cousins, her mother's sister's children, a pair of boys who, the last time they visited, had destroyed her dollhouse by sitting on it. She came awake then in a flash. The cousins were here! They were down the hall, they were yelling, they were breaking things!

Then reality crept to her. It was dark in her room, it was Saturday night, and the voices she heard belonged not to children but to her brother Abe, who was yelling.

She was in her bed, the head of which was pressed against the wall of her room. Behind her, down the hallway, was Abe's room, and in the other direction her parents' room. Both of the doors to her room were open. The voices came from Abe's end of the house.

Abraham, yelling. A torrent of words, words like animals, leaping through the house. A crash, the quick squeak of a window being pulled open. Her father, his voice streaked with panic: "Abraham, what are you doing?"

"I am trying to save her! I have to save her! She's my grandmother, there is no one left to save her!" A distant crash, then another. Was he hurling things out the window?

"Abraham, stop it, stop that!" yelled her father. Ruby imagined him reaching out to his son, trying to grab something from his hands.

"Josef!" Her mother, maybe reaching out for her father, pulling him back from Abe.

"Who are you?" Abe screamed, a desperate scream, a scream like Ruby had never heard. "Leave me alone! You are not my father! Don't touch me!"

Ruby's father, his voice shaking and shocked, now soft, "Abraham! I am your father, stop it!"

"You are not my father! You killed my father! You're a murderer! *You killed him!* You are not him!"

They were moving now, the voices coming closer. Ruby imagined Abe, her parents trailing behind him down the hallway. She could see the expressions on all of their faces, she could hear their expressions in their voices, even as she stared at her ceiling from her bed, the moonlight thrown across it in long, thin rectangles. The lines of light were on her ceiling and she was looking at them but she was seeing her brother Abe, crazy in the hallway behind her, screaming, her parents following.

"Murderer!" yelled Abe. The word cut through the dark house, very close now, taking on shape, twisting in and out of rooms, expanding, shrinking, occupying space.

"Murderer!" Time slowed, the word rose and fell, magnifying itself. "Murderer!" yelled Abraham, the oldest son.

Did he believe what he was saying? What was he saying? Who did he think was his father? Who did he think *he* was? Ruby's heart was loud in her chest; it felt as if it was growing, it was growing too large to be contained. What could she do? She tried to stay still.

"Abraham! Stop!" yelled her mother, panicked, desperate.

Then they were in Ruby's room. All of them, the imaginary lurking bodies were standing in her room. Ruby looked up from her bed and there was Abraham, standing beside it. Her parents moved in behind him. She looked from Abe to her parents and back. She had the covers pulled up around her chin. Abe was silent, his face almost gentle, settled into a vague smile as he looked down at her, but his eyes were far away. Her parents looked ravaged. Her father's gaze was fixed unwaveringly on Abe, his whole body tense, her mother meeting Ruby's eyes with sympathy, helpless and apologetic and scared. Ruby stared at Abraham. Her heart was in her throat.

"Little sis," Abe said gently.

"Come on, Abraham," said her father, "let's leave Ruby alone."

"All right!" said Abe, holding up his hand to their father. "I just wanted to see her, that's all." He turned to the door, and his gaze fell on the spelling bee trophy, which she had moved next to the bookshelf by her closet. "Cool," he said and crouched, peering at it, letting his fingers rest on the top of it, where the fake gold woman's arm was thrust into the air. "Liberty," he mumbled, "yes!" Then he stood, and turned, flashed Ruby the peace sign with a wide grin, and followed her parents from the room, shutting the door.

Ruby could hear them moving down the hall behind her, and then her mother was at her other door. "Ruby," she said, one hand on the doorknob, about to pull it closed, "why don't you go to Nathan's room until this is over." Ruby's father and Abe were in their parents' room now. Ruby heard Abe say, "No! No! I said so!" and her father: "Why?"

"I love you, honey," said her mother. "Go to Nathan's room. I called Abe's doctor, an ambulance is coming. It will be over soon." She closed the door.

In Nathan's room, everything was quieter, as if they were a lot farther away. He was a lump in the bed. A door connected his room to their parents', and through it came the sound of more windows being opened, and then Abraham's voice hollering out into the night.

Ruby crept close to the bed. Nathan didn't move. It was strange that he had been in here the whole time, hearing everything too. What did he think of it? Was he scared? She thought of Wally, the dog, the only other witness, trapped downstairs where she slept, and had to fight the impulse to sneak down the back stairs and gather the dog into her arms. She was probably frightened too, her little legs knocking into each other; she should be with them. But Ruby couldn't go now, she couldn't risk being caught out in the path of the drama in her nightgown.

She stood over Nathan, suddenly timid. His shaggy rug was a little rough on her bare feet. When was the last time she and Nathan had been in a bed together? She didn't know. She lifted the corner of his comforter. "Mom told me to come in here," she said, her voice almost a whisper.

He moved over and she climbed in. Beneath the covers it was warm with her brother's heat.

They didn't speak. The voices continued in the next room, though they were muffled now. She felt better, stretched out next to Nathan, welcomed into the heat of his bed. She wondered what he was thinking but couldn't bring herself to ask. They lay next to each other, the quilt pulled up around their bodies, the darkness of his room stretching off to the left of them, through the wall to the muffled voices on the other side. They lay and listened, the action of the house outside the room like a distant play.

Soon, there were other voices, male voices, and Abe's voice rose again. "What's this?" he yelled, then "You can't take me alive!" and "Murderers!" The last high-pitched and desperate, almost a squeal, lingering in the air. Ruby tried to imagine the action of the hallway, men on the stairs, her parents at the top. Men in uniform, putting their hands on Abe?

Everything was silent. Ruby and Nathan lay still. In the absence of noise, the house felt deserted. Had they been left behind? Suddenly it felt like this was all there was, the two of them clustered together in Nathan's single bed, the house around them full of silent fear. Time would freeze, time had frozen: they would lie there forever. It would always be dark, they would never speak again, and this was the only place it would be warm.

Then her mother was at the door. "Kids," she said, coming into the room. "It's okay now. He's gone to the hospital." Ruby suddenly felt very small, lying before her mother so close to Nathan, whom she couldn't even see. "Dad and I are going to follow the ambulance there and check him in," she said. "Why don't you two come to our room and get in our bed until we get back. We shouldn't be long."

Neither one answered. "Come on." Their mother gestured toward the door with her head. Ruby could tell she was trying to keep the emotion out of her voice. "We have to go, kids."

Ruby pushed back the comforter and got up. She and Nathan shuffled out of his room and followed their mother next door to their parents' bedroom. She pulled back the covers on the bed and Nathan got in on their mother's side, Ruby on their father's. Her mother pulled the covers up around them and leaned over the bed to kiss each of them on the forehead. Ruby closed her eyes, and as her mother leaned over her, for a second, it was just as any other night, and she was in her own bed and her mother was wishing her good night.

"I love you both," their mother said. "We will be back soon. Try to sleep."

Then she was gone, and the house was silent. Ruby could sense it around them, all the activity emptied out of it, leaving so many noiseless rooms. She lay next to Nathan in their parents' bed. The quiet filled the house, the room, seemingly the whole world.

"Nathan," she said, forcing the words out through the stillness. Her voice was a whimper. "I'm scared."

For a moment she wasn't sure he would answer. Then she felt his arm come up and around her head. She moved her head, and Nathan slipped his arm under her shoulder. It was awkward, and hurt her neck a little, but it was the most affectionate gesture she could ever remember from him. This was not the way they ever were together, not the way Nathan ever was.

"It's going to be okay," he said, pulling her to him. "I'm here. I promise. It will be okay."

Did he believe this? She didn't know, but it didn't matter. They lay huddled together in their parents' bed, surrounded by the thick and menacing silence, their parents somewhere out in the world. Their bodies together were, for now, like a shield. Ruby tried to let her brother's words comfort her, and tried not to cry. His arm under her neck was uncomfortable, but she hoped he would never take it away. She lay on it like a pillow.

They didn't speak again. After a time, Nathan slid his arm from beneath Ruby's head and turned from her, onto his side. Soon she could hear his deep breathing; he was asleep.

How could he sleep? She thought she might never sleep again. She lay in the dark in her parents' room and the hush rose up and around her. Even with her eyes closed, she could see the room: the bed in the center, the headboard of thick wood carved in a subtle design, round wooden leaves that she'd loved to trace with her fingers when she was little, taking naps in the afternoon as her mother read to her; the bookshelves along the far left side of the room, one whole shelf packed full of family photo albums; and on the right, her mother's dressing area, a bureau with a glass top built into the nook. In front of the bed, her father's heavy wood bureau, the brass handles loose and floppy, so that the noise they made when he pulled open a drawer was as familiar to her as the bureau itself—the *clackclackclack* as the brass hit the wood and settled. This was her parents' space. She tried to allow the room to comfort her, even in their absence. Their books, their clothes hanging in the closet, her father's squash bag by the door, even the art on the walls—two pencil drawings of reclining women, done by a friend of theirs—and in a sense, it worked. Everything was fine. She was in her parents' bed next to her sleeping brother, who said it would be okay. The house was silent, it was night, she was safe.

But each time, as she began to drift off, her head sunk into her father's pillow, the familiar smell of him—a little bit sweet, a touch of his aftershave and the masculine, almost nutlike odor of his body— rising off the pillowcase, she would be jolted awake by the sound of Abraham's voice yelling "Murderer." "Murderer!" she would hear, or think she heard, clear and strong, cutting through the silence of the house. She heard the word, the crack in the voice as it reached its highest note, its most desperate tone, and then the echo as the word filled the house and lingered there. And then she would be awake, staring up at the ceiling of her parents' room.

Nathan was snoring next to her. She was thankful for his body, its warmth calming her, the sound of his snores filling the room with something other than her imagination. He was there. She listened to his snores and tried to align her breathing with them. She told herself that her brother's untroubled sleep was proof that things were all right. She tried not to feel that he had abandoned her, by sleeping, by leaving her alone in the dark, and she tried to resist waking him, or pulling his arm around her shoulders again.

There was nothing to be afraid of—see? Nathan was asleep.

She must have drifted off, for at some point later she was woken by a kiss on her forehead: her mother, leaning over her, whispering gently, "Ruby, we're home."

Ruby was wide awake immediately, though disoriented. Her father was standing next to her mother, head down, as if waiting for a subway train. "Come on, Ruby," whispered her mother, "you and I are going to sleep in Aaron's room."

Next to Ruby, Nathan stirred, rolling over, but he didn't wake up. "Your father's going to sleep in here with Nathan," her mother said.

Ruby allowed herself to be coaxed from inside the cocoon. She held her mother's hand and sat up, swinging her legs over the side of the bed and slowly standing. In the dark, her parents' shapes were eerie and foreign. She stood for a second and looked up at her father; his face was expressionless. He bent to kiss her. "Good night," he said. "See you in the morning."

Her mother led her from the bed, and she turned to see her father taking his pajamas from under his pillow. His shoulders were stooped with exhaustion. He slipped off his shoes while unbuttoning his shirt. It was strange to see her father in the dark, doing something so methodical.

Her mother led her across the hall to Aaron's room. His bed was a single. Why were they sleeping here rather than in her room down the hall? She didn't know, but in a way she was glad for it; she didn't feel like going back to her room. "Get in," her mother whispered. "I'm just going to get my pajamas."

Ruby lay in Aaron's bed, where she had never lain before, and waited for her mother to come back. She could hear her across the hall, whispering something, and the thud of a shoe as it hit the floor. Then she was back and she lay down beside Ruby, on her side with one hand on Ruby's shoulder. She didn't say anything. Maybe she thought Ruby was already asleep.

"Mom, is he—"

"Shhh," her mother replied. "Everything's all right. Just go to sleep now. We'll talk in the morning." She leaned over and kissed Ruby's temple. "It's over. Go to sleep."

But Ruby was awake again. Her father and her brother lay in her parents' bed across the hall, and she and her mother lay huddled together in Aaron's. The moonlight cast two long shadows across the ceiling, where Aaron used to have a poster of Wade Boggs from the Red Sox. She thought of Aaron, asleep in his college dorm room, as on any other night.

The house was still again, but it felt different. She heard her mother's words—"It's over"—in her mind like a skipping record. She wanted to believe it, she wanted the words to sink into her bloodstream and relax her into sleep, but she couldn't help but feel that they betrayed the opposite: it had just begun. The events of the night, of the last few days, were like a wave that had lifted her family and moved them here, to these curious sleeping arrangements, her mother's arm around her waist, Aaron's clipped photographs of air force planes surrounding them as they lay curled together. She thought of her empty bed down the hall, of Abe flashing her the peace sign with a toothy grin, of the frogs they had drawn together, the peace frogs, now sitting on her desk, of the way he had bent to touch the trophy she had won. It was all so mysterious, all of it, and she knew her mother wasn't asleep, she could tell from her breathing, but she could hear Nathan's snores and maybe that was a comfort to all of them.

She lay beside her mother and tried to keep her eyes closed and to think of happy things. She tried to count sheep, which sometimes worked for her, and when that didn't work she thought of vocabulary words, pulling the letters apart and lining them up next to one another, reading the words back and forth until they were not words anymore, or letters, but abstract symbols, lines and circles, giant curving symbols full of mysterious meaning, and then she was asleep.

———

The next morning, before they got out of bed, her mother spoke to Ruby plainly about what was happening. At this point, she said, she and Ruby's father understood very little about what had happened to Abe. He was sick, she said, very sick, they didn't know why, but it was an illness just like any other. They would find out more from the doctors, she expected, but Ruby shouldn't worry. He was in the hospital now, which was where he needed to be.

"Of course it's up to you," her mother said, her head propped up on her hand, her salt-and-pepper hair falling down behind her fingers, "but I'm not sure if you should tell your friends about what happened." She traced Ruby's hair along her forehead and tucked it behind her ear. "There is nothing to be ashamed of, that's not what I mean, it's just that your friends are so young, I'm afraid they won't understand. I wouldn't want you to suffer unnecessarily. If they knew, they might not want to come over to play, and then you'd be hurt." She paused, tucking and retucking Ruby's hair, and Ruby could hear the murmur of her father's voice across the hall. Was he saying the same thing to Nathan?

Ruby looked up at the ceiling, allowing her mother to stroke her hair. Was it true that her friends wouldn't understand? The mention of her friends at that moment was a surprise to her; it was as if she had forgotten their existence, and the thought of them—she was supposed to be in Hebrew school this morning!—seemed out of place. Why would her mother think of this, first thing in the morning? "Of course it's your decision," her mother said, "but you might want to wait before you tell anyone."

And so she did. For four years Ruby told no one. She left Abe at the hospital, where he was diagnosed (the closest they could come, the doctors said, though it was not exact) with schizo-affective disorder, where her parents took her to see him, on the locked ward, where he stayed for two months, where he insisted that he be called Dave, and where he picked her up by the waist and held her up to his face, grinning wildly, so he could "look at her." She learned to leave her family at home, her parents talking in hushed tones in their bedroom at night, her father crying in the easy chair in the den—the first and only time she had ever seen him cry—unaware of Ruby in the kitchen, peering around the wall to see him in her mother's arms. She learned to distance herself, to make two Rubys: the Ruby at home and the Ruby elsewhere; the Ruby who saw sad things and the Ruby whom the world saw.

1992

How to Remember

R uby sat on the windowsill of an apartment in Prague, as if it was a bench in a train station and she was preparing to spend the night. This was her pensive pose: she didn't belong here, at fourteen, with her parents—she was an artist, she was an alien teenager on an island of parents and she was sending her alien energy out into the world. She was in a tower of her parents, she thought, and imagined the street full of young people in trench coats, coming in a wave and reaching up.

It was late afternoon and Ruby was in the apartment alone; her parents had gone out for a walk. She had been there, in Prague, with her parents, for almost a week now, and had been cultivating, more and more as the week went on, the feeling that they were flying along on parallel tracks at different altitudes.

In December, over a meal of crispy-skinned chicken, rice, and peas, Ruby's father had declared that he was ready to go back to Czechoslovakia. There was no prelude; they weren't speaking of the topic, and as far as Ruby knew, this was also the first her mother had heard of it. Until then it had always been "Why go back?" and "There's nothing for me there"—a topic closed before it had even opened. Her father had never expressed any interest at all in his home country and, if pressed, would say he considered himself more Israeli than Czech. But sure enough, there it was, just after Ruby's mother had risen from the table to take her plate and the remaining chicken over to the sink. "Ellen," he said, angling his head in her direction, "I've decided. I'm ready to go back to Czechoslovakia."

Ruby's mother stood still for a moment, then turned from the sink to face him. She smiled. She had been waiting for this, Ruby supposed; maybe all these years she had known this would eventually happen. She hardly seemed surprised at all, though she raised her eyebrows, tucked her hair behind her ear, and leaned against the counter as if she needed support.

"Really? You're sure?"

He nodded. "Yes. I'm sure. I'm ready. I want to go."

Ruby's mother nodded back. "Okay, then, we'll go."

They planned the trip for the beginning of June, after Ruby finished with school. She'd be the only one to go with her parents— Aaron had to work, Nathan was taking a summer school class, and Abe was in no shape to leave the country. Her parents organized it; they would stay in Prague, and from there they would take mini trips to the places they wanted to visit: Brno, the city where her father was born, and Terezin, where he was held, as well as a few small towns where his grandparents and cousins had lived. From Prague they would then go to Poland, where they would see Auschwitz and Krakow, and then head for home.

The magnitude of the trip was present and constant, though they barely spoke about it. Ruby and her mother went shopping for a suitcase for Ruby, and it was there with them in the department store while they wheeled the bags around on the tiled floor: this bag would come with her to the concentration camps. Ruby wanted to speak about it, but what could she say? Would her father suddenly remember the horror he had so long forgotten? Nothing would be known until they arrived. One night, sitting on the side of Ruby's bed, her mother told her that she should try not to have expectations, for it was highly possible he would still remember nothing. Ruby felt the oncoming confirmation of a subject she had long been obsessed with, questions she'd never been able to articulate, topics she had never known how to address. She tried not to elevate it in her mind— They were going to the camps! The camps were real! Her father was a survivor! Gas chambers, barracks, Nazis, little yellow stars—and did her best just to focus on school, and to pack her suitcase as if they were going on vacation to Maine.

They boarded the plane and flew to Prague. They spent a week seeing the city, which Ruby loved; Prague suited her, she felt, it was old and literary and full of secrets. On the second day, they went to the old Jewish cemetery in the section of Prague called the Jewish Quarter, a designation that in itself was a clue to the grand difference between these streets she stood on and her faraway home. *The Jewish Quarter?* A place in a city where only Jews lived? How was this truly a reality, how was it that for people who grew up in this town the Jewish Quarter was as normal as the return addresses they wrote on their envelopes? She knew no equivalent to this. The stones in the cemetery were tall and flat and crumbling, covered with a cloudy Hebrew, and they leaned toward each other, often touching, forming a crowded chorus of ancient death.

There was a mental leap required in this country, an understanding of oppression that Ruby wasn't sure she was capable of. What did she know about anti-Semitism? It was an abstract concept, a bolt of historical lightning that touched her life but that she couldn't see. These people buried beneath her feet were all Jews; she was a Jew; okay, so what? She could know this as a fact, but she had trouble making meaning of it. What did it really mean, to be Jewish? What did it mean that she belonged in this part of this city, in this cemetery, or with the people buried beneath her feet? What was it that marked her as a Jew, and what was it that made all of them—*Jews,* even the word was odd to her—different from the rest of the city's occupants? As they pushed through the gate on their way out, her father shook his head and said, softly, so Ruby wondered who he was speaking to, "We were never Czechs, we were always just Jews."

She was the only one of her father's children to see this, the chosen witness, though she couldn't fully grasp what she was witness to. At times, while the three of them sat at the table drinking tea before they went to sleep, the teacups hanging on the wall of the kitchen in the apartment struck Ruby as unreal, and she looked at her father and wondered how it was for him, his birth language returning after all these years, hearing it spoken all around him, seeing it written on street signs and newspapers and brochures. At night they planned their next day, and he was tireless and excited but not at all emotional or reflective. So far, though, they had not gone to the heart of the trip: Terezin.

After her parents left for their walk, Ruby explored the apartment, which they had rented for the two weeks that they were in Czechoslovakia. It belonged to a family named the Caneks—this was all the information Ruby knew. Her parents thought it would be cheaper and more fun to stay in an actual apartment—"to really have a home base," as Ruby's mother put it—so the result was that Ruby and her parents overlaid themselves on another family's home like stickers over a photograph. It was strange, and gave Ruby a dreamlike feeling, a sense of confusion about which of them were the more ghostlike people—the family who had created this space, whose belongings were stashed into drawers, or she and her parents, who would pass through the apartment and never return.

Ruby went slowly from room to room, opening drawers, trying to pry open locked cabinets. In the top drawer of the dresser in her room, where the Canek daughter also slept, she found a nearly full pack of cigarettes, slid one from the pack, and placed it between her lips. The smell of it was intoxicating: it smelled of deviance, of privacy, of Europe, of home.

The first time she'd ever had a cigarette was the day before Featherton's eighth-grade graduation last year, when Keri Grange, the first girl in their class to have a boyfriend, had all the popular girls over to her house to spend the night. They had walked around Harvard Square in a big group. It was drizzling, and Keri wore a blue raincoat with a huge hood. She carried multiple packs of cigarettes in her pockets, and offered them over and over to everyone ("Take your pick," she said, holding the pocket open), long after they all stopped wanting any, so that finally she was the only one who kept smoking.

Ruby didn't feel comfortable in the group, and was sure that her being invited was some kind of fluke; she didn't feel that these girls were really her friends, except maybe for Jill Krist, tall and blond and messy, with big breasts and loose-fitting sweaters and a quick laugh, who for some reason had never intimidated Ruby and whom she was slowly beginning to trust. Ruby had never been popular at Featherton since entering at the beginning of seventh grade; the transition from her old school had been hard for her. Her diligence about her schoolwork was no longer a novelty at private school, in a population of kids on the whole far more privileged than the people she knew in elementary school. Zoë Creswell, her best friend at Featherton, didn't trust the popular girls, even Jill Krist, and told Ruby so loudly and with aplomb every chance she got.

Several weeks before Ruby came to Prague with her parents, she'd smoked pot for the first time with Jill. It was one of the few times they had spent together without any other girls, and the lingering novelty lent a sense of excitement to the day even before the drugs came into play.

Drugs had always been vilified in the Bronstein household—both Ruby's parents claimed to have never been drunk—and Ruby never thought she'd try any substances. When her father came across Nathan and his friend Chris listening to Bob Marley's album *Catch a Fire* one afternoon in the den, he caught one glance of the album cover, with a picture of Marley holding a thick joint to his lips, grew solemn, and told Nathan that he must cut the joint from the picture if he was going to be allowed to keep the record. Nathan and Chris cut the joint out and thought it was hilarious, the picture of Bob Marley holding a fat hole to his mouth.

Ruby and Jill smoked pot near Jill's house in Quincy, sitting underneath a train bridge on two rocks among the tall grasses. Jill had gotten the pot and the little pink pipe from her sister, Tara, who was four years older and did a lot of drugs. Tara had tried to kill herself earlier in the year by swallowing an entire bottle of painkillers stolen from their father's medicine cabinet. The first time Ruby slept over at Jill's house was a few weeks after the incident, and Jill told Ruby about it—reluctantly at first, in the dark, and then more freely. Just knowing about the event endeared Jill to Ruby. Most of the girls they went to school with had fake-perfect home lives—neat houses with couches you weren't supposed to sit on, flowered wallpaper and dressing tables in their bedrooms, parents who wore pressed khaki and seemed never to raise their voices. Knowing that things in Jill's house were imperfect and difficult, and that she didn't mind if Ruby knew about it, allowed Ruby to trust her.

That day, sitting beneath the train bridge, Ruby felt nothing from the pot but felt closer to Jill than ever. She liked the foreignness of her and of the smoking, the newness of this activity and this friend. "Take it into your lungs and then hold your breath before you let it out," Jill told her, and Ruby watched how she did it, thinking there was so much Jill knew that she didn't.

Jill spoke of Tara and the stash of pot that she had ransacked as if it was as commonplace to her as a toothbrush. "She'll never notice," she said with a wave of her hand, and then, softly, "she doesn't notice much these days." She took a hit, held it, and as she blew out the smoke added: "except every little thing my mom does." She laughed.

Jill told Ruby about Tara's eating disorder, and about the way her mother bought Tara nonfat foods and allowed her to eat only carrots for lunch and dinner. She told Ruby about Tara's new boyfriend, who brought more and more drugs into the house, how their parents tried to make rules but Tara would laugh at them, a laugh full of hate. Jill made jokes about everything, but still she let the stories roll off her tongue, and the way she let them come was a revelation to Ruby.

Here, then, was how Ruby first broke the silence that had begun with Abe's breakdown. Before she knew it, she was sharing her own stories. They rushed from her; she pushed them out like the smoke in her lungs. Her brother Abraham was sick too, yes, a different sick; he'd never tried to kill himself, not that she knew of, she tried to stay out of his life as much as she could. He lived in an apartment now in Providence with a friend of his from music camp, which she knew was a bad idea because of how her parents spoke about it, how they called the friend a "lowlife," how they pleaded with Abe on the phone to clean the place, how her mother offered more than once to go down there and clean it for him, and had tried a couple different times and always came back depleted and upset. Abe had a job as a dishwasher and repeatedly burned his hands.

"My mom didn't want him to go live there," she said. "She told my dad she didn't think he was well enough, and they shouldn't let him go, but my dad said they had to let him try to live his own life. I think he just didn't want him at home anymore." Ruby hadn't been aware that she thought this until she heard the words come from her mouth. She looked up at the train bridge, the long grass that was growing over its side, hanging down like knotted hair. "I know I didn't."

Jill was attentive, and she said "yeah" and nodded, looking down between her legs at the pebbles beneath them. She picked up a few and threw them, one by one, across the little stream under the bridge to the matching ridge on the other side.

"My parents fight about it still," Ruby said. "My mom wants to bring him home but my dad says as long as he can hold a job they shouldn't."

She stopped and handed Jill the pipe. "I've never told anyone about my brother before."

"Really?" Jill brought the pipe to her mouth with one hand and lit it with the other. She shot Ruby a quick glance, holding in the smoke.

Ruby nodded. "Yeah."

"Wow." Jill exhaled.

Ruby picked up some pebbles and let them fall through her fingers. "I mean if you meet him you can pretty much tell, but I've never really officially told anyone. When people ask, I generally just say he's 'trying to figure himself out'"—she brought her fingers up as quotation marks—"or something like that."

Jill turned the pipe upside down and hit it against her leg. Evidently it was finished. "I think you said that to me before."

Ruby laughed, surprised; being caught in the reality of this embarrassed her. "I did?"

"Yeah. I came over once, last year I think, and I met him, and I remember when I asked you about him you just shrugged it off. I figured he was just superweird and you guys didn't get along."

Ruby felt suddenly very sad. The thrill of letting her secret out was reined in by the feeling that there was still more to it, that there was so much more, and that her friend, even if she heard it, even if she could in some way relate, didn't and couldn't really understand what it meant. She wanted to tell Jill more, she wanted to tell her everything there was to tell, everything she knew, and at the same time she wanted never to speak again. She wondered if it had been a bad idea to say anything; she felt a quick pang of guilt, and resentment—at Abe, at Jill for being so blasé about what she had just been told—and then it passed.

"Do you feel anything?" Jill asked. She was looking at Ruby and smiling.

It took Ruby a second to realize she meant the pot. She thought about it, looking around at their surroundings. The grass hanging down off the train bridge seemed a little sharper, maybe, like she had just gotten a slightly better prescription on her glasses, but the light in the sky was dimmer now, and she couldn't be sure of anything. "Not really," she said. "Maybe a little bit sharper, but I might be making that up."

"Yeah," said Jill. "Sometimes it takes a couple times to feel it." She looked up at the bridge and put the pipe back in the little knitted sack in which she had carried it. "Trust me," she said, "when you feel it, you'll know."

Ruby thought of all this as she sat on the windowsill in Prague, taking a few tentative puffs of the cigarette, blowing the smoke quickly out the open window, and then snuffing the cigarette out on the cement of the building and letting it drop down into the street.

She went to the bathroom to wash her hands and brush her teeth. A few minutes later she heard her parents turning the key in the lock. She was nervous, coming out of the bathroom, but they didn't notice. They were in good moods and came in holding each other by the arm and laughing, even though the day before they had fought bitterly in a crowded open square and had had to separate for a few hours, Ruby's father going off to who knows where, and Ruby and her mother—after a period in which Ruby's mother cried, and cursed her father, and said things like "I don't know, Ruby, I just don't know"—walking quietly through the streets, her mother commenting on stores and architecture and trying to pretend that she wasn't still seething and preoccupied.

They hadn't fought over anything important—it started with the guidebook, and Ruby's mother reading information from it about the castle in the square, where there were two soldiers, the kind who weren't supposed to move no matter what. Ruby's father was irritated for some reason, it was starting to rain and they didn't have an umbrella and they had been walking all day, maybe he was just exhausted, and he said he was tired of that guidebook, he was tired of her being so married to that goddamn guidebook, couldn't they do anything without that thing? Which was a fair point, Ruby thought, because she was getting a little tired of the book herself, but her father was mean about it, and he snapped, and her mother was hurt and defensive, and came back at him, saying, Well, what did he want to do, and maybe if he made more of an effort to plan what they were doing, and here they were in *his* goddamn country but she was doing all the work, and why didn't he *try* a little bit, she was only trying to help, and let's see how far he got without her and her guidebook.

The fight had gone on longer than it should have, it had escalated and grown much larger than any of the tiffs they had had the rest of the week, and her mother had been trying to control herself, they were in a public square, she was standing stiff and clutching the guidebook in her fist, but finally she had yelled "I can't take it anymore!" and "I don't even want to see you anymore!" and turned and walked away, and when Ruby didn't follow for a second she turned back and said "Come *on*, Ruby!" in a voice that was shaking. Ruby looked to her father, who watched them, his own fists curled, his camera bag over his shoulder—Where would he go? Would she rather go with him?—and then she ran to catch up to her mother.

It wasn't unusual for her parents to fight, nor was it unusual for them to fight in front of her. Neither of them would ever give in, and though they always made up, Ruby never understood how it happened. She was pretty sure they rarely apologized; certainly her father never apologized to *her* when they fought, never. Ruby had always had difficulty relating to him, but in the last few years, as she grew, it had gotten worse. None of her friends had fathers who came to "inspect" their rooms two or three times after they cleaned them, who insisted they be home every Friday night, who made them set the table though their brothers never had to, who would allow them only two hours of TV a week. None of her friends had fathers who never came to their sporting events but who attended all of their violin recitals; who would never let them out of Hebrew school, ever; who wouldn't let them go to the mall on Saturdays. Her father had no idea what it was like to be her! Many pages of Ruby's journal were covered with her furious scrawl, the words *I Hate You* ripped into the pages from pressing so hard. She'd always feel guilty afterward and try to cross it out, writing *no I don't* in the margins just in case someone ever read it.

She rarely felt this way about her mother, but Ruby was her mother's baby; after three boys, she was the gift her mother had always wanted. And just by being an American, and by being a woman, and by having had two parents her whole life, Ruby's mother was able to understand more about Ruby than her father ever could. Like her father, her mother had come a long way from home: she was Jewish now, whereas she had been raised Catholic; she had money now, whereas she had not when she was younger. As Ruby saw it, both her parents had come from nothing to something—her mother from a four-room apartment with five occupants and her father from a kibbutz with a house full of other young people (not to mention the concentration camp, or the Israeli army barracks)—they had come from other worlds where they had learned the value of the life they lived now in the land of suburbia, and the value of the life they gave to their children. But in Ruby's opinion, her mother's changes had made her softer, while her father's had made him anything but—a steely survivor who had very little tolerance for a young girl's weaknesses or wishes.

For as long as Ruby could remember, her parents had occasionally fought, though since Abe got sick their fighting had grown worse, the fights louder, more frequent, and more drawn out. At home, it was often frightening. She could remember more than one night when she lay in bed and listened to them, their voices carrying to her room in two streams: through the dining room, up the stairs, and through the door at the far end of her room, and out the kitchen windows, into the driveway, and up to the window next to her bed. She had learned to be more frightened of the fights that were short and intense, and ended with a long silence—these were made up of real anger—whereas the other ones, with prolonged arguing, arose more from a desire to disagree and to be proven right.

That fight in the square in Prague would be the last fight Ruby would ever witness between her parents.

———

The next day, a taxi took them from Prague to Terezin. The driver, whose name was Ivan, met them on the curb by the bus station, where the air was sour and thick with dark smoke. Ivan was a small man with pale hair and a mustache, dressed in jeans with a jean jacket. He shook hands with Ruby's father and mother, and then bent at the waist to shake hers. The ride took almost an hour. The cab smelled like coconut and aftershave. Ruby and her mother sat in the backseat, her mother's hand occasionally reaching over to the middle to rest on Ruby's. In the front, Ivan and Ruby's father spoke quickly to each other, a constant stream of prattle that Ruby's father frequently turned around to explain. Ruby recognized by now the expression in her father's eyes when he was speaking Czech, animated with the excitement of his original tongue.

She was becoming accustomed to her father's first language. Strange, guttural sounds, strung together with dips in inflection, entire phrases without vowels coming from his mouth—these were new noises, noises she was hearing in the present though they betrayed a link to a distant past. Czech, this language her father automatically understood though he had not spoken it in nearly forty years, was flowing from his mouth as smoothly as from the mouth of their cabdriver, who had lived in Prague his whole life. It was difficult for her to grasp. Perhaps more than anything else on the trip, this string of noise was proof to her of the journey that had begun here, with her father as a child, these sounds filling his tiny head. The language made it real, even more so now as they headed toward the camp Ruby had been trying to imagine her whole life. While they were in Prague she had managed to distance herself from it, this was just a trip she was on with her parents, she was safe inside their parental orbit, she could put her headphones on and listen to R.E.M. and think normal teenage thoughts—but as she sat in the cab on the way to Terezin listening to her father speak Czech, she could feel the trip shift inside her chest. Suddenly she was aware of the power of that cab, rolling through the countryside now with its cargo, her father traveling back to a place from which he had come so far, which maybe seemed as unreal to him as it did to Ruby, and Ruby and her mother in the backseat as witnesses, his women, flanking him, tuned in to his every movement as human thermometers for memories or for pain. Everything else drifted away: Terezin was real, her father's past was real, and they were traveling toward it.

"He says his grandfather was Jewish," her father was saying over the seat. "He married a non-Jew to the disgrace of his entire village and moved away."

He looked back to Ivan, who was emitting another string of guttural consonants. "He says he's always sympathized with Jews because of his grandfather," her father translated, watching Ivan as he spoke. "Now the entire village he lived in is gone. Not a single Jew left."

He shook his head and said something to Ivan that he did not translate, a brief phrase that fell from his mouth and lay in the air of the car. He turned and looked out his window.

The trip wore on, and her father grew silent. The countryside passed by, wooded and dry. Off the highway, they drove along narrow country roads, passing small stores and cottages, and occasionally apartment buildings a few stories high. The landscape was bright with sun, but it seemed to Ruby that there was an air of sadness about the streets. They passed a few people, all old, walking slowly with their heads down. Where were the children? Everything she saw was a shade of brown or gray. She thought of her father, coming out of the cemetery gate saying *We were never Czechs, we were always just Jews.*

Ivan spoke, and her father turned to the backseat to tell them they were almost there. Ruby looked at him, trying to read the level of tension in his shoulders. Was he nervous? Did he feel a knot in his stomach? What was he thinking of?

They drove between what looked like two identical houses on either side of the road, their roofs covered in a thick brown grass. They seemed to have passed into another town just like the ones before it, although even more empty. After a few more minutes they pulled over to the right-hand curb, in front of a central town square with a manicured lawn. "Here we are," her father said. His voice was curiously void of expression.

"Theresienstadt," said Ivan, looking ahead.

• • •

Throughout her life, Ruby had pored over photographs, history textbooks, Hebrew school pamphlets, and documentaries, any images or texts she came across that could enlighten her as to what her father had faced as a boy. Knowing as little as she did, she placed him in the face of every small child she came across. Children holding on to their mothers' hands, waiting for trains, or peering out through barbed wire; children, their heads shaved, screaming as they were torn from the arms of their parents, their faces distorted in perpetual wails, their arms reaching toward the receding figures of the people who loved them. Real children, children who died, children who survived, actors, the children of stories and novels and history books, each one of them became her father, and yet she never lost hold of the painful reality that none of them were.

Gradually, even the very fact of her Jewishness came to seem strange to her; at times even the word, *Jewish,* seemed to connote something foreign and far away. In synagogue on Saturday mornings, she sat next to her father and heard him singing out, and though she did not herself feel connected to the words, she let her father's history imbue them with meaning. When she was bored, she took her father's hand in her lap and played with the veins that snaked over the surface of his skin—poking them, trying to push them together, to understand their determination to flow underneath her pressing fingers.

She knew, because her mother had told her, that her father had proclaimed himself an atheist. But where, then, was the explanation for his firm insistence on the traditions of Judaism, and for the glow that would surround him when he arrived at synagogue, freshly shaven, in a newly pressed suit? What could he remember, and what did he force himself to forget? Ruby looked at her father as if at a curtain over a movie screen—trying desperately to see the images behind the fabric, waiting for the moment when the sides would part and the mystery be revealed. His Judaism, his life story, was a mammoth statue that sat at the entrance to their lives. His Judaism had changed her mother's life, it had made her mother into the committed Jew that she was; it was an accepted part of all of their lives, and yet there was little talk of God, or really of belief at all. The only consistent tenet of Judaism that Ruby heard her father espouse was one she found both inspiring and confusing: "Life is the highest good," he'd say, as he caught spiders and flies and beetles and released them outside. "Whenever it is possible, choose life." This fit with his revulsion from guns and violence of all kinds, but how did it fit with his insistence on her learning to say the mourner's Kaddish?

For most of her childhood, it was her mother Ruby clung to; her father was uninterested in her, she felt, he never wanted to hear her stories or see her drawings, he just wanted her to get good grades and clean her room and stay "seen and not heard." It was only on this trip, for the first time, that Ruby began to truly be friends with her father—that they began to laugh together, to have private jokes, to share—and that she began to feel connected to his past, to believe in it, and to understand the way it was connected to the man she knew. It was only on this trip that she began to feel the way her father loved her, and to feel that maybe someday his secrets would make sense to her.

Once out of the car, Ruby was able to identify how Terezin was different from other towns they had passed through: there were no freestanding houses. All of the buildings she saw as they circled the square on their way toward the museum were huge and sprawling, nearly dilapidated, seemingly out of place against the backdrop of the square, with its close-cropped lawn and occasional trees. As they walked around it, her father told them that the Nazis had planted flowers there—"So many flowers, I remember them here"—for when the Red Cross was coming to "inspect." "They brought us out and paraded us around like we were at summer camp," he said, his eyes fixed on the grass.

At the head of the square, they entered a building with a sign outside that said GHETTO MUSEUM; one room with its walls plastered with photographs and information about the concentration camp, maps showing where the different barracks used to be and who their occupants had been. Terezin, they learned, was now an army base, home to hundreds of Czech soldiers and their families. Most of the barracks had been renovated, turned into conventional apartments and army housing. They were not to venture off the main path, the woman at the desk told them. These were people's homes now, she said, people lived here now.

People lived here now? Ruby couldn't wrap her mind around this fact. This was a town that people lived in?

"We'll see whatever we damn well please," Ruby's father said as soon as they were out on the street. He was holding their maps. "I didn't come all this way just to walk on paths."

They stepped off the curb and rounded a corner, walking for a while in silence. The street was empty and bathed in sunlight; there were no cars or noises, and they walked in the middle of the cracked pavement. On either side of them rose buildings, each a few stories high and a block long. Occasionally Ruby saw, or thought she saw, blank faces peering at them through thick windowpanes, but whenever she looked more closely they were gone.

As they walked, she felt the past swirl around them. She was walking—her feet were in front of her, her arms swinging by her sides, her parents ahead of her—and yet she was sure that, in a way, she was not here, on this street, in her body. If they were all here, she felt, now, walking on the empty street, then they had all just as surely been here fifty years ago. Thin bodies struggled around the corners, Jewish bodies, women with sagging breasts under light dresses, children with holes in their shoes, men in uniforms with swastikas on their arms and guns over their shoulders: countless ghosts passing them as they made their way down the street. Yet even as she saw them, even as she felt their presence and their pain, Ruby was aware that they were her own constructions, images lifted from books and planted, in her mind, on the sidewalk. She didn't know what it had been like then; even if she tried she couldn't imagine it. All she heard were their footsteps on the gravelly pavement; all she saw were her parents, and the street, and her own body moving along it.

They walked down a few streets, her father rarely looking at the map that he carried. He seemed either determined or dazed, Ruby couldn't decide. They saw no one, only the tall concrete buildings, each one a different drab color, and an occasional sad and lonely-looking tree. Above them, the sky was blue and beautiful, but it seemed to Ruby that the light didn't reach them down on the ground.

Finally they crossed a street and came to a round, reddish building with high, pockmarked walls. None of the other buildings they had passed had been round; this one reminded Ruby of the Colosseum. Her father slowed to a stop.

"What is it?" asked her mother.

"It's—" he started, and then stopped. His eyes were fixed ahead, through the gate at the entrance, where two men, both in uniform, stood talking.

"What is it, Josef?" Ruby's mother said again, this time standing next to him.

Ruby looked at her father. His eyes were narrowed, as if he were trying to see through time.

"I think," he said, taking one step closer to the gate, "I'm not sure, but I think this might have been where we first came, when we first got here. I just have this feeling. I don't know."

He took another step. "Wait here, I'm going to talk to them."

Ruby watched as her father approached the uniformed men and spoke, gesturing to himself, the gate, and the space behind them. Her mother started to follow him, then stopped herself and came back to Ruby.

The soldiers looked at each other and then shook their heads slowly. Quick, choppy sounds came from their mouths. Her father gestured out to the street, his arm wide, and his voice rose. The men shook their heads faster. One of them raised his hands, palms up, by his shoulders.

When her father came back, he was visibly agitated. He spoke through his teeth. "They won't let me in. They said only the soldiers that live there are allowed in. Soldiers and their families. Can you believe that? They live there now, so they won't let me in."

Ruby's mother's jaw dropped. "That's outrageous. Did you tell them who you were?"

He paused, looking back at the men. He seemed to have barely heard her. His voice was a strained whisper. "They don't even know what this place *was*. Can you believe it? That's why they don't want us walking around here. I tried to tell them, and they looked at me like I was speaking another language. I am just some *foreigner* to them."

He put his hands in his pockets and took them out again. "I'm pretty sure," he said, shifting his feet and looking down. "I remember waiting in there when we first got here. I just have this feeling." He shook his head. "I'm sure I remember. There were all these people, everyone was milling around, there were suitcases and we had to wait a long time. That's where they separated me from my parents."

He looked at Ruby's mother, who had an expression on her face Ruby wasn't sure she'd ever seen, except maybe when she was sick and her mother was bending over her to take her temperature. His words spit from his mouth. "They're trying to protect the poor soldiers and their families from what really went on here. It's sick."

"There must be a way in," said her mother gently. Ruby could tell she didn't know what else to say. "Tell them we won't leave until we can go in. You've come all this way, Josef, it's not right."

He looked down at his feet, thinking, for what seemed to Ruby a long minute. Then he turned and walked quickly back toward the men. When he reached them, the sounds came fast from his mouth, his arms quick pinwheels at his sides. Ruby, watching her father, imagined his hands when he was a boy; how small and empty they must have been when his parents' hands were removed from their grip. What would they have held on to, those hands, after that?

Finally, the men stepped backward, and one of them reached down to open the gate. Ruby's father turned back and gestured for them to come along. He looked stern and impatient.

They went through the gate. Inside, there was a brief tunnel, a dim staircase going up to their left, presumably to the apartments, and to their right a round, paved courtyard surrounded by the walls of the building. Ruby wasn't sure she'd ever seen a building like this, the inside gouged out and exposed to the elements. What was the point, really, in having a huge courtyard that was hidden from the street? It was like a gladiator arena, she thought, and as they moved past the guards and into the open space, she imagined a lion charging at them. Was it a trap? Ruby looked up at the building around them, and caught the eye of a woman with a scarf wrapped around her hair leaning from a window. Before Ruby and her parents arrived, what had this woman been looking at? She watched Ruby with no expression.

Ruby's mother was watching her father. He stood still, his hands in his pockets; in the wide, empty space, he appeared small, as he rarely did.

"Well?" her mother asked him after a few minutes.

He shook his head, slowly, his eyes wide. "Nothing," he said. "I don't remember a thing."

• • •

Back outside, they walked on, turned a corner and walked two more blocks, Ruby's father occasionally consulting his map. The lower levels of all the buildings they passed were darker and seemed slightly more weathered than the upper floors, and Ruby's father said that the concrete of the first floors was the original, the upper floors additions. Ruby wondered, if the buildings had been renovated, why were the other floors weathered too? All of the buildings were crumbling, as if there had been earthquakes here, as if there had been shoot-outs in the streets.

At the next corner was an enormous gray building, easily the biggest they'd seen, extending for what looked like many blocks. At the front of the building, its towering gates were held together loosely with a rope. "This was the men's barracks," her father said, consulting his map, then folding it and putting it in his pocket. He stood before the opening in the gates. "This is where my father was."

They peered in. Just inside the gate there was a narrow entryway with a guard booth on the left-hand side; past that, an enclosed concrete courtyard opened up, about the size of half a football field. The entryway was dim and the booth was deserted. The courtyard was bright with sun.

"Let's go in," her father said. He moved the rope and pulled on one of the gates, and it creaked open just enough for them to slip through.

It was more of a stadium than a barracks, its inner courtyard similar to the round apartment building's they had just been in. Everything was perfectly symmetrical: from under the rounded doorway of the entryway they could see across the courtyard to an identical doorway on the far side, which then opened up onto an identical courtyard, to another doorway, and so on, for what could easily have been miles. All along the walls were windows, evenly spaced and crumbling, looking out from who knew what sorts of rooms. The pale yellow of the walls was stained with water damage, in some places so severely that it was a dark gray. Clumps of weeds thrust through the crumbling concrete floor, which was divided almost perfectly in half by deep shadow.

The effect was dizzying. Every wall looked the same, each window vacant and desperate. Silence hung over the barracks. They stepped into the courtyard, the three of them, and the crunch of their feet on the gravel covering the concrete reverberated across the space.

"I remember," Ruby's father said, his words tentative, as if he was unsure his voice would penetrate the silence. "We used to play soccer in here."

He paused, looking up at the windows on the sides of the courtyard. "Yes," he said. "We used to play down here, right here on these stones. I remember the men used to watch us from up there." He pointed to the second story, where there was a length of open landing. "I remember my father watching me." After he spoke, his gaze lingered on the upstairs windows.

Ruby watched him watch them, imagining her father as a boy— dark curls, shorts, skinny legs, knees like knobs—running in a group of other boys (identically dressed, forced to look alike) after a deflated ball that danced over the concrete. She tried to hear the sounds from fifty years ago—the shouts of boys united by sport, playing not because they wanted to but because they were told to, guards watching from the sidelines. She tried to imagine the tug in her father-as-a-boy's heart when he noticed his father watching from the window; she tried to feel the connection between father and son as it was felt then, over a great distance; the way the sounds of the game would change for the son as he played (slowing, maybe, swirling), his father's gaze a filter through which all of his movements would pass. How he must have wanted to yell to his father, she thought; how he must have wished he could feel his arms around him.

Her father raised his eyebrows and lowered his gaze once more to the courtyard. The moment was past, she knew. He would say no more.

"Let's go in," her father said, gesturing to one of the doorways on the side, through which they could see stairs. They followed him into a dark stairwell and up into a long hallway with doorways opening off both sides. It was like the hallway of a long-deserted mental hospital, Ruby thought, with secrets hanging thick in the air. Their footsteps echoed through the darkness. She tried to hear the sounds of a building full of men—shouts, snores, insults, even whispers—but heard only their own footsteps.

She looked into the rooms as they walked by. The white walls were crumbling, the windows looked out onto the deserted courtyard; in some rooms there were metal bunks with thin, striped mattresses. Ruby's father stopped in the doorway of one of the rooms, and Ruby and her mother stopped behind him, peering in. The sun cast a parallelogram of light onto the mattress on the bed.

"I came up here once to visit my father," he said without turning around. "I came only once. It was the last time I ever saw him."

Ruby couldn't see her father's face, but over his shoulder she could see the bed. Her mother was standing next to him, and she had her hand on the underside of his elbow. "All I remember," he said, "is that he was lying on his bed, it looked just like this, and the light was coming in the window. Everything was very noisy, but in the room it was very quiet. He looked very thin and very sick. He was wearing these socks with holes in them, and flies were buzzing around his feet."

He stopped, still staring at the bed. "That's all I remember. Just those socks and the flies." The memory dropped into the stale air of the barracks hallway and lingered there. For a moment, there was a figure on the bed, and there were noises, and there were flies, and then there was nothing.

The three of them looked into the room. Her mother moved her hand to her father's shoulder. Quickly, he turned and said, "Come, let's go," and they were walking away.

———

Later, as they returned to the main square and the waiting cab, they walked along the stone fortification enclosing the camp, overgrown with brown grass and eager weeds poking through the stones. It took Ruby a fair distance of walking along the wall to realize that it encircled the whole town, and that earlier, when they had passed through those two identical "houses" on either side of the road, they had been crossing into the camp. When her father was imprisoned here, there had been no such way out. What would it be like, to go for a walk from where you lived and come to a wall? What would that do to a child, to her?

Ruby walked next to her father. Her mother walked on the other side of him, looking ahead, and Ruby briefly thought of them as his guards, moving him through this perilous place of memory. This man next to her was her father, she thought—his blood flowed in her veins—and this strange place was familiar to him as from another life, a bad, reoccurring dream. Her father had been imprisoned inside these walls when he was a young boy. The man with the socks with holes in them was her grandfather, who sang in the local synagogue, the man who, before he lay on that mattress with flies buzzing around his feet, had been a leader in the Jewish community with a promising, healthy son: her father.

She repeated these words to herself and looked around her—the street, the buildings, the sky—trying to burn the reality into her brain, trying to understand it all before they left this place forever. Her father as a boy; her father imprisoned; seven years old; eight, nine, ten, eleven. She tried to imagine him walking the streets, drinking milk, a young Jewish Czech boy, not a word of English in his head, not an inkling yet of his future, of what he would become, of her mother or their house or their four children. She thought of herself at those ages, trying to conceive of how it would be to be fourteen, her age, and to have come out of this place just three years before. How would she feel about anything, then? How would she feel about humans, about the world, about Judaism, about God?

It was impossible; she could not make the leap. She was herself; she had not been here as a child, but he had. She looked at him, walking next to her, a fifty-eight-year old man, and thought of how proud he was last year when she was Bat Mitzvahed, grinning wildly, hugging her tight. Was all of her father's insistence on Judaism a way to get back at this place, to live determined not to give in to the wasteland of that courtyard where he played soccer with a barely inflated ball to the ridicule of soldiers, not to give in to the ideology that killed his father and destroyed his family? He had kept Judaism, she supposed, just as it was, except he had cut out God. Was this an act of revenge? How could you come through this place and still believe in your prayers, the praise you sent to an unknown entity in the sky?

She looked down at her legs, walking next to her father's. In a few moments she noticed with a shock that her strides were almost the same length as his. When had this happened? She watched with sudden amazement the way her father's leg would come out just a few inches in front of hers, and then the two of them—her leg and his—would return in sync to the backs of their bodies.

She turned her head to look up at him, and saw that he too was watching their legs. He seemed to be observing them with curiosity, and she felt he was seeing them as they were: strong and full of life. She allowed this observation to bolster her and tried to speak through the layers of years. "Dad," she said, looking up at his face, "how . . ." She tried to think of the right question and said the first one that came to her. "How do you feel?"

For a second he looked surprised. He took his eyes from her legs and looked down at her. "I . . ." he began, smiling at her, then stopped and looked away. He shrugged. "I don't know." She thought she saw him struggling, thinking of what to say, his bushy eyebrows furrowed. Then he shook his head. "What can I say?" It seemed to Ruby that his accent was suddenly thicker. "It's just life, you know? Life is very strange."

He shrugged again and smiled down at her, as if from a joke they shared. He reached over to take her hand and gestured to her legs with his head. "You're getting so tall," he said, giving her hand a squeeze, and then looked back at their feet.

Three weeks later, he was diagnosed with the brain tumor that would kill him.

1994

Robot, Now Fly

I t was May, the Sunday before the junior prom, and Ruby was in her bed talking to her friend Tim on the phone. The sound of his voice calmed her. She closed her eyes to concentrate, trying to visualize his voice, trying to make it big and wide. She wished he would just talk; she wished she could hear him talk on and on; she wished she could dive into his voice, ride his voice like a slide, from her house to his, from her bedroom through the phone and down his throat, into his body, into his normal life. She wished he would tell her stories, endless stories, the sound of his voice moving through her body like a warm liquid.

He was telling her about his cat, Bobo, who had just given birth to kittens. "It had been three days since anyone had seen her. We started to get worried," he said. *"Naturally."* She could hear him smiling.

Ruby laughed. Tim's house was notorious among her friends for its animals. His family had a dog and two cats, a gerbil, and a parakeet that hung in their kitchen in a cage so crowded with toys and dishes of food, a white slab for beak sharpening, and two mirrors, the bird barely had space to move. When Ruby looked in at the bird obsessively staring into the mirror, she always made the same joke: "Oh, he definitely doesn't need company. Look! There are two other birds in there!"

Tim's house was generally overcrowded, even though Tim had only two siblings and the house was large. The TV in the living room was almost always on—Ruby and her friends joked that it was "tired, oh so tired"—and anything perishable in their refrigerator was usually well past its prime ("Wait! Smell that first!").

"We *searched* the house and couldn't find her," he was saying. "Then my brother found her under the couch, dude, the one in front of the TV, and she had seven little babies around her, all wet and gross. Can you believe that? It's like a freaking animal show over here now."

Ruby laughed. Something like that would never go unnoticed in her house, and not just because there would never be a cat in her house in the first place. "Wow. I can't believe that. I mean, you must have known she was about to have babies, right?"

"Well yeah, sure, of course! But we didn't know she'd go under the couch to do it!"

They laughed. This was what she and Tim did most often together.

"Well of course," she said.

"Yeah, anyway," Tim said. "It actually was pretty cool. They're so small, you know? I've never seen anything so small and alive."

She imagined Tim and his family lifting the skirt on the couch to peer underneath, pulling out the whimpering kittens and holding them in their palms. The luxury they had, she thought vaguely, of being able to examine that moment of new life.

"Yeah," she said.

Ruby liked to talk to Tim just before she went to sleep, with only her bedside light on, or with no light at all. Just before she called him, almost every night, she brushed her teeth and climbed between her sheets. Most nights she talked to him while looking out the window at the moon. It made her feel she had something secret, while she talked to him, something all her own. Talking to Tim when she was supposedly sleeping was a secret from her mother; looking out at the moon while she talked to him, cherishing his voice, was a secret from Tim.

"So," she said, lying on her side, the phone resting on her ear, "you got any ideas about who you're going to take to this prom thing next week?"

"The prom?" Tim answered quickly. "Oh, I don't know"—she could hear his smile again—"I was thinking, maybe I won't even go."

She heard the squeak of his desk chair as he leaned back in it. "I think I might just stay here with my parents. You know, make popcorn?"

"Yeah," she said. "That will be a lot more fun."

This was classic Tim. The junior prom was Friday. She knew they would go together—at this point it was too late to go with anyone else—but she didn't want to be the one to ask. This was the kind of thing Tim always did: avoiding the issue until the last minute, when she brought it up.

"Anyway, I don't know," he said. "I'm still mulling it over."

"Well, you better mull fast, my friend, or there won't be anyone left to ask."

"Right." He laughed. "Gotcha."

They hung up, and she lay down in the dark and closed her eyes. This was the part she had been having trouble with since Nathan got sick, almost a month ago, and especially since he'd entered the coma five days before: the moments just before sleep. She closed her eyes and willed her body to calm, trying to concentrate on her breathing—in, out, steady. She thought of the prom, and of Tim, and wished he could just know everything: about how it felt to be her now, under her blanket, willing her eyes to stay shut, trying not to think of Tim or of Nathan in the hospital or of Abe down the hall in

his room or of her dead father or of her mother across the hall. She
didn't want to have to tell Tim anything; she wanted him, she wanted
everyone to just know, and at the same time she wanted no one to
know. If people knew about Nathan, then it might be real, what was
happening, another member of her family close to death. She refused
to believe it; it was not real, it couldn't be real, so she wouldn't tell.

She thought of school tomorrow, of walking into her homeroom
with everyone milling about, how it felt to see Tim first thing in the
morning when he was the last one she spoke to at night. She imagined
him now, climbing into his bed and turning toward the wall. She
focused on this thought and tried to eliminate the others. She pictured
her thoughts as a tunnel, a technique she had read about recently in a
book on meditation, banishing all of them to the sides as she focused
on her breaths. Thoughts jumped toward her, and she swatted them
away like tennis balls.

———

Ruby had known Tim Dane since seventh grade, but they'd never
been close before last year. He lived next door to Zoë Creswell, her
best friend in middle school, so when she'd sleep over at Zoë's, the
two of them would lie in Zoë's room in the morning and listen to the
sounds of Tim and his brother playing street hockey, whooping and
hollering, yelling "Car!" when someone drove by and they had to
move to the sidewalk. At the time, Tim didn't seem to dislike her and
Zoë, he just didn't seem particularly interested. He was in his own
world, Ruby could see that even then; it was what made her curious
about him.

She didn't quite know how her friendship with Tim had come to
pass. At this point he was her closest friend aside from Jill, and she
barely even spoke to Zoë anymore, a shift of allegiances that still
bewildered Ruby when she thought of it. One afternoon in January

of their sophomore year, in front of the math building as the sun was setting, Zoë had gotten angry at Ruby for hanging out with Jill and had picked a fight, saying "Let's just see how well you do without me!" and storming away to her parents' waiting minivan. She told Ruby she had been holding her resentment in because she knew Ruby's father was sick—because she didn't want to add to her pain. "But I can't do it anymore!" she said. "You just have to take the consequences for your actions! I can't spare you!"

Ruby had thought Zoë was being a bit dramatic about Jill—why couldn't she be friends with both of them? She'd never asked Zoë to hold anything in. Was she supposed to feel guilty that her father was sick and slowly dying? She resented the implication that her pain was a burden on anyone, or that she had brought any of her pain—even the tiniest, smallest bit, even any at all—into her relationship with Zoë, into any of her relationships. Zoë had no idea about her father, not really, and what, now she was supposed to feel guilt about that too? Spending time with a new group—a group that included Jill and Tim—going to parties, smoking pot and the occasional cigarette, having conversations with people she'd thought she would never speak to, ever—all of this helped to mitigate the seemingly endless deterioration of her father over that year.

Tim, for Ruby, had been a growing light in an increasingly dim world. Throughout sophomore year, their friendship grew, and there was an unspoken element of attraction between them although they never acted on it. Ruby felt incapable of acting, unsure of what Tim wanted, and in her self-consciousness assumed he just wanted to be her friend. Everyone knew about her dad, who lingered on for most of the year at a local hospice, unable to speak.

Tim never bored her; he was himself in a way she had not known anyone, except maybe Nathan, to be. There was virtually no self-consciousness in him; he wore his hair in brown curls like a helmet around his face, sweatshirts he found in the lost and found, pants that billowed out around the waist. He once described his wardrobe to Ruby as a system set up solely on the concept of warmth. "I look at a piece of clothing and all I see is a thermometer," he said. "All I think is, How warm will this keep me?" She had the sense, when she was around Tim, that the whole world would be funny if she only looked at it the right way.

At school, he was constantly performing: putting ketchup packets in his mouth and pretending he was bleeding; making announcements in assemblies about clubs that didn't exist ("The TI-82 club! Calculate this!"). He was elected to student council with a three-point speech about the Red Sox, a soft-serve ice cream machine, and his promise to wear tights to assemblies. He gave the speech dressed in a pair of his mother's black tights, a pair of too-small blue shorts, and a white T-shirt on which he had written the word *win* in black Sharpie.

Her father died in August, just before the beginning of junior year, and by then, Ruby knew she had seen parts of Tim that no one else had. When there were people around, he was always on, making jokes, throwing his arms out and taking bows, but when he was with Ruby he was calm. After school, when he drove her home, he relaxed in the car as if he were an actor settling back into his skin after a play. He talked to her about things he thought of before he went to sleep: black holes in the universe, sucking in the stars. "I wouldn't tell anyone else this," he said; "You know no one else knows this." She carried what he shared with her as if it were top secret, and when she watched him at school or at parties, making other people laugh, the secret dissolved inside her.

They knew about Nathan's tumor for only three weeks before he hemorrhaged and entered the coma. One day in early April, almost a month ago, after Ruby got home from school, Nathan came in the kitchen door with a duffel bag. Her mother had picked him up at the train. It was spring break, not that warm out yet, but he was wearing shorts and one of his Hawaiian shirts. He had a collection of these—he and his best friend, Rob, had started collecting them at the beginning of their freshman year of college ("The array of Hawaiian shirts! It's infinite!" Nathan had once exclaimed).

Ruby greeted him at the door. She had been looking forward to his arrival all day. "Rubalski!" he cried, as he pulled his duffel bag free from the doorframe. "Spring break is here!"

He was looking at her funny; Ruby noticed immediately. His head was angled a touch away from her, so that he looked at her more from the sides of his eyes than head-on. It was as if looking at her was covert, as if he was whispering something to her with his eyes that he didn't want the person next to him to hear. Even when he bent down to greet the dog, letting Wally put her front paws around his neck and hugging her to him like she was a child, Ruby could see his head was tilted slightly away.

He dropped his duffel bag. She hugged him. "It's good to be home," he said.

That night they had dinner, the three of them, Ruby and her mother and Nathan—Abe sat it out in his room, saying he had to "get used to" Nathan being home, and Aaron was living in Chicago—and the way Nathan looked across the table at Ruby was unnerving. He said he needed glasses, that was all, he'd been having some trouble studying lately, it was probably all those hours looking at the computer screen—yes, of course that was what it was. He was home again, for a little while, and this was what mattered. Later, Ruby lay in bed and heard him talking on the phone in his room, and the sound of his voice was like an anchor pulling her into the house and securing her in her bed.

In the months since her father's death, after Nathan had gone back to college and Aaron to Chicago, it had been difficult for Ruby to feel connected to them. She knew they must be grieving but

couldn't fathom how. Things were going back to normal, she supposed, they were all to move on, but sometimes she resented what
she imagined was an easier transition for Nathan and Aaron, away
from the house where they couldn't see the results of the loss, their
mother having tea at the table alone, the silence at the end of the day
when her father never arrived. And they didn't have to interact with
Abe, who was now permanently home and seemingly oblivious of
what had taken place, an increasingly ghostlike character at his end of
the house. When she spoke to them on the phone they seemed fine,
they had the usual short and casual conversations, and there may
have been a gentler-than-usual tone to their voices when they asked
her how she was, but that was about it. They asked her about their
mother and about Abe, and she took on the role of point person
("She's okay, I think"; "Yup, still crazy"), but as a consequence she
felt more and more removed from them. Increasingly, she felt her
brothers were distant, unreachable islands. As long as they were
away, she was alone.

Over Christmas break, the first time they'd all been at home
together since the funeral and the shivah, Ruby had gone into the bathroom one night after dinner and heard Nathan crying in his room:
deep and halting breaths. He had been playing his cello—she could
hear him from downstairs, where she was watching TV—the cello
had been ringing deep and sultry, and then it had stopped. The door to
his room from the bathroom was cracked open, and as Ruby entered
she could see him sitting on his bed with his head in his hands. His cello
lay next to him on the floor.

He was at the tail end of his cry, she could tell, his breathing slowing and growing calmer, and he hadn't heard her come in. She had
never seen Nathan cry like this, and the sight paralyzed her in the
bathroom. Should she go in and try to comfort him? Should she
retreat so he wouldn't know he'd been seen? He was wiping his eyes.
Ruby left the bathroom before he saw her, but the experience gave

her an added tenderness toward him, so that, although they never cried together, she could feel, when she cried alone, that she had something in common with him.

When she heard Nathan's voice in the house again that April, her relief was palpable. She was happy to see him because she missed him, because he always made her feel better, because his presence calmed her—but a new relief accompanied his arrival this time, as if she had been afraid he would never come back. Seeing Nathan reminded her of him again, reminded her of all the things about her family that she loved, all the ways she had always thought her family special and herself lucky to belong. The way it had been with Nathan before he left home, before her father got sick, before, even, Abraham: the two of them left in the house, Nathan her protector in the other room. She lay in bed now and listened to him on the phone, laughing (pacing the thick brown carpet, she knew), and though his voice kept her awake, she hoped that he would not stop talking. She felt a release in her chest, to hear him talking and laughing through the wall.

But a few days later Nathan went to the eye doctor, and the man took one look in his right eye with his light and straightened up fast. He sent Nathan to a neurologist, and the next day they had the diagnosis: brain tumor, glioblastoma, the deadliest kind, the same one her father had had. They couldn't explain it, said the doctor, this type of tumor was not necessarily hereditary, it was just one of those freak things. What could he say, it couldn't be explained.

The night Ruby found out, her mother picked her up at school. It was her night for car pool, and they had to drive Faith Kominsky, who was a year older than Ruby and lived five minutes away from the Bronsteins in a new, slick wooden house. Faith was a tiny girl, her skin suctioned to her bones, with the kind of gigantic eyes that protruded from their sockets. You could see most of Faith's eyeballs at any given time; Ruby was wary of her.

The two of them got into the car, and Ruby's mother drove away from Featherton. The sun was setting. Ruby could tell immediately that something was wrong with her mother. Her smile was too eager as she asked, "How are your parents, Faith?" into the rearview mirror. Since when did she care about Faith's parents?

After Faith answered, Ruby asked, "Mom, is something wrong?"

Her mother dropped her eyes to the road ahead and blinked. She gripped the steering wheel, struggling with what to say. "It's okay," she said finally.

"What is?"

Her mother's eyes flipped quickly to the rearview mirror and then back to the road. "Let's talk about it after we drop Faith off."

"What?" said Ruby, her heart beating faster. There was a liquid feeling inside of her. "Talk about what?"

"Ruby, I'm serious. Let's wait."

"Why? What's wrong?" Ruby was surprised by how frantic she was getting. "Mom, just tell me!"

"It's okay, Mrs. Bronstein," Ruby heard Faith say.

Her mother's mouth became very small and pursed—Ruby recognized the expression from fights she used to have with her father, when her mother knew it was futile to argue but felt strongly that she was right.

"What, Mom?" Ruby asked again.

Her mother kept her eyes on the road. She took a deep breath and let it out. "Nathan went to the eye doctor today."

Ruby's throat constricted. Nathan! Oh, God. Not Nathan.

"The eye doctor told him to see a neurologist." She swallowed, her hands gripping the wheel. "He has a brain tumor, Ruby."

There was a silence. It was as if someone had hit a cosmic pause, as if the car had stopped moving and the three hearts in the car uniformly stopped beating, the blood stopped flowing, the earth stopped turning. The car, a Toyota Previa, round like a teardrop, paused on a road, three stunned bodies inside it looking ahead, clouds holding in the air. Nothing moved—no insects crawled on trees, no birds chirped or pecked for food, no humans took any steps or blinked any eyes, no thoughts flashed in any minds, no lights turned green or red. Ruby felt as if she had swallowed a stone. Would she ever move again, would time ever unfreeze? The stone sunk slowly through the thick, paused contents of her body, and nothing else moved.

Then, just as quickly, they were moving again. The sounds came back: the tires on the road, a honk somewhere outside.

"What?" Ruby said, because it was the only word that came to her mouth.

Her mother didn't respond.

"What?" Ruby said again, louder now. "What, Mom?"

Her mother nodded, just barely, but still said nothing.

"But that's impossible, isn't it? I mean, isn't that impossible?" Her voice was rising.

"It may be impossible," her mother said, "but it's true."

"But it's not serious, is it? It's not . . ." She ran out of voice. She was looking through the windshield. Now it was dark, pitch dark. There were no lights.

"It's the same kind that your father had."

But even with this information, of course, there was no awareness, no belief, nothing except the dark road in front of them. How could there be? No one is programmed to believe the worst, to really believe it, at least not before the worst happens more than once.

"But it couldn't happen again, right?" said Ruby to her mother. Tears had come to her eyes, and her throat felt thick. Not Nathan! "I mean, it couldn't happen again!"

"I don't think so," said her mother. "I don't think it could happen again. But I don't know."

Faith sat behind them in the backseat and was silent. Ruby could feel Faith's gigantic eyes boring into the back of her neck, boring into the windshield, she could feel her thin presence in the backseat, and Ruby wanted to pull her over her knee and break her in half, she wanted to throw her out of the moving car into the darkness, she saw her body hitting the pavement and breaking. She deserved it, for daring to sit back there, for daring to be silent, daring to witness this.

"Ruby, please," her mother said, her eyes darting to the rearview mirror as Ruby's voice rose, as she wailed "It can't happen!" But Ruby didn't care, she could rip Faith apart with her disbelief.

When they reached Faith's house, Faith pulled the back door open, she used her whole body to roll it open, and she put her hand on Ruby's shoulder and Ruby wanted to tear it off of her wrist, it took all her strength not to grab it and twist.

"I'm sorry, Ruby," she said. Ruby did not reply. Her mother said, "Thank you, Faith," and Ruby wanted to kill her mother for conceding that much, for even conceding that this was real enough that there would be an apology and a thank-you.

By the time they arrived home, Ruby was calmer. There was nothing to do but enter the house. What could they do? They sat in the driveway for a few minutes and her mother told her: Well, they didn't know, what could they know? Nathan was home now, he would start chemotherapy. She didn't think it could happen again. What could they do?

What could they do?

They entered the house. The sound from the television could be heard as they came in. Nathan.

Ruby went through the kitchen and stood in the doorway of the TV room. Nathan was lying on the couch watching *The Simpsons*.

Wally was lying in front of the couch, and Nathan had one hand on her back, as if touching the dog somehow could hold him in place.

"Hey, Nate," said Ruby, looking down at him.

"Hey Rube," Nathan said, his eyes on the TV.

She came around to the front of the couch and climbed onto it, positioning her body so that she lay behind him, her head on his shoulder and the top of his right arm. Nathan. What was there to say? No words would work.

They lay still. On-screen, Homer Simpson had a heart attack. His family gathered around his hospital bed, and he gave them a weak smile. Even *The Simpsons* were in on this, Ruby thought.

She lay next to Nathan and felt the presence of something evil growing inside his body. This was Nathan, her protector; beneath her head his warm body alongside hers was the same as it was yesterday and the day before, when he had picked her up in a bear hug and lifted her over his head. But now there was something foreign in here, something dangerous growing, even now, even right now.

She remembered games they used to play together, when Nathan would allow his body to be her toy, letting it go limp, letting her control it for him. There was Raggedy Andy, when Nathan's body would be a doll, limbs flailing, and Ruby would prop him up, or use her hands to move his arms, move his jaw with her small hands in order to make him talk. "I am Raggedy Andy," she would say, moving his jaw with her hand, his head leaning back against the couch, "I am a doll." She would feed him cereal, sometimes, like this, putting the Cheerios into his mouth in a handful and then moving his jaw with her hand, the crumbs spilling everywhere, and though Nathan's eyes would sparkle and wrinkle at the corners with his effort not to laugh, he never would, no matter how the Cheerios would spill onto his shirt or pants. "I can eat Cheerios! I'm hungry!" Ruby would squeal, stuffing the cereal into his mouth.

There was the Robot, where Nathan's body would be stiff, perpetually in one position (head down, arms held at a ninety-degree angle, legs tight) until Ruby would type a command on the imaginary keypad on his back, and the Robot would come to life to perform robotic feats. "Robot," Ruby would say, poking her fingers lightly onto his back in a diagonal formation, "move to the couch!" And the robot would straighten up and, in slow, jerking movements, make his way to the couch, where he would stop and lower his head, waiting for the next command. Nathan never said a word during any of their games—even if Ruby gave him an impossible task ("Robot, now fly!") he would attempt it (arms out straight, ramming headfirst into the wall). Sometimes Ruby would try to move between games, instructing Raggedy Andy to become the Robot or vice versa ("Robot! Be a doll!"), but Nathan would never break character until, for him, the game was over.

Behind Nathan's body on the couch in front of the TV, she could feel his heart beating through his arm. That was his young body, that was hers, and now here they were. On-screen, Homer Simpson's heart pumped and then stopped, and then pumped again.

"Oh, Rubalski," Nathan sighed, and it was as she suspected, the TV was on, but were they watching it? The TV was holding them, stationary, connected to their former lives, but something evil was growing.

Ruby brought her arm up and let her hand rest on Nathan's arm, next to her head. She said nothing. There were so many words, but none of them would do. Nathan, Nathan, oh, not Nathan.

After that he was home for three weeks with the knowledge: a tumor, the deadliest kind, was growing in his brain. She tried to imagine how it was for him, she tried to leap from her body to his, but it was impossible. She was not him. She went to school and Nathan started chemotherapy. He sighed a lot, and shook his head. Ruby moved around him cautiously, watching him keenly, noting every detail of his whereabouts, but she didn't know what to say. He sat in chairs at the kitchen table or in the backyard, reading a book about healing and miracles that their mother had bought. She could not imagine how to be twenty-one and know what he knew. She was aware of him always—the sound of him in the shower almost broke her heart—and obsessed with what he must be feeling, but she didn't want to dignify the reality with words; it was real, and there were no words that were real enough to match it. She hugged him, and felt the gap between them: for her, the knowledge; for him, the presence of the thing in his brain.

Three weeks later, he entered the coma. He was supposed to have surgery, they were supposed to remove the bulk of the tumor from his brain, but instead something ruptured. Nathan was home alone and he started to feel disoriented and called a family friend, Bruce, who used to play tennis with their dad, and Bruce came over and called an ambulance and took Nathan to the hospital, and by the time they arrived he was unconscious. Ruby imagined it, the blood exploding through Nathan's brain like those plastic ketchup packets when you stepped on them, the way the boys in her class loved to do, hopping on them, the ketchup splattering over the carpet and walls, the way Tim put them in his mouth, biting down so it looked like he was bleeding. The blood seeping through the passageways in Nathan's brain, seeping, seeping, evil blood, blood in places it shouldn't have been, and Nathan, sitting in the leather chair in the living room, reading, trying to stay calm, the words starting to swim, the room starting to move just slightly, his heart starting to pound. What strength it must have taken for him to find his way to the phone, the phone numbers dancing, for him to think of Bruce, to find his number, to dial, the strange white object in his hand connecting him, the panic in his chest, and to say to Bruce, as she learned later that he did, "Bruce, something's wrong, can you come over please."

That morning, before the hemorrhage, as Ruby was getting ready for school, she'd crossed from her bedroom to the bathroom to take a shower, and as usual, the door from the bathroom to Nathan's room was open, and she reached to pull it closed, peeking her head in to see, just for a moment, Nathan asleep in his bed with his back to the wall. She always loved this moment of privileged intimacy, this glimpse of her brother she was given without his knowledge, but that morning she cherished it. It made her feel in control, to reach in for the door-knob and see him asleep, peaceful, comfortable; it made her feel that somehow he trusted her, having left the door open, knowing that she would see him this way. And she would not violate the intimacy, she would respect her sleeping brother, his curls against his pillow, his face gone slack with sleep, his body turned off to the world. This was a moment they shared, a mutual acknowledgment of sorts, a subtle contract. Nathan loved to sleep; there were few things he loved more. It made Ruby happy to see him doing something he loved.

Later, when she thought of it, she would be nearly convinced that as she reached in for the door that morning she had felt something else, something stronger, a premonition. She was sure that she had for some reason lingered there, with the doorknob in her hand, look-ing at her sleeping brother with a tumor growing in his brain. How could she have known then that this would be the last time she'd see him at home? She couldn't have. Perhaps these premonitions are always products of retrospect. Perhaps, the night that her father died, when she'd felt a distinct sinking in her stomach at 11:00 P.M., only to arrive home at 11:15 and learn that he had died fifteen minutes earlier, perhaps even this was a product of what she now knew. Add these to the list of moments that grow, moments that transform, moments that become somehow legendary in the mind of someone who lives after someone else dies.

The night of Nathan's hemorrhage Ruby went with Jill to a Red Sox game; the seats were just behind home plate. They went straight from school and sat next to a drunk man in a wife beater and khaki shorts and his girlfriend, who wore a baseball hat. The two of them were loud and raucous and fed Jill and Ruby bags of peanuts.

"Aren't peanuts really bad for you?" Jill asked the man, who was massaging his girlfriend's thigh. He turned to her with surprise.

"Nuts?" he yelled, so loud that Ruby was sure the players at the plate could hear. "Nuts? They're not bad! They're nuts! They're full of protein!" He grabbed the bag his girlfriend was holding and thrust it at Jill. "Here!" he said. "Have more!"

His girlfriend squealed, "Ronny, hey!" but he just patted her leg. "I'll get you more."

Ruby and Jill looked at each other, their laps covered in peanuts, and laughed. Ruby had told Jill, on the way to the game, about Nathan's tumor—the first person she had told. Jill had pulled the car over and hugged Ruby, and said, "It will be okay, it has to be okay," and Ruby had replied, "I know it will." Now, next to two ridiculous strangers, strangers who did not have cancer, strangers who were watching the ball game and eating peanuts and drinking cheap beer, part of Ruby relaxed, and she and Jill laughed until their stomachs hurt.

But when they pulled into Ruby's driveway at the end of the night, it was full of cars. Immediately, guilt washed over her— Nathan. While Ruby had been laughing with drunk strangers at a baseball game, something had gone wrong. Jill and Ruby sat in Jill's car for a minute, as the night darkened, and Jill asked, "Do you want me to come in with you?" and Ruby said no.

Jill's headlights were on her as she got out of the car and walked to the house, feeling ashamed, brushing a peanut flake from her T-shirt, and in the kitchen she found her mother and a table of her friends sitting around her. Her mother's friends, most of whom had been her father's friends too, the people Ruby had grown up seeing at dinner parties and on high holidays and who had given her generous gifts for her Bat Mitzvah, were now all sitting around her mother, without her father, at the kitchen table, their faces turned to her with helpless expressions and their eyebrows furrowed.

"Ruby," her mother said, standing up at the head of the table, and Ruby could see her face was stained with tears.

———

The Monday before the junior prom was Nathan's sixth day in the coma. Aaron came home on Sunday, but Abe was too out of it to process what was happening. When their mother asked him if he wanted to go with them to see Nathan, Abe waved her away with his hand. "I'll see him when he gets home," he said decisively, loudly, a big smile on his lips. Ruby was relieved.

For five days, Ruby had gone with her mother and then with Aaron to sit next to Nathan's hospital bed, where he was attached to a respirator that breathed for him. The breaths it gave him were deep and even, spread unnaturally across long seconds. Ruby watched his chest rise and fall, filling and then releasing the air. She waited, holding her own breath until his chest rose again. She tried to align her breathing with his—deep breath in, out, then pause—and felt the unpredictability of the respirator. How did it choose when to release the air? Why should it get to choose? There was something evil in the way it staggered its gift. Her brother lay peaceful and calm and the machine injected air into his body; it was violent, a violent, life-sustaining gift. The respirator fired—*deep breath in*—Nathan's chest rose—*wait*— his chest fell, there was the sound of a deep sigh—*wait, wait*—then a shot of air was fired, there was a noise like a snore, and his chest rose again.

His body looked the same to her every day, though she was aware of the expectation, just before she entered his curtained area, that it would somehow be different. Each time Ruby arrived at the waiting room, she pressed the button on the side of the locked door to the Intensive Care Unit, and a disembodied voice said "Name" and she leaned into the speaker and said "Ruby Bronstein," and then the door buzzed and she pushed through and into the unit, which was a long hallway with a series of curtains hanging in front of beds on which lay a series of people close to death.

She walked down the hall and tried not to look to her left, where the thin curtains were floating, airy and white like ghosts, thin membranes that were all that separated her from strange dying bodies. But of course she looked, of course she had to look, and behind the curtains she saw lumps in the end of a tucked-in bed, the outlines of a person's feet, a hand holding a remote control, or sometimes, a face, thin and drawn, with its eyes closed. The hallway was long and evenly lit, the cubicles of sickness one after another, the desk for all the nurses, and the constant smell of sharp antiseptic and the lotion that they rubbed on the immovable bodies thick in the air.

Every day, some of the cubicles held healthy people. People were gathered around a bed, people were holding each other's hands or talking loudly or wearing birthday hats, and in the middle of them, as Ruby walked by, there was a pair of feet, lying still at the end of the mattress, attached to a body that was dying. She noted these things, this hallway was alive inside of her now, and though she tried not to notice the other families, the other tragedies, the other hearts full of worry and hope, she knew she was just one of them, one of the constant stream of humans who passed through this hallway as on a conveyor belt, passing through with love and fear filling their chests. But Nathan was here, and so as much as she was like the others she knew she had much that they didn't have. Every day, as she made the trip, a feeling in her chest mounted, an anticipation, for in just one second she would see her brother, she would be near her brother in his hospital bed. It would still be him, Nathan was at the end of the hall, silent Nathan with a tube in his throat.

There was the hope, of course, that one of these days his eyes would be open, that she would arrive to find him sitting up and smiling, but more subtle than that was the hope of a twitch—an upturn of the mouth, a wink of a closed eye, a quick squeeze of her hand. She sat with his body and watched it for signs of life.

It was warm, and sometimes that was enough.

Jill was the only person Ruby had told. In the moments when she thought the words might come, they didn't. The illusion remained: nothing was changing. This could not happen again. Another horrible thing was not happening, not to Nathan, not to her.

At school, she tried to banish images of Nathan from her brain. She carried her grief like a backpack she could remove. She was called to the blackboard in math class and as she raised her arm, chalk in hand, she saw him; the board was glass and Nathan was standing behind it, smiling, and she was raising her arm to him. She forced her hand over the blackboard, forced her eyes to see the board as dark and opaque, forced her brother back into his hospital bed and her mind back to math.

She smiled at her friends, and laughed, and made jokes, and mostly, it worked. She was distracted. She was a teenager and her school books held facts and the classroom walls had posters she could read over and over: MARTIN LUTHER KING, JR.: "I HAVE A DREAM," or ATTITUDE: A LITTLE THING THAT MAKES A BIG DIFFERENCE. She breathed deep and regular and tried not to think of Nathan, the way his tongue was dry and cracking next to the tube in his mouth.

With Tim it was hardest. She felt she was betraying him, somehow, by not telling him, and yet she savored the way he looked at her without knowing, his eyes wide and smiling. She savored how he expected nothing from her but a response to him, how he looked at her and saw an unchanged version of herself—a person who had no reason to change. She did not want to see, yet, the pity in his eyes; she did not want him to treat her differently. Not yet.

"Well, obviously we're going together," he said to her on the Tuesday before the prom, when she brought up the dance over lunch in the cafeteria. He was eating wet and floppy string beans off a white plate.

The cafeteria was crowded and loud, with people milling around the salad bar and going through the buffet line and shouting to each other from across the long wooden tables that lined the room. The population was segregated by group: the jocks always sat with the jocks, the AV crew with the AV crew, the black people with the other black people. Tim and Ruby were sitting at the end of a table by the back, next to a tall window that looked out over grass.

"Oh, is it obvious?" she said. "I hadn't realized it was so obvious." She raised her glass, full of fruit punch, to her lips, trying to hide her relief.

"It's obvious," Tim said without looking up. "You know it's obvious."

Two boys, underclassmen whom Ruby recognized but didn't know, slid into the seats next to them. "Hey, Tim," the one next to Ruby said. He was wearing a white hat with a perfectly curved brim; he had probably worked on curving that brim for weeks, Ruby thought, putting it in the dishwasher, holding the curve overnight with rubber bands.

"Hey," said Tim, flashing the kid a smile. The two boys started talking to each other about a test, and Tim leaned forward, gestured to the one next to her with his head, and mouthed, "Golf."

Ruby nodded. The noise of the cafeteria was a curtain of sound

surrounding them. She was eating a chicken patty sandwich with let-
tuce and ketchup.

"Well anyway," she said, "come on then. I still want to be asked
to this thing. You can't just make assumptions, you know. I might not
say yes." She smiled at him, chewing.

"Oh," he said, smiling back, raising a fork of green beans to his
mouth. "You'll say yes."

"Try me," she said.

"Okay," he said, putting his fork down. "Do you want to go to
the prom with me?" He held his hand out to her. "You can't say no."

For a second, when she looked at Tim's hand reaching for hers
over the wooden table, Ruby thought of Nathan, his hand limp
against the white of the hospital bed. She blinked, and the image was
gone. She took Tim's hand. It gripped hers tightly. "Obviously," she
said.

Tuesday afternoon, when she arrived at Nathan's bed, Nathan's best
friend Rob was there, sitting next to the bed and reading to him from
Tuck Everlasting. Rob and Nathan had been captains of the wrestling
team together at Featherton, and now went to the same college. On
his own, Rob was shy and restrained, serious, awkward with women,
a hulk of a man with sunken eyes; but with Nathan he was goofy and
reckless, a naughty child. Ruby's mother told her—the night after
they found out about the tumor, while Nathan was on the phone with
Rob in the living room and Ruby and her mother were on the couch
in front of the TV—that Nathan had told her he thought Rob was his
soul mate.

"He said that?" Ruby was surprised. "Soul mate?"

"Yeah"—her mother nodded, looking at the television—"soul
mate."

Ruby remembered getting a ride to school once in Rob's car, a huge Chevy Suburban, during his and Nathan's last year at Featherton, when she was in seventh grade. The two of them were chewing tobacco and spitting into a soda can that they passed to each other, laughing garrulous laughs, throwing their heads back and slapping the dashboard. Ruby sat silently in the backseat, hesitant as if she were witnessing the feeding ritual of lions. Rob stopped at all the green lights ("Green light! Oh shit! Green light!") and went on the red ones, and the two of them roared.

"Hey, Ruby," Rob said now, when she came through the curtain. His eyes were tired. "How are you?"

"Okay," she said, coming around to the other side of Nathan's bed and putting her hands on the bed rail. When she saw what book he was reading to her brother she felt a part of her chest open with affection. Why hadn't she thought of that book? It was the perfect book to read to someone you loved who needed to live.

Nathan's body was between them. "How are you?"

"Okay." He closed the book.

Ruby thought Rob looked very small in the chair next to the bed, smaller even than Nathan. How long had he been here, reading to his friend?

"That's a great book."

Rob nodded, looking at Nathan. "Where's your mom?" he asked suddenly, as if he'd just realized she wasn't there.

"She's coming," she said. "I think she's talking to the doctor."

Rob nodded at Nathan. "He's looking okay, don't you think?"

Ruby looked at her brother. His tongue was peeking out from the opposite side than it had been yesterday, and it looked a little more moist. The respirator fired air and his chest rose. "I guess."

"Yeah." Rob sighed. He stood up and took Nathan's hand. "Well, I guess I should be going. See ya, buddy," he said to Nathan. "You take care of yourself, okay?"

He released the hand reluctantly, laying it gently back down on the white cotton blanket, and gazed at it after he'd let it go as if trying to memorize the image. "If I don't see your mom, tell her I'll see her tomorrow."

"Okay," Ruby said. "See ya, Rob."

She watched him leave, pushing the curtain to one side and stepping out into the hallway, and she noticed his Birkenstocks and khaki shorts, the roundness of his calves, the way his back curved from shoulder to shoulder beneath his T-shirt. He was so out of place here, in this hospital with knobs and tubes coming from the walls, white and sterile, the thin curtains hanging from the ceiling, the only sounds hushed and murmured or electronic, always so methodical and controlled. A body so young and so full of blood and muscles and strength did not belong here.

She looked down at Nathan and thought of his body next to Rob's, the way they used to look side by side in their puffy jackets in the wintertime, so similarly built. She thought of the two of them in their wrestling uniforms, the straps long and reaching down to their stomachs, exposing their chests, the spandex shorts hugging their thighs. She had always thought wrestling uniforms were the strangest articles of clothing; even the strongest of boys looked weak in them. She had to hold back laughter when she was around Nathan in his uniform, which of course made him keep it on as long as possible and try to interact with her as much as he could.

She thought of Nathan on the wrestling mat; she had a sudden full image of the gym during a match: the deep smell of sweat in the air, the feel of the thin grooves of the metal bleacher on her thighs, the grunts of males on the mat before her, their shoes squeaking against the rubber as they pushed against each other with the balls of their feet, their arms reaching and pushing each other's sweating skin, and then Nathan, his body pale, pulling his opponent's arm out from under him and flipping him onto his back. She saw the gym, she saw Nathan in his uniform, and she saw him after a match, emerging from the locker room with a smile, his hair wet and his shoes slung over his shoulder, their laces tied together with a knot.

The room was hushed, save for the noise of the machines. The *beep, beep, beep* of Nathan's heart in a jagged green line on a screen, and the respirator, pausing, waiting, and then firing. She was alone with Nathan, aware of the brevity of the moment, her mother somewhere close by. She watched his body for signs of movement. Were his muscles thinning? What happened to muscles if they no longer had to move limbs?

She thought of her father, the way his body had thinned and dwindled, the way that by the end he didn't look like himself, and yet there was always something about him that was familiar. By the end, his body was so fragile they needed a machine to lift him into his wheelchair, which was specially padded so as not to harm him. Even his wheelchair could harm him then; his wheelchair, if not properly padded, could give him sores, could rot his skin, could tear him like a piece of paper.

She had never seen her father like this, though; in all the time he was dying she never saw him unconscious, he had never had machines to help him breathe. There was something so different about this. It was still Nathan, still fully Nathan there before her—no dramatic scars, no thinning—there was only the presence of the machines, only the curtain and the whiteness and those perpetually closed eyes.

She resisted the urge to climb onto the bed and lay her body next to his. Did he know she was there? She wanted to speak to him, but what could she say? She wasn't sure he could hear her.

She brought his hand up and touched it to her cheek. It was soft and warm, and she ran her thumb over the back of it. She wanted the hand to dissolve into her face; she wanted to possess the hand and its warmth; she wanted Nathan's hand to be something she could swallow and keep. She closed her eyes and pressed it to her.

"Hi, Nate," she said softly, pushing the hand against her skin. The hand did not respond.

At the bottom of the bed, his feet peeked out. Nathan didn't like to sleep with his feet inside blankets ("What can I say, I just don't like to feel *confined*"), and on the first day he was in the hospital Ruby had objected to his feet being tucked in; it looked wrong, to see him like that, his feet those hidden lumps. She had pulled her mother's arm— they were standing by the foot of the bed together, the machines were making their noises. It was the first time Ruby had seen Nathan, and something was wrong, something besides this room and the tube in his mouth and the way he was silent and serious, and then it occurred to her—the feet—and she touched her mother's arm and said, "Mom, his feet, his feet should be free."

Her mother looked at the bottom of his bed, nodded, and said, "You're right," and went out to tell the nurse. Now Nathan's feet were always free. Nathan's feet were free, and that meant that this was Nathan, that these were Nathan's feet.

Ruby looked at them now—his toes, the light tufts of hair before the knuckles, the toenails square and pushing out against the sides of skin, the dots of black in the corners where the skin was callused and hard—and recognized them: her brother's feet. The same feet that stepped next to hers on the grass up in Maine, tan and tough in the summertime; the same feet that Nathan loved to shove in her face while they watched TV to make her surrender the remote.

How could a body be in so many different places, she thought, and always look the same? How could it carry its happy memories with it to its worst places?

She lowered his hand to his side and moved to the end of the bed, reaching out to touch the hair on his left big toe. She looked to

Nathan's face for a reaction, half-expecting him to giggle as she ran her finger gently over his toe.

He did not move.

————

So far, it had just been her mother saying the words: *brain tumor, cancer, coma, respirator, resuscitate, vegetable, life support.* Her mother and the doctor she took Ruby and Aaron to see, a neurologist who spoke of Nathan's brain in technical terms—*medulla oblongata, glioblastoma*—and told them that the chance of anyone surviving this was nil.

"Unfortunately," the doctor said, his hands clasped together on his knees, his thin glasses pulled down low on his nose, "I understand you already know this. This is the deadliest kind of tumor."

It was strange in the doctor's office, so different from the sterile, fluorescent hallways and waiting rooms of the hospital, where the furniture was all hard, flat wood jutting out from textured fabric cushions. One minute they were walking down the hall, away from the ICU and Nathan's beeping monitors, and the next they turned a corner and went through a door and they were in a completely different sort of place, a large office filled with dark wood bookshelves stacked high with medical textbooks, journals, and paperbacks; a desk piled with papers and a dim reading light; and three leather, stiff-backed chairs, regal, as if they'd been taken from a British monarchic estate. Ruby was suspicious of it all. Somehow it didn't seem right, that a man should have an office like this just off that hallway out there, that bright conveyor belt for nurses in cotton smocks and squeaky shoes, poking their heads into so many rooms of sickness and death. Ruby felt that she was in some sort of theater set, that this room had been orchestrated so families might have a comfortable place to receive bad news.

And then there he was, this doctor, wearing a blue button-down shirt and khaki pants, a hospital ID clipped to his right breast pocket. Who was this guy anyway? What did this guy really know? Where was his white coat, where was his surgical mask, his paper cap to cover his hair?

He was youngish, his hair was clipped short, his fingers were long and slim against his thighs. His wedding ring gleamed. How could this man know anything about Nathan, so far away down the hall? She had never seen this man before, not near Nathan or anywhere else. Ruby wanted to be with Nathan, her brother, not here in this man's office. She longed for Nathan, to be holding his warm hand.

Her mother sat in the chair facing the doctor, then Ruby, then Aaron, in the big padded chairs, and the doctor said: "I'm afraid he will not survive. You can keep him on life support as long as you want, but the fact is that he will not wake up." He paused, and then he said, "For this kind of tumor, there simply are no survivors."

Survivors. The word echoed in the room, bouncing off the wood furniture, the shaft of light on the desk. What did that word mean, anyway? Her father had been a *survivor*, but now he wasn't anymore? Could someone be a survivor and a *no survivor* at the same time? A survivor who was not a survivor. Did one survival affect another? If you survived something terrible but could succumb to something else, what did survival even mean? *He will not survive*. This was not a statement she thought her father, at least, would have believed.

If her father had once survived Terezin, who was to say that Nathan couldn't survive this? Even if no one had ever woken up, even if it had never happened before, who had the authority to say it wouldn't happen now? There was always a first time for everything; their parents had taught them this. Never say never, nothing is for certain, anything is possible, there was always a chance. Life is the highest good, always choose life. It was ingrained in them, their father had worked and survived and worked and survived for them to know this!

But there was her mother, sitting next to the doctor and looking at Ruby and Aaron, and she was saying, "Nathan didn't want to be a vegetable, kids, he told me so." Her mother was saying, "I wanted you to meet with Dr. Glasstone so we could all decide together what to do." Her mother was looking at Ruby, and Ruby knew she wanted her to give in, she wanted her to hear "no survivors" and give in, she wanted her to believe in this statement just as she had always believed in the possibility of its opposite. How could her mother believe this, how could she ignore the significance of that word? Where was the choice for life? Nathan's life, *Nathan's life!*

Her mother was reaching over, her mother was holding her hand, and Ruby didn't take it away but she wanted to. She felt betrayed by her mother, the hand that was holding hers was a foreign hand, it was speaking a language she didn't understand. Ruby averted her eyes, she looked down at the carpet blurring into a thousand blurry diamonds, and she didn't want to be in this room anymore, she wanted to be with Nathan, she wished it was Nathan's hand that was holding hers.

Her mother was saying something that Ruby barely heard; her mother was saying, "Ruby, please," and something about two weeks, a compromise, and her mother was crying now too, and Ruby barely noticed that Aaron had hold of her other hand, both her hands were being held now but she felt as if a fist was gripping her throat. There was still a sliver of hope like a bolt of bright lightning in her heart, she felt it and she didn't want to give it up, why should she have to give it up, and how was it possible that no one else felt it? She felt a long rope leading from her chest to Nathan's bed; *I won't give up on you*, she thought, reaching out to Nathan along the rope as her hands were held. The two hands holding hers were fists, they were shackles holding her to this chair, her family had become wardens, they had signed a contract with this thin impostor doctor and she didn't understand why. How could they all be ready to let Nathan die? Nathan was alive, Nathan was warm, and this meant that there was light, that there was life to choose, but this doctor was shaking his head and her mother was saying two more weeks, and then Aaron was standing and shaking the doctor's hand. Through her tears Ruby stood and let her mother's hand fall and followed Aaron from the room. Nathan had no advocate but her, and she was as helpless as he was. Everyone wanted to let him die, everyone wanted to let his warm body grow cold.

———————

On Thursday, the day before the prom, Ruby took Jill to see Nathan. It was an act of elongation, an attempt to draw out the end of her brother's life with another pair of eyes. Someone who had known Nathan only as Ruby's big brother needed to witness him now, on his back in the white pillows of a hospital bed, so helpless it took a nurse and a moist towel to wet his lips. This was reality, this was the way it was for Ruby and her family, this was what she was dealing with. See all of this, yes, but then touch him—he is warm.

As long as Nathan was warm it was all still a reality, the hospital room and the waiting room and the routine, driving there with her mom and sometimes Aaron after school, meals in the hospital cafeteria. As long as it was still happening there was no death, no pain, no tragedy to process. They were suspended there, in the room with the warm body, in the time between living and dying, and please let them remain there for now. This was why Ruby told no one but Jill, and why she brought her to the hospital.

Ruby was waiting in her homeroom after school for her mother to pick her up, and Jill was there, reading a chapter in her biology textbook with a pink highlighter poised like a cigarette between her lips, and Jill asked her if she was going to see Nathan, and she gave Ruby a weak smile and shook her head as if to say she couldn't imagine, having a brother in a coma. It was something in Jill's smile that did it, that weak smile that said *I can't possibly understand, you are so brave, your world is so separate from mine*. Ruby saw that smile and a flash of anger lit up inside her and then, before thinking, she said, "Do you want to come?"

Jill's eyes widened—she hadn't been expecting this—and Ruby knew, no, of course she didn't want to come, but at the same time this was Ruby, who had stayed with her and slept in her bed after her sister had attempted suicide for the second time. "Do you want me to?" she asked.

"Sure, if you want to," said Ruby, and then they were in the car with Ruby's mother and Featherton was receding from view.

It was a warm day. Shouts and whistles blew in through the car's open windows as they passed the playing fields surrounding the school. If Ruby's mother thought it odd that Ruby was bringing a friend to the hospital, she didn't say so. The minivan door had opened and there was Jill, climbing in the back just as if her mother was taking the two of them to the movie theater.

"Mom, I invited Jill to come," Ruby said as she climbed into the front seat, "is it okay?"

"Hi, Mrs. Bronstein," Jill said, settling into the back.

"Oh! Okay," Ruby's mother's replied. "Hi, Jill."

The car rolled along back roads to the highway. Ruby turned on the radio, a Led Zeppelin song.

"Where's Aaron?" Ruby asked.

"He's already there," said her mother.

The road swerved and rose, they passed big houses separated by brick walls, houses with wide porches dotted with white pillars. Ruby looked out the window and did not think. Nathan's body waited for her, his skin warm beneath the cotton blanket on his hospital bed, his heartbeat sounding from the monitor next to his head. Nathan was alive, at least for now, at least for today, and she was in a car moving toward him.

At the hospital, Ruby and Jill sat together in the waiting room, an enclave of uncomfortable chairs just outside the monitored door. Her mother had gone in to get Aaron; the nurses didn't like more than a few people visiting at a time, and she wanted to let Ruby bring Jill in alone. Jill was flipping through a fashion magazine that had been lying on the chair she sat in. It was a well-worn *Glamour*, Ruby knew, the same one that had been circulating around the horseshoe of chairs all week, the pages crumpled and torn, the colors of the photographs on certain pages fading and peeling like sunburned skin. She had held this magazine before, a few times, and had thought about the river of hands that had done the same, all the hands belonging to bodies waiting, waiting, waiting for the fates of people they loved beyond that door. Jill's hands on the magazine were untainted and free. Ruby watched her fingers flip the pages.

"Can you believe the prom is tomorrow night?" Jill said, looking absently at the magazine.

Ruby shook her head. "Nope."

"Are you definitely going to go?" Jill looked at Ruby, her hand flat on the page.

"I think so," Ruby said. "Hopefully. Tim doesn't even know about Nathan."

"You'll tell him when you're ready. Maybe it will be good to go to the prom and try to forget."

Ruby looked at the ICU door. She thought about Nathan beyond it, down the hall in his bed, his feet free and sticking up. The thought of the prom prompted a wave of unease in her stomach. She shouldn't go, she shouldn't go. Nathan. How could she go?

"I guess," she said.

It was strange, walking with Jill down the hallway toward Nathan's cubicle. Ruby felt as if Jill's eyes were somehow her own, as if she were seeing all of this for the first time.

She felt as if she were showing Jill a dream she'd been having, as if she had opened a window in her brain and allowed Jill to peer inside. *This is what I see,* she was saying, taking her friend down this hall, walking her past the other patients toward Nathan at the end. *Can you believe it? Can you believe I have to deal with this?* There was the nurses' station, with the bottle of vanilla lotion that stood handy by the computer monitor; there were Jill's Doc Martens with their purple laces treading on the ICU's waxed linoleum floor.

As they approached Nathan's curtain, Ruby said, "He's in here." She pulled it to the side, and they both stepped in.

Nathan lay before them as if on an altar.

Ruby heard Jill inhale quickly. They stood at the foot of the bed. Ruby looked from Nathan to Jill. Jill's forehead was furrowed; she looked pained, like she was puzzling over a math problem she knew she could never solve. She shut her eyes and shook her head slightly. "Ruby," she said softly.

Ruby looked back to Nathan. "I know."

They stood still and gazed at Nathan, the respirator firing and his chest rising. Nathan's face was at rest. Save for the tube in his mouth, he could have been asleep. They could have been in his bedroom, the two younger girls sneaking in to catch a glimpse of a boy at rest, about to tickle him and flee with peals of stifled laughter.

One night toward the end of Ruby's freshman year, Nathan was home for a vacation and had friends over while their parents were away. Jill slept over, and she and Ruby stayed up in Ruby's room while Nathan and his friends sat out on the screened-in porch, listening to music and smoking. During the night Ruby and Jill snuck down the stairs and crawled, shushing each other, the few feet from the last step to the door of the living room, where they could see out onto the porch. The glass doors were fogged up with smoke. It seemed, from where they crouched, peering around the doorframe, that Nathan and his friends were sitting in a rain forest thick with fog. Ruby saw Nathan sitting in one of the stiff wicker chairs with the thick flowered cushions, his head against the back and his eyes closed, a smile on his lips. "Is Nathan asleep?" Jill whispered, laughing.

Now, standing at the foot of Nathan's bed, Jill said: "He looks so . . . alive."

"I know." Ruby took a step closer to the bed, and put a hand on Nathan's right foot. "Feel him," she said, turning back to Jill. "He's warm."

Jill hesitated. Her eyes flickered to Ruby's face, and Ruby saw a flash of fear. She didn't want to touch him, Ruby thought. Suddenly she was completely aware of the strangeness of the situation; for an instant she floated above the room and saw the two of them, teenage girls, she with her hand on her brother's warm coma foot, gesturing for her friend to touch it. Was she crazy to have brought her friend here? Was there any way anyone could ever understand this? She felt confused and overwhelmed and oddly lucid, crystal clear. Her knees wobbled.

"Come on," she said to Jill, and she heard the slight pleading in her voice, and she was embarrassed and angry for it. She was desperate for Jill to touch Nathan, she realized; she would be furious if she didn't.

Jill stepped forward and reached out. She laid her hand on Nathan's foot, touching his pink toe, her hand just next to Ruby's.

Their eyes met over Nathan's foot. Jill's eyes held Ruby's, Nathan didn't move.

Ruby looked down first, at the cotton blanket that began at Nathan's ankle. "Wow," she heard Jill say, but the sound seemed to come from behind her, and she was unsure what the word referred to.

Later, at home, Ruby ate dinner with her mother and Aaron while Abe watched a video in the TV room. The video was called *Visions of Death,* a black-and-white short film that, from what Ruby could gather, had something to do with a crazy old professor-type who wore suits stained with chalk and invented monsters. Abe had a series of unusual movies like it—some about fighter pilots in World War II, some about fantasy worlds with giant flowers that dwarfed humans—that he bought at the supermarket and left around the house in unexpected places: on top of the banister leading upstairs, in the drawer beneath the kitchen telephone, on top of the coal stove in the living room.

Ruby and her mother were used to finding the videos, as well as other strange artifacts with which Abe peppered the house—his railroad cap, illegible or nonsensical postcards, old tapes. When Ruby found a remnant of Abe, so stark, always, against the sanity of her mother's household, it was like finding a bread crumb he'd left in his meandering wake. What thought pattern would lead him to place this movie on the mail table, or to perch it precariously in the medicine cabinet next to nail polish and expired bottles of aspirin? There was no following the logic, and they had learned it was easier and less harmful for them not to try (Ruby tried, though, she couldn't help it, she always tried). Joking about it, turning the house into a treasure hunt for craziness, leavened the reality of Abe's illness just a bit. It was the only way; there was simply too much to handle otherwise.

Now, in the TV room, Abe watched *Visions of Death* and

laughed raucously at something on-screen. Ruby, her mother, and Aaron ate in silence, dwarfed by Abe's presence in the other room. Abe had already consumed a plateful of food, stuffing rice into his mouth, jamming his fork, which he gripped in his fist, down against his plate so that it made a *clink* noise every time, and picking up his chicken leg and devouring it in three bites. Then he pushed his chair back from the table and carried his plate over to the counter by the sink and left it there, the remnants of his meal strewn across it, and bounced back toward the table to say "Thanks for the grub, Mom," before disappearing into the other room. When he was gone, Ruby's mother sighed, her fork paused against her own plate, and shook her head, and Aaron looked at her and then at Ruby, but none of them said anything. When they heard the TV turn on they resumed eating.

Ruby's mother's friend Priscilla had brought the food. The day before yesterday she had come by with a home-cooked meal and told them that she would be bringing meals by every night for however long they needed. Tonight, when they got home from the hospital, the food was in the mudroom just inside the door, with Post-it notes telling Ruby's mother that all she needed to do was warm it in the oven. Ruby remembered people doing this for them when her father died. For weeks after the funeral, they ate other people's food. All of these tiny details were echoes; it was strange and yet familiar for them to be happening again.

"You know I'm going to this prom thing tomorrow night, right?" Ruby said now, looking at her mother. She picked up her glass of water and took a sip.

Ruby's mother looked blank for a second, as if she had registered that words had been spoken but had to replay them in her mind before they were heard. In the other room, the TV blared. Ruby heard a voice say, "World domination!"

"Oh," her mother said, "that's right, I had completely forgotten." She gave Ruby a forced smile. "Of course."

"Prom?" Aaron said, and he reached over to poke Ruby's side. "You've got a prom?"

Ruby looked back at him and smiled shyly. "Yeah."

"Are you going with a *boy*?"

His tone of voice was the one that he used when he spoke to Ruby about anything related to her being a girl. It was the same tone he used when she got her period while he and Nathan were driving her back to camp the summer their father got sick. It had mortified her to tell them, but she'd had to, and they had stopped at a convenience store so she could get, as Aaron said, reaching his arm around the front seat to playfully pat her leg, "*feminine* products."

"None of your business," she said, poking him back.

He grinned at her. "When I went to the prom I crashed Dad's car," he said. "Remember that, Mom?"

Their mother looked at him, deadpan. "Of course."

"Really?" Ruby said.

"Yeah. Dad lent me his good car—you remember the one that talked?"

Ruby remembered. The night her father had gotten that car, they had all gone out and sat in it in the driveway so he could demonstrate its features. She remembered climbing into the backseat next to Nathan and Aaron (Abe was already in college), their mother in the front passenger seat, the strange excitement of being in the driveway at night, in her nightgown, with her family in an unmoving car. They all exclaimed about the new car smell, about the leather interior and the lights on the dashboard, and then, when they were all in and settled, their father said, "Are you ready? Are you all ready? Listen," he said, and then he opened his door, and there was a pause, and then from somewhere at the front of the vehicle a computerized voice said: "The door . . . is ajar."

It took a moment or two for them to figure it out—had the *car* just said that?—but then they howled with laughter, and made him close his door and open it again. The car said other things too—"Please fasten your seat belt," and apparently it would tell you when it was low on gas—but "The door is ajar" was everyone's favorite. They repeated it, after the car said it they would all repeat it back, trying to imitate the exact way it had sounded—"The door," flat and even, "is a *jar*," with a slight rise in pitch at the end—and then Nathan would shout "No it's not, it's a door!" and they would all laugh. They sat in the driveway doing this for who knows how long, opening the doors and laughing, until finally their father said, "Okay, that's enough"; the switch had flipped in him and it was time to go back inside. "Best car ever," Nathan said as they climbed out the left side. "Definitely," said Aaron.

"Of course I remember," Ruby said now. "Best car ever."

"Right, until yours truly borrowed it. I promised Dad I would be good—it was such a big deal that he lent it to me—and I didn't even make it to the prom before I crashed it. I didn't even make it *off our street*."

"Really?" Ruby looked from Aaron to their mother, who was smiling and shaking her head at her plate.

"Yup. I was running some errands that day before I went—Dad lent me the car in the morning, so I had it for the day—and I rolled right down the hill and into a truck that was turning onto our street. Maybe . . . *three* minutes after I left the house with it."

"Wow."

Aaron was nodding and laughing. "And then I tried to play it off like it didn't happen."

Ruby couldn't believe this story. It was like a remnant from a distant past, a story vaguely familiar from a book she'd once read. "What?" she said, her mouth open.

Aaron looked at their mother, then back at Ruby. Ruby's mother was still laughing; it was good to see her laugh.

In the other room, Abe clapped three times, big claps, and said "Yeah!" There was a sound from the television like a bomb dropping on a cartoon, a high-pitched squeal getting lower.

"I came home and parked it in the driveway. There was a huge dent in the side, but I parked it so that side was facing the basketball hoop."

Their mother joined in. She looked at Ruby. "Then he just goes upstairs like nothing had happened—didn't say a *word*—and starts to get ready for the prom."

"Oh, my God," said Ruby, shaking her head.

Aaron shrugged. "I thought I could get away with it, at least until after the prom. So my friends come over, and we're getting ready for the prom, it's like three or something and we're supposed to leave at six. And then Mom sees the dent."

"Uh-oh," said Ruby, smiling. It was difficult, but she felt herself giving in to the shared joy of this moment.

Aaron nodded. "Yeah. Mom sees the dent, and she calls me downstairs and starts *chewing* me out about it, about how Dad is going to be so *mad*, about how that car is Dad's *baby*, oh my God, how could I be so irresponsible, the works." Aaron was into the storytelling now. His eyes had a spark in them that she hadn't seen in a while. "Then Dad comes home around six-thirty. I'm just about in tears at this point, I'm all worked up and guilty and *freaking* out, and he sees the car and he comes in the house and he is . . . cool as a cucumber."

He stopped.

"*Really?*" This was not what she expected. Ruby looked at their mother, who was still smiling at Aaron. She liked hearing him tell this story.

Aaron nodded, slowly. "Totally. He's completely calm. He just says something like 'We'll talk about it tomorrow, go to the prom and have fun.'"

"No."

"I know! I couldn't believe it. Mom had built me up so much."
Aaron flashed a smile at their mother, who said, "I was totally caught
off guard! I couldn't believe he wasn't more mad." She looked at
Aaron. "After you left, he basically said something to me like 'Boys
will be boys' or something, and that was it."

She paused, then picked up her fork, shaking her head. "Your
father was *completely* unpredictable. Completely. Just when you
thought you could predict exactly what he would do, he would do the
exact opposite."

Aaron nodded, and picked up his fork too. "It was pretty
amazing," he said.

Ruby looked at her own plate, and the sounds from the TV came
back into the room. Abe said, "Ha!" and clapped. No one looked up.
They were silent again, eating Priscilla's food.

On Friday, Ruby got dressed for the junior prom while her mother
cried in the kitchen. She could hear her mother crying; the sound was
choked and desperate, gliding up through the hallway, up the stairs to
her room. She couldn't hear Aaron, but she was sure he was down
there too.

Ruby stood in front of the mirror over her dresser and looked at
herself. She imagined her mother at the kitchen table, her head in her
hands, Aaron standing behind her with his hands on her shoulders,
gently rubbing. Her mother was crying because Nathan was dying.
Ruby thought this as she straightened a necklace around her neck.

She wore a light blue dress with darker blue flowers that she had
bought a year ago for a cousin's Bar Mitzvah. The dress narrowed at
her waist and then fell in waves to the floor. Her hair was pulled up off

her shoulders into a tight bun. She decided she did not like it this way and pulled out the pins that held it in place. Her hair fell loose, the dark curls slightly frizzy from having been so contained.

She looked at herself, and listened to her mother cry. The image in the mirror shifted: she was herself, she was looking at herself, she was not herself, she was looking at a girl in a dress. Her face was serious and pale and familiar. Her mother's wails were growing softer. *Nathan is dying*, she thought. *I am going to the junior prom.*

When she went downstairs, her mother and Aaron were at the table. Aaron was sitting in the chair next to her mother, both his hands wrapped around a cup of tea. Wally, her tail wagging, got up from the floor and came to Ruby, who bent to pet her.

"Oh, honey," Ruby's mother said, wiping her eyes. "Oh, honey. You look beautiful."

"Yeah Rube, you look great," said Aaron.

Ruby stood up and looked at the floor. "Thanks," she managed. She felt silly before the two of them, so dressed up. Did they think she was ridiculous for going, did they think she was selfish, did they think she was doing something wrong? They had a coalition against her, she thought, the two of them with their cups of tea.

She raised her eyes to her mother. "Are you okay?"

Her mother sniffled and wiped her nose with the back of her hand. "Yes," she said, standing and pushing back her chair. Aaron didn't move. He took a sip of his tea. Why did that little gesture make Ruby angry? Somewhere in that gesture, she thought, in that little sip of tea, was the whole difference between them.

"I'm so glad you're going tonight," her mother said. "Really, Ruby. You deserve it. Try and have a little fun, and try not to think about any of this. Everything will still be the same when you get back."

She came over to Ruby and put her hands on her shoulders. Ruby didn't want to look at her mother's tearstained face, at the red rims around her eyes. She found she couldn't look up, she couldn't look at Aaron, she could do nothing but stare at the floor. She felt her mother's hand smooth the hair on the left side of her face.

"I'll go get the camera," Aaron said, pushing his chair back and starting for the door.

"No," Ruby said, a hint of panic in her voice, turning quickly from her mother toward Aaron's retreating back. "Aaron, no. Don't bother."

He stopped and turned. "Why not?"

"I don't know," Ruby said and looked back at the floor. She thought of her father behind the camera in the backyard, taking the annual family photo on Rosh Hashanah, the tripod balanced on the grass. He would direct all of them, as they sat in formation at the top of the backyard hill (three of them sitting on the white metal outdoor chairs, three of them standing in back), from behind the lens—"Ruby, move a bit closer to Abe, Nathan put your hand on your mother's shoulder, Ellen, come on, smile. What's the matter here? All of you, smile!"—and he would set the timer and then jog back to them, flushed and excited, while the camera made a rapid beeping sound, and then they would all stare at the camera anticipating the flash ("Here it comes, just a second, just a second, just a second").

"It just," she said, "it doesn't matter."

"Of course it does," her mother said, but Aaron didn't move. Her mother came toward him, so she was standing between them. She turned to Ruby. Her arms looked helpless, hanging, useless objects at her thighs.

"Of course it matters, honey," she said again.

"No." Ruby shook her head, still looking at the floor. Tim would be there any minute. "Really, Mom," she said and looked up at her. She made her voice hard and strong. "*Please*. Don't get the camera. I don't want any pictures."

• • •

Tim pulled in to the driveway in his father's Lexus. Ruby was waiting at the door for him, and when she saw the car pull up she went quickly outside. As she stepped out the door, she willed herself to leave her family behind. She would focus on Tim; she would focus on the night. The house and its inhabitants dissolved behind her. Her thoughts were a tunnel.

"Who needs a limo?" Tim said as he got out of the car, holding his hand out toward it like a game show host. The sight of him, smiling wide, dressed in a tuxedo, flooded her with relief. She stepped toward the car, and the urge to run and put her arms around him was strong. She wanted to hug him, she thought for sure that if she hugged him the two of them could lift off the ground and rise into the air.

She held herself back. "Hi," she said, and gave him what she knew was a shy smile.

"Hi," he replied, and came around the car. "You look nice," he said, also shy. He was holding a clear plastic box in one hand. She looked at it. "Oh, right. This is for you."

He held the box out to her. It was a wrist corsage—a huge one, made of tiny purple flowers. She was surprised by this gesture—Tim wasn't one to follow traditional rules. She tried to slip it onto her wrist, but it was too big; the flowers flopped off at an angle and the thin metal piece beneath them dug into her skin.

"Shit," he said. "I knew it! I should have had my mom come with me. How was I supposed to know what to get? I didn't even know I had to get one before my mom told me!"

Ruby laughed. "It's great," she said. "It's great."

He shook his head, but he was smiling. "No it's not, it blows. Sorry."

They stood for a moment, looking down at the corsage.

"Where's your mom?" said Tim. "I took so much shit at my house for not taking pictures, seriously. My mom wanted to come over here with me so she could see us both."

"Oh," said Ruby, with a quick flash of fear—should she lie? "She's . . . she's inside. I told her I didn't want any pictures."

"Really?" She could see he was confused by this. Did he want to have pictures taken of them, or was it because he could tell she was nervous about it? "She let you do that?"

Ruby shrugged, still looking at the corsage. She felt sure that her mother and Aaron were watching her from a window. Was Abe watching too?

"Anyway," Tim said, "why don't you want pictures? Are you embarrassed or something?" He gestured to himself, his body stuffed snugly into his tuxedo. "Does this body embarrass you? You embarrassed to be seen with this?" He made a sexy model pose, pouting his lips.

She laughed. "Come on, let's get out of here." She turned toward the car door.

Just then, Aaron came out of the house holding the camera. "Hold up!" he called, walking toward them. Ruby stood by the car door and looked at him in horror. Her stomach sank. This was not what she wanted; didn't anyone care what she wanted?

But she was trapped. Aaron was grinning. He went over to Tim's side of the car and held out his hand. "Timothy," he said in his big brother voice, "good to see you again, sir."

"You too," said Tim with surprise. He would be wondering, Ruby knew, what Aaron was doing home. Now she'd have to make something up.

"Ruby told me not to, but I'm sorry, Rube, the moment must be documented. Come on over here, stand up here by this tree, you two."

Ruby walked reluctantly after Tim toward the tree, her mouth tight, anger and shame running through her. When Tim put his arm around her shoulder, she wanted to melt into it; she hoped when the picture was developed she would be invisible, it would be Tim with his arm around a column of air.

"Say cheese!" said Aaron, holding up the camera. "No, wait, say prom!"

"*Junior* prom," said Tim, smiling.

Aaron pushed the camera button and the flash went off. Ruby knew Aaron loved his pictures almost as much as their father did; her straight mouth would be his punishment, she would not smile. It was the least she could do.

The prom was in the ballroom of an upscale hotel in the center of Boston. Tim's father had given him money to park the car in the garage; as they got out of the car, the sound of their doors closing echoed across the cement floor.

She followed Tim to the elevator and they took it to the top floor. They didn't speak. Ruby was fighting the growing feeling that something was terribly wrong, that something was missing. The thought had begun to creep in: *You can't do this, you don't belong.*

Just keep going, she told herself over the other voices. *You are fine, don't think.*

They stepped out of the elevator onto a plush carpet with a diamond pattern that led them to the ballroom. They entered down a wide staircase. The room was lit with chandeliers, and there was a disco ball hanging over the dance floor in the middle. A number of people were dancing awkwardly on the shiny wood of the dance floor, and some were seated around it at round tables. There was a balcony that surrounded the room, and a few people stood on it, leaning on the railing and looking down.

"Wow," said Tim as they stepped in. "Fancy-town."

Ruby watched her shoes as they descended into the room. They were blue patent leather, with heels. There was something off about them, she thought, about her feet in shoes like this. She felt distant from her feet, as she watched them. Were those really her feet? Was she really walking, on those feet, in those shoes? She had worn heels only a few other times in her life—her Bat Mitzvah, she remembered, had been the first time, her shoes had had little mini-heels, and she had loved wearing them while she mingled with her parents' friends, just a little taller than she normally was. But now, looking down at her feet, she felt like a fraud, like it wasn't just the shoes that were foreign but those ankles too, those moving calves, the feet tucked daintily into the leather. She looked at Tim, descending the stairs next to her, his tuxedo jacket pulled tight over his chest. His eyes were straight ahead and he looked excited, he looked like himself. She imagined them being announced—"Countess Bronstein and Timothy Dane"—and straightened her shoulders and raised her head. *Don't think.*

They found their friends, seated at a table to the left of the dance floor. Jill, wearing a long green dress with a halter neck, smiled at Ruby from across the table, where she sat next to her boyfriend, Tom, his hair slicked back against his head. "You look great, Rube," she said. She had told Ruby that tonight she would have sex with Tom for the first time. They were not going with Ruby and Tim to the after party—instead they were going to Jill's mom's house, where no one was home. Jen, sitting next to Jill in a low-cut black silk dress, nodded and agreed. Jen's date was Ralph Hunters, whom Ruby liked; he looked like a Jewish JFK Jr. and had a good sense of humor to boot.

"Thanks," said Ruby, "you guys do too."

She tried, but she couldn't seem to shake the feeling that she didn't belong. She couldn't engage. She didn't feel she looked good, she felt like someone else was wearing her dress and she was curled up inside. She was uncomfortable and she couldn't hide it; Jen and Jill were beautiful and at home in this room, in those dresses that looked perfect on them, hugging their beautiful breasts and tiny waists; Ruby was too flat-chested to even fill the space where her dress wanted her breasts to be. Jill was going to have sex tonight, Ralph couldn't wait to get his hands on Jen, and Ruby and Tim were so awkward they could barely speak. Tim didn't want to touch Ruby, she knew it, he wouldn't touch her, and Ruby's brother was in a coma across town from them right now—*right now,* as they sat there, talking about that new movie with Alicia Silverstone, a tube stuck in his throat was giving him breath.

Ruby watched the dance floor and resentment swam in her. She couldn't think of anything to say to her friends. Where was she, and where did she belong? Was she here, or was she in Nathan's hospital room, or home with her mother in front of the TV?

Dinner was served—chicken with mustard sauce and mushroom ravioli—and they ate. Around the table, her friends brought forks and crystal glasses to their mouths, her friends in formal dress, sitting upright, their faces fresh and shining under the crisp chandelier light. They were speaking as if they were sitting around after school in their homeroom—"No way! You're such a fucking liar"—but their silverware was clinking and their lipstick was making mouth prints on the rims of their glasses. What was this strange custom, that brought these people who bought ASICS sneakers and polo shirts in waves, one after another, who knew one another from the days of the black middle school miniskirt, into this room to act like their parents and speak like themselves? Was she crazy, that she felt they should be speaking of something wildly different in this setting or not speaking at all? She felt like yanking the forks from their mouths, standing and yelling, tearing the dress from her body and ripping it to shreds, anything to wake everyone up.

She couldn't eat much. Finally she abandoned the effort. She needed to get up from the table; maybe all she needed was to breathe some other air.

Tim turned to her as she pushed her chair back. "You okay?" he asked.

"Yeah," she said, "I'm fine. I'm just going to the bathroom."

"You sure you're all right?"

He was looking at her with real concern. She loved and pitied his genuine eyes. "Yeah," she said, "I'm sure. I'll be right back." She stood up and made her way toward the ladies' room.

The restroom was clean and bright, with a long marble countertop and four stalls with pristine white doors. She went into the handicapped stall, which was huge and had its own sink, and shut the door with relief. She had the whole bathroom to herself. The only sound was the hum from the lights and the dim bass coming from the prom.

She stood in front of the sink and looked at herself in the mirror. She saw herself, she recognized herself, but around her was whiteness and she could find no anchor there. She thought of Tim, and the fact that he didn't know about Nathan colored her image of him, dimming the outlines, so that it faded and grew blurry. When he knew, would it erase any possibility that he might touch her, ever? When everyone knew, would she be forever marked by what she already felt inside?

The thought of Nathan caused a sharp pain in her heart. She shut her eyes and put her hands on either side of the sink, leaning forward. *Don't think. Don't think. You are fine.* There was not room in this building, in this dress, in this restroom, in this night for thoughts of Nathan.

She opened her eyes and straightened. She wondered if she

might be cracking up—right here, right now, she thought, she was losing it, as Abe once had. She didn't want to go home, she couldn't imagine getting in a car with her mother or walking in her front door, she couldn't see Aaron or Abe, she didn't know what would happen to her if she saw Abe right now. But she couldn't go back into that room, either.

She heard the door open and the click of heels on the marble. "Rube?" someone said gently.

It was Jill.

For a second Ruby didn't answer—the surprise of having someone enter this space and then call her name took her a minute. Was it real? But then the heels came closer and Jill said her name again: "Ruby?"

"Yeah." She spoke tentatively.

"You okay?"

Ruby was grateful for her friend, but frightened too. There was an ocean of feeling just beneath this blue flowered prom dress, and with Jill here she felt it might break over the levees that held it back.

"Yeah," she said. She opened the door. Jill was standing just outside, looking concerned. Ruby tried her best to smile. "I just needed to get out of there for a second."

Jill nodded. "Yeah," she said, "me too. It's pretty weird, huh?"

Ruby laughed. "It's *so* weird."

"I saw you weren't really talking at the table," said Jill. She came into the stall. "Wow, this is so nice."

"I know," said Ruby.

Jill moved in front of the mirror and looked at herself, smoothing the hair behind her left ear. "Just thought I'd check on you," she said, turning to face Ruby.

"Thanks." She smiled hesitantly. "I appreciate it."

She didn't want to talk about Nathan or about Tim; she hoped Jill wouldn't ask.

Ruby could feel Jill's eyes on her as she looked down at the shining floor, sweeping her shoe over the bright shapes reflected in the marble. There wasn't a speck of dust on the floor; how many times a day did they have to clean it for it to shine like this? She imagined for a brief second that she could live inside this floor, that she and all the people in the ballroom were living inside a shiny marble floor like this. If they lived inside something so sparkling they would have to dress up all the time, she thought, they would have to always be clean. Maybe they would see one another's true natures, living in something so reflective.

"Can you believe the skank that Henry Judds showed up with?" said Jill.

Henry Judds was a big football player who had been particularly mean to Ruby for a time in middle school—he used to call out "Shut your hole" at her in English class, a class Jill had been in as well. Ruby *had* noticed his date tonight, a girl who did not go to their school and who was wearing a tiny red shiny dress that was way too small for her body. Her flesh spilled out of it like unrisen dough, the tops of her breasts rolling over the cups of the dress, her thighs bulging from the line of material just beneath her ass. Ruby had seen them on the dance floor with his knee stuck between her legs as if it were a hobbyhorse.

Ruby laughed. Jill was pulling her back, she could feel herself coming back to her friend, it was as if she were a balloon floating in space and Jill had begun to pull the cord to bring her back to earth. Jill understood how to help; Ruby was grateful and relieved.

"Who is she?"

Jill shrugged. "No idea," she said. "Some skank. He probably hired her for the night."

"Totally."

Jill shook her head, but she was smiling. "Sometimes I really hate our school."

Back in the ballroom, people were dancing. At the abandoned table, Tim and Tom were sitting next to each other as Ruby and Jill approached, a sight that softened Ruby. Their two boys were waiting for them; they cared about them and they were waiting together for their girls to return. Seeing the boys like this, from a distance, she could just about believe that she and Tim had a love comparable to what Jill and Tom had, that Tim was waiting for her just as Tom was waiting for Jill.

"Hey," she said, putting her hand on Tim's shoulder.

"Hey!" he said. She took the chair next to him. "Where've you been? We're missing the good stuff."

She laughed. "Right. *Real* good."

"*Real* good," repeated Tim, even louder. "You already missed the Humpty Dance, man. We really might as well just go home."

A slow song was starting. Jill and Tom, holding hands, were moving toward the dance floor.

"Sorry," said Ruby.

"It's cool," said Tim. "But you better be ready now." He took a sip of his water and pushed back his chair.

"You ready?" he said. Ruby nodded and stood.

They made their way to the dance floor and through the couples to a spot near the middle. The song was "Forever Young," one Ruby knew without remembering how. The lyrics filled the room: "Forever young, I want to be forever young. Do you really want to live forever, forever and ever . . ." They stopped, and faced each other for a second, and Tim gave her an awkward smile, and then they stepped close.

Ruby, her arms around Tim, looked over his shoulder and saw

the dance floor full of couples, the people she knew all dressed up and holding each other, heads resting on shoulders, hands clasped around necks and backs, bodies close and swaying, eyes shut, eyes open, people talking and laughing, their faces close. The light from the disco ball was dancing across the familiar people; the light was reflected, a shape here and then gone, a shape there and then gone, light cast across a forehead or suit back, across a calf or oxford shoe. She held on to Tim; his body was between her and the room. *Forever young,* said the music, *I want to be forever young,* and the bodies danced and swayed.

It was too much; it was beautiful and tragic and shining and too much. Tim was close, so close, his body was pressed against hers, his neck was just by her face, she could feel the coolness of his ear on her skin. She closed her eyes and concentrated, being present, present, in this moment. Tim was holding her; they were dancing. His body was solid and real, holding hers. She felt the solidity of Tim's body—the way it came up from the floor like a strong, soft pillar. She rested her head on his shoulder, closed her eyes, and tried to sense all the places where her body was touching his: his arms around her waist, her breasts against his chest, her chin on his shoulder, his ear against the side of her head. She concentrated, trying to hold on to the moment, trying already to remember what the moment felt like. She was amazed by the heft of him, the force created as their strong bodies were gentle with each other.

After the prom, they went to their friend Joe Pott's house. Joe's parents were supervising from the basement, and there were two kegs of beer outside on the porch. Ruby and the girls changed out of their dresses in one of the upstairs bedrooms, but their hair and traces of their makeup still gave them away. The beer, someone yelled, might be nonalcoholic, because no one was getting drunk.

The night passed quickly—Ruby smoked pot with Tim and Jen and Ralph out on the porch, and they laughed for a good half an hour about a garden gnome that Tim swore he saw move (he crouched down beside it and peered at it, insisting they were communicating), and before she knew it, people were drifting off to the bedrooms and pulling out the couches. Tim and Ruby had put their stuff in the same guest bedroom when they first got to Joe's. After she brushed her teeth, she found Tim at its door.

"Hey," he said.

"Hey." She went in and sat on the bed, suddenly nervous. What was expected of them now? She was frankly surprised that they were going to sleep in the same bed; it seemed to have come about by coincidence rather than by design.

Tim stood in front of her for a few minutes, looking around the room. He seemed nervous too, she thought. There were a few picture frames on the bureau by the window and Tim peered at them, saying softly, "Look at these people, man." Ruby felt as if her body was cemented in place. She thought of Jill and Tom, surrounded by flickering candles, in Jill's mother's flowery four-poster bed.

Finally, Tim turned around to look at her. He gestured to the carpet next to the bed. "I can sleep on the floor," he said hesitantly.

She knew it; he wanted to sleep alone. She shook her head. "Don't be silly," she said. "It's not a big deal."

She pulled back the covers and got in the bed with her clothes on. She turned from him so he wouldn't think she was watching him; she could hear him taking off his pants next to the bed, the sound of his belt buckle opening. In a minute she felt the bed move as he got in beside her.

"Good night," Tim said, and then there was silence. She wondered what he thought about having her next to him, if he was thinking at all or if he was falling straight to sleep. It was classic Tim to be oblivious; she envied his peace.

Ruby lay on her back in the dark and felt the heat from Tim's body creep slowly over to her. As always lately, before sleep her thoughts started to move, they spun quickly through her mind, flitting like the light of the disco ball. She was still a little stoned, and alone with her brain now, she was aware of how quickly her thoughts were moving. Tim was next to her, his body was warm and close, his heat enveloping her. She tried to concentrate on it, banishing the other thoughts to the sides and only feeling the heat. It raised the hair on her arms; she imagined the hair reaching out to Tim, trying to absorb his energy into her skin.

She couldn't help it: she thought of Nathan in his bed right now at the hospital, his body warm under the cotton blanket. *Don't think,* she told herself, but she saw him: now in his hospital bed, now in his bed at home before he left, now playing his cello, his body wrapped around it and swaying. *Don't think.* She saw her father, in his last wheelchair, the salt-and-pepper hair on his chest curling out of his V-neck undershirt; she saw the dance floor at the prom, covered in young bodies holding each other; she saw Jill leaning against the sink in the restroom at the hotel in her long green dress, her head tilted with concern; she saw Abe in his train conductor's hat; she saw Tim leaning over the garden gnome, holding his hand next to his ear to listen. *Don't think,* she thought. *You are fine. Your thoughts are a tunnel.*

She turned her head to look at Tim. He was lying on his side, with his back to her, his torso swelling beneath the blanket like the curve of a bell. She stared at his back and fought the urge to reach out to him, to touch his silent, peaceful body. His breaths were calm and steady. Even if he had been thinking about her, he must be nearing sleep by now.

She felt longing rise up in her like a wave. Her body was a shell for the longing; as she looked at Tim the longing filled her up until she was full. She tried to keep her breathing slow, but the feeling was welling in her chest, expanding and constricting over her heart. Longing, longing, desire, feeling; she wanted, she wanted, she needed, but she could not have. She felt the need to touch his hair, to run her hand down the length of his arm, to watch his face as she gently touched his stomach. She wanted to be enclosed by his arms; she wanted him to turn to her and swallow her whole. She wanted to be inside his body, peeking out. Her body did not move, but she could feel every cell inside her reach for him. She felt she was being strangled by longing.

"Tim," she said at last, the word like a gasp.

"Hmm," he answered, almost asleep.

"Tim," she said again, a little louder, forcing the word out, the feeling contracting in her chest.

Tim rolled toward her, onto his back. "What is it?" he asked.

But she didn't know what to say.

Fifty-two Rubys

Ruby and Michael lay on the metal dock at the shore of the lake, looking up at the sky. Their feet were on the soft ground at the edge of the water, their backs on the metal. They were quiet, looking at the stars and listening to the frogs in the grass somewhere off to their right. Every night, this croaking—*uhh, uhh, uhh, uhh*—the methodical and disenchanted sound of frogs that were, as the rumor went, fucking. Was that what they were doing? Ruby wasn't sure she believed it, but she imagined a whole series of them anyway, lined up on the shore, mounted on top of each other, thrusting their froggy organs into each other one by one, on down the line. *Uhh, uhh, uhh, uhh, uhh,* the groaning was constant and relentless, the tone never altering. The frogs had deep voices and they were deeply bored, Ruby imagined, even as they copulated. *Uhh, uhh, uhh;* yeah, yeah, yeah.

The frogs added a bit of humor to Ruby and Michael's vigils at the lake, which had become serious and frequent, almost nightly. One of them would utter a terribly sad or deep statement about life, about their feelings, a statement they'd never uttered before to a single soul, and they would look at each other, and there would be the frogs— *uhh, uhh, uhh*—to point out how seriously they were taking themselves. One of them, usually Ruby, would be crying, and asking Michael *Why, why, why,* and then there were the frogs, answering her back: *Uhh, uhh, uhh.*

Perhaps this was why they went back to the lake every night. It had become their spot of choice, though before they'd landed there they also spent a few nights in the amphitheater, where the camp gathered on Friday nights for Shabbat services, a few nights in the green wooden sukkah on the path by Ruby's bunk, and one night on the steps of the Chadar Ochel, the dining hall, where they never returned because they had seen a skunk cross in front of them. Now, when Ruby met Michael outside her bunk while the rest of the girls got ready for sleep, there was no discussion about where they would go. They met, their legs moved over the ground, and then they were there.

They were still shy with each other, despite (or perhaps because of) the increasing intimacy of their nights together. During the day they were camper and counselor—Michael was twenty-one, the head of Ruby's kerem, the name of her age group, the oldest kids in camp, and Ruby was sixteen, just one of the many campers in Michael's charge. At night, though, they spoke their saddest and most puzzling secrets to the balmy night air. Ruby shared herself with Michael as she never had with anyone, and it became more and more difficult to repress the way she felt about him, to align their relationship with those of her other friends.

The agam—the waterfront: during the day a sun-bleached territory, the only patch of shade back at the boundary of the sand where groups of campers lined up before they entered the lake and Estelle, the woman in charge, gave a speech about being respectful and behaving, *"Bevakasha, bevakasha, BEVAKASHA!"* Campers hot and cranky, campers itching for water, towels around their necks and laps, the lumpy beginnings of breasts and chests and private parts throbbing and restricted and longing to be touched and explored and submerged. The docks patrolled by counselors in red bathing suits, their feet slapping against the metal and echoing, the sound of campers running, *slap slap slap slap,* and counselors walking after them, yelling, *Don't run! I said don't run!* People standing and dripping and looking out, people touching each other's wet skin and giggling, people brushing sand from the soles of their feet, from their calves. Little kids shaking their heads and crying, pulling away from counselors; the youngest kids in the shallow section, with yellow plastic puffs on their arms, grown women sitting around them in water up to their waists.

Ruby didn't like the agam. She never liked spaces where she couldn't escape the sun, and she resented forced swimming, it was just slightly worse than swimming at all. She associated the agam with the sun rashes she'd suffered as a kid, with her father making her take swimming lessons, someone holding her body in the water, with feeling awkward about her body, with feeling vulnerable, and with sputtering and confusion and embarrassment. She didn't like swimming in a lake, where soft and unknown things sometimes brushed against her legs. She wasn't very good at it, unlike all her girlfriends who wanted to be lifeguards and spent the afternoons lying on the sand; she didn't really see the point in swimming back and forth in a lane between two metal docks. She never understood why her father thought it was so important, why he used to write her letters at camp that said, *How's the swimming? You know I think it is very important to know to swim.* She looked forward to when it rained and swimming was canceled and they gathered in the Chadar Ochel instead and watched movies about water safety, lying on the dirty floor in the dark on their towels. She even looked forward to when she had her period and she could give Estelle the look that said so and could sit on the shore and read her book, or write letters to her friends, anything to keep her clothes on and stay out of the water. Sometimes, especially this summer, she'd even lied about it: she'd given Estelle the look when it was not true, she didn't have her period, just because she could, or when she did have her period it rained and therefore her period was wasted and she was owed this day off, she was owed it.

At night, though, with Michael, the agam was magical and serene, it was like some sort of romantic painting they could sit inside. As they approached the familiar area, the lake emerged before them as if from a fairy tale, the sign posted at the entrance that said THE AGAM IS CLOSED like a warning from an enchanted palace. Ruby could feel it calm her, as they approached; the air was pure and cool, the heat of the day dissipated along with the bodies and the noise. The lake sat peacefully, all of the activity let out from it like air from a tire. There were the frogs, making their groaning sounds, and the moonlight on the water, on the raft that bobbed out beyond the farthest dock. The water rippled, there was the faintest noise of it moving, just the faintest rippling sound as it rolled over itself.

This was when the water was inviting to Ruby. She imagined, lying next to Michael on the dock, that she could walk out on the water, that she could lie on the water and pull it over her body like a blanket, that this water could rock her to sleep. She imagined the water a perfect body temperature, she imagined submerging her face and feeling the water against her eyelids, soothing her mind, the water entering her ears and flowing through her brain and washing it out, washing all of it out, giving her sleep. She imagined the two of them, herself and Michael, out on the raft; she imagined Michael pulling his body up and onto the raft, reaching out for him to take her hand, the moonlight on his body as he flopped onto the raft, his skin glowing silver, the water rolling off of it as off of a fish's slick scales. She saw the moonlight on both of them, out there on the raft, the moonlight and the water across both of them, uniting them, the raft lifting and falling, through the water, the two of them just lying there next to each other on the raft and the raft falling through the water and then rising up, flying through the air, still submerged, somehow, in moonlight and water and always, the air like the water, their bodies air and water and flesh and peace.

————

Ruby had met Michael Fischer at the beginning of the summer, though she'd heard a lot about him before camp began. He was the first cousin of one of her best camp friends, Noah Baum, whom she had known since Hebrew school and who was part of the reason she had started coming to camp three years ago (that and the fifty dollars her father had paid her). Michael was notoriously smart and likable and good-looking, and had been a camper too, part of Kerem '89, reputedly the most fantastic kerem that had ever been until now, until her own. A few months before camp he had sent a letter out to her kerem that impressed Ruby; it was well-written and smart and just a bit idealistic. He recommended that everyone read *As a Driven Leaf*, which no one did, but Ruby loved any man who suggested reading anything.

It was the last week of June when her mother drove her to camp, almost three weeks after Nathan died. There had been discussion— Should she go? Would it be too hard? Was it too soon?—but for Ruby there was never any real question. What was the alternative? Miss her final summer at camp to stay at home and think about what had happened? She couldn't help the timing, she couldn't help any-thing, she could only go on as best she could. So she went.

They pulled through the gates of camp that first day, and as usual there were people to greet them, people wearing white shirts with the camp insignia on them, people with bright smiles who leaned in through their windows and said hello, and welcome, and told them where Ruby's bunk would be, where to park to unload. Ruby was happy to be back; the people were familiar and healthy and they said

"Hey Ruby!" when they saw her, and as soon as she and her mother pulled through the gate she felt at home. This was where she was known apart from her family and its tragedies; there was a freedom she found here that she never had with her friends at home, even with Jill or with Tim, who knew her as a person who went home to her house every night after school, and who emerged from it in the mornings. Here she was only Ruby, a person completely independent of a family or even of a home.

She and her mother were pulling up the path, past the office, toward the dining hall, when a man jogged toward them, smiling, wearing the white camp shirt and a whistle around his neck on a thick black rope, and he held up his hand for them to stop. He came around the car and leaned in Ruby's window.

"I'm Michael Fischer," he said. "I've heard so much about you; it's so good to finally meet you." His arms were tan on the car windowsill, and his eyes were a piercing green, and he said, "It's going to be a great summer, I'm so glad you came."

They said they were glad to meet him too, and Ruby looked at the skin on his face, so smooth and full of color, and then her mother pulled the car on down toward the bunk and they watched Michael grow slowly smaller in the rearview mirror. Ruby's mother said, "Well, he was cute!" and Ruby felt a warmth inside of her; she had made the right decision, the summer was ahead of her like a pile of wrapped birthday presents.

That night, after her mother helped her unload the car and put the sheets on her bed, after her mother had hugged her tightly and kissed her cheek and told her that she loved her, and to call if she needed to; after Ruby and her friends had dressed for dinner and lined up at the flagpole for the first time and eyed all the boys to see who was looking the best this summer; after they ate dinner, which was fish sticks and tartar sauce; and after Rebecca, the camp director, made her first post-dinner announcement of the summer, saying how happy she was to see them all again, and for everyone to give a special round of applause to Kerem '94, who were the oldest campers this summer; after the camp applauded them, because this year they ruled the camp—after all of this, the entire camp streamed out of the Chadar Ochel and onto the playing field for a campfire. Some of the counselors were already there, the wood was set and ready to be lit, and the camp gathered around it, counselors moving their bunks into groups and sitting them in ascending order, smallest kids in front, shushing them, organizing them into a wide circle. Someone lit the fire, the flames flared up and everyone cheered, and slowly, slowly, the sun went down, and everyone grew calmer, the feverish talking ceased, and the sparks from the fire floated through the air like bubbles, up, up, in wild directions, wayward and quick, then popped.

It was dark. There were crickets chirping from the woods next to the field and mosquitoes buzzing around her ankles and the air was just slightly cool, and Ruby sat with her friends and put her hands behind her and leaned back. She angled her face to the sky and shut her eyes for a moment and breathed deep and let the sounds wash over her: the sounds of this familiar camp full of Jewish people gathered around a campfire. Someone started a song; it was in Hebrew, and the counselors joined in first, and slowly everyone began singing, the sound of the fire was drowned out but the flames still leapt from the center of the circle. Ruby didn't sing; instead she raised her head and watched the fire. Over the heads of the campers in front of her she watched the flames, like some kind of transparent and upward-flowing water. Her gaze zoned out into the wavering and incessant red, the sound of the singing camp entering the movement of the fire. She saw the flames, and noticed the way their edges were flared and tentative, fading at the ends. She had just started to wonder about this—was there something to this fading, metaphorically speaking?—when she felt a tap on her left shoulder.

She turned around to see Michael Fischer, crouching on the grass behind her. "Can I talk to you for a second?" he said gently.

Her heart fluttered, she nodded, and then she and Michael were walking away from the fire and the crowd of voices singing, away from the flames traveling up.

They walked out onto the playing field behind the campfire. Just a few steps away, it was suddenly much darker and hushed; the sound of the voices seemed to come from a much greater distance. Michael led the way, striding fast, and then suddenly he stopped and faced her. She caught his eye in the moonlight, and he smiled at her. "Hi," he said.

"Hi," she whispered. She felt very shy, as if he had just asked her to dance.

He looked back to the fire. "I just wanted to say something to you, Ruby," he started. "I'm sorry to single you out like this, but I didn't really know how else to do it." He turned to her. She tried to keep her eyes on his face but felt her cheeks flushing warmer and had to look down.

"I just wanted you to know," he said, "that I know what's happened in your family and that I am thinking about it. I wanted to tell you that I'm here for you, to talk, or really for whatever you need. I can't imagine how it must be for you to be here now"—he paused—"or how it must be for you in general."

She looked up at him and their eyes met. She felt sure that there was heat coming from him, as there had been from the fire. It was suddenly warmer out here in the dark with Michael than it had been with the fire on her face.

"I also wanted to tell you that I"—he stumbled—"I lost my father when I was at camp, when I was fifteen." He shifted his feet in the grass, reached his right foot out as if to touch something. "He had a heart attack, while I was at camp. It was very sudden."

Ruby thought of two summers before, the day her father was diagnosed, when she had left camp for two days. Adam, the boys' counselor, had picked radishes from the garden he had started and pressed them into her palm just as Nathan and Aaron pulled in to pick her up. She remembered the call over the camp loudspeaker—"*Bevakasha, bevakasha,* will Ruby Bronstein please come to the office for a phone call?"—and how she just knew what the call meant, her father had been strangely sick for a couple weeks and he was never sick. She remembered the way her stomach dropped into her toes when she heard the announcement, right there on the basketball court, and then the trip down the hill to the office with her stomach in her feet.

Michael was looking at her. The voices from the campfire rose, they were singing a song now that Ruby knew, part of her brain was following the words although she didn't know what they meant. "That is not to compare our situations, at all," Michael said, "but just to let you know that I can understand. I want to make this summer as easy on you as possible, Ruby, I mean it. I'm glad you're here, and I'm here for whatever you need. I hope you won't be afraid to ask for anything at all." His skin in the darkness looked smooth. "That's all."

Ruby felt a sudden, strong realization: she was at camp; she was standing on the playing field with Michael Fischer, whom she did not know but who knew about her family, which meant that it was real. Nathan was dead, and her father was dead, and her mother was at home with her crazy brother Abe, Aaron was somewhere in Chicago, and Ruby was here, on this field, with a campfire off to the right of her shooting sparks to the sky. She was suddenly completely present in her body, as if she had been shot down into it from somewhere above herself. Here she was, standing here, when who knew where she was before. Her knees were weak. The sky was full of stars. Her body was hot and she could feel grass on the tips of her bare toes. She was looking at Michael and he was waiting for her to speak.

"Thank you," she finally managed, the feeling passing. "Really, thank you."

Michael nodded. "I mean it," he said. "Anything. If you ever want to talk."

"Thanks," she whispered, because she wasn't sure if she could speak louder and not cry. She tried to smile. "I'm sure I will."

Sure enough, the very next night, she did.

———

Her father was diagnosed when Ruby was at camp, two summers before, just three weeks after she and her parents had returned from their trip to Czechoslovakia. Because of that trip, therefore, because of who her father was and what they had just seen, because of where she had been, at this Jewish camp, Ruby had put her trust in God.

Every morning, before breakfast, the camp gathered in the Ben Tzvi, an all-purpose room across from the dining hall where they held all their services and performances, and everyone gathered around the portable ark and sat on benches that were long and uneven and wobbly and had names carved into them, and they prayed. The prayers were the same every day, every summer—the Shema, the Amida, the Viahavta—prayers that Ruby had memorized but couldn't translate, prayers she had been saying all her life in some capacity: on occasional Saturdays with her family, in Hebrew school, at Bar and Bat Mitzvahs, and then, for three summers, daily at camp.

Generally, during morning prayers, before the day she was called down to the office over the loudspeaker, Ruby had chanted the words mindlessly and thought about what she would eat for breakfast and whether it would rain that day and if swimming would be canceled, about how good it felt when Ari Nussbaum put his arm around her waist when they sang "Rad HaYom"; but then there was her father's diagnosis, her father in the hospital bed, too full of life and fire to belong there.

She went home for two days. She went to the hospital with Nathan and Aaron, who had flown home, and saw her father straining against the bars of his bed and begging to be taken home. Her father told her to go back to camp; he looked at her mother and told her Ruby should go back to camp, and Nathan should go back to school, and Aaron should go back to work. So they did.

When she returned to camp, the prayer for the sick had been added to the morning service, and suddenly, maybe this meant something, all of it, maybe this whole ritual was meaningful, just maybe. Ruby heard her father's name murmured by the rabbi, her father's name bracketed by a minute or two of steady Hebrew, and everyone stood and said "Amen" with their heads bowed. Everyone in the camp sent their pleas to God to heal Ruby's father, who was at home with a brain tumor, and she felt sure that if there was a God, He would have to hear. A camp full of people was praying for her father, who had gotten her to come here in the first place, to this Jewish camp; it had to help. If it could help, it had to. She heard her father's voice, *Life is the highest good,* and she knew that what she was doing was for him: choosing life. The whole camp, around her, chose her father's life.

Every morning for the following three weeks she had come to prayers with an extra awareness, the sleep wiped from her eyes, ready to send her prayers up to God, ready to believe. Her recent trip to Europe was part of all this—when she arrived at camp that summer the experience was still with her, and the idea of this camp full of young Jews, privileged and free, celebrating Judaism, living the rhythms of a Jewish life, lifting their voices in unison to the sky, had a new poignancy for her because of what she—not her brothers, only she—had recently seen: the small towns of Czechoslovakia wiped completely clean of Jews; the gas chambers; the ovens she had peered into to try to glimpse human remains; the prisoners' uniforms with their still-attached yellow Jewish stars. Here, in this camp that she had taken for granted, was the proof that life went on, that Judaism continued; this was why her father wanted her to be here, why he was so happy that she wanted to come back. She understood, now, she thought, what he couldn't, what he didn't need anymore to explain. There was power here, she was witness to it—the power of generations, the power of history, of the past, the power of memory.

So when the prayer for her father came around, she closed her eyes and imagined it as a long and twisting rope of words, billowing out the top of the Ben Tzvi and rolling straight up, into the sky, beyond where she could see. She imagined her father as she had last seen him, in his hospital bed, so big between the rails, his hands on either side, and she concentrated on the hope that the prayer would stay tight and strong all the way up to God. She hoped that God would receive the twisting words, that God would receive them and unravel them and pay attention to the unified pleas of the people in the room, this gathering of Jews asking for the health of her father, *hers,* Ruby Bronstein's, all these prayers for one special man. If God was up there, He would hear this prayer, and He would respond. She imagined that all of Jewish history was praying, that in the prayer of this camp was the prayer of all the Jews who were missing from where she had just been with her father, all the Jews who wondered where God was then. Here was His chance to show Himself, to avenge the horror He had already permitted.

Everyone at camp told Ruby that they believed—everyone said, "I just know he'll be all right," and hugged her—and when camp ended in August and Ruby was going home, she was a little scared that without the camp's daily prayer the string to God might weaken, or maybe falter, and then what? But the rabbi pulled her aside on the last day and told her that he would keep praying, that they all would, and that God would not forsake her, no matter what, and she took his words into her heart and she told herself they were true. God would not forsake her. God had forsaken her father once already in his life, God had forsaken her father and her grandfather and the Jews. He would not forsake him twice.

But the following August, Ruby's father died, and from then on, she told herself, it was over between her and God. It was like a promise to her dad, whom God had forsaken: she would not believe. She would not give God the dignity even of feeling sad about His absence, of believing that He had ignored her prayers, the prayers of all of them; she would believe, instead, that He did not exist, that the prayers had been useless and blind, airplanes heading into thick fog. She imagined the prayers, the thick spiral, heading into the fog and dissipating, splintering, fraying, and splitting apart, airplane fuselages, metal flying through the air, wings breaking off and falling. There was no one to receive them; there never had been. She had chosen life and life had been taken away. She passed into the season of her father's death with a steeliness bred from this anger, the resentment of being abandoned and overlooked.

This was her mind-set when Nathan got sick in April; if she had decided after her father's death that it was over between her and God, then this summer, after Nathan, her feelings for Him were so empty and confused that she could not even access them. The words of the prayers she said or the songs she sang were nonsense words, disconnected from any meaning at all.

One night, weeks after the campfire, when their routine had grown solid and reliable, Ruby and Michael were at the agam. Ruby's eyes were on the stars, the frogs were croaking, and Michael lay beside her. They often had long stretches of silence before they spoke, marking the transition between the energy of the day and the contemplative night.

Ruby watched the stars. The more she looked at them, the more appeared: some of them bright and distinct, others clustered and smudged, as if they had been rubbed over by an eraser. She imagined the stars as a curved ceiling, the round cover of a snow globe closing her in.

"Do you think that everything is preordained?" she said, her words slicing into the night.

Michael didn't answer. She could sense him thinking. "What do you mean?" he said finally. "Like that everything that happens is already going to happen? That it's all planned out?"

"Yeah," she said. "Sometimes I wonder about that."

"Me too. I don't think it is, though."

"Sometimes I think," said Ruby, still looking at the stars, "that maybe there's a whole series of parallel realities—that each of us has a whole deck of possible realities. That it's like 'Choose Your Own Adventure,' you know, and we just happen to be inside *this* reality, but at this very moment there are fifty-two other Ruby Bronsteins living in other possible versions of my life."

Michael laughed, then stopped, considering this. "Yeah," he said.

"Like, for every given moment, there are all these other possible ways the moment could go, and when it goes one way for me, it spins out into all these other parallel realities for the other Rubys. I don't know. Sometimes I think about that."

"Well, then there would be a whole lot more than fifty-two Rubys."

She smiled. "That's true, I guess. There'd really be an infinite number."

Across the lake, a dog barked.

"It's weird to think about," said Ruby. "Because then you start to wonder, why am I *this* Ruby, you know? Why am I the one that lives through *this* moment?"

"Yeah. And is there any possibility for transition between Rubys? Can there be any movement?"

"Right."

Michael's body was close to hers in the darkness. Ruby could sense the heat of his arm, just an inch from hers.

He said: "I think the harder thing to grasp, though, is that there's only one of us. Everything we experience, everything we feel, it's all just ours."

Ruby didn't answer, but she felt the sudden weight of this. The stars, the whole dome of the sky seemed to drop a few stories closer to her; it all hovered very close.

"That's really why we think of other possibilities, you know?" Michael said. "Why we think of parallel selves, or enlightenment, or even God, any of it. Because the other alternative, the *reality*, is so unbearable."

His words traveled up into the hovering sky. Despite Michael's nearness, she felt terribly alone, as if she were the only real thing and all the rest was a movie set, carved from cardboard.

The next night, at midnight, when everyone else was asleep, she lay awake in her bed, a few feet from her friend Amanda, who was awake in hers. Amanda was the first person Ruby had met at camp, a bubbly girl whose friendliness had surprised Ruby—there was no one like that at Featherton, so trusting and open. Meeting Amanda that first day across the table in the dining hall had been the reason she'd thought she might like this place.

Beneath their covers they had on sweatpants and sweatshirts. They were waiting to sneak down to the boys' bunk to see Noah, who was Amanda's boyfriend, and Karl, who had climbed into Ruby's bed one night a few weeks ago.

"When do you think we should go?" whispered Amanda.

"Just a few more minutes," Ruby whispered back. "When Elisa starts to snore."

They faced each other, waiting.

The first time Noah and Karl came to them had been a cold night; Karl was wearing his fleece, and when he got into Ruby's bed he was shivering. Noah's visit, as Amanda's boyfriend, was no shock, but the appearance of Karl was a complete surprise. Ruby was half-awake when she realized he was standing over her, in his red fleece and sweatpants, already taking off his Tevas, and it was almost instinctual for her to move her body closer to the wall to make room for him. "It's freezing out there!" he whispered as his body entered her warm bed, and she put her arm around him and felt him shivering. He smelled clean and sweet, like shampoo.

"Freezing," he said again.

She rubbed his arm, the fleece soft against her palm. "Warm up, warm up," she whispered. He had his arm around her waist. He shivered and then lay still.

She had known Karl, like all the other boys in her kerem, since her first summer. The two of them had never been good friends; in fact, she couldn't remember thinking much of him until this year. But this year, almost on the first day of camp, there he was, as if they had been close for years.

This was how camp worked: alliances shifting, bonds forming and growing without any awareness or understanding, people you had known for years suddenly brand-new to you, crushes rising and falling, people impressing you less or making you feel somehow newly and inexplicably safe. Now, Karl always sat next to her, Karl took her aside to confide in her about how annoyed he was with people, Karl even began to tell her about his home life, about his "buddies," about the crazy girlfriend he had left behind who was nearly suicidal because he had left her for a whole summer. But the thing about camp, Ruby felt, was the way your home life became distinctly unreal and distant—as if they were all floating on an island in the middle of a vast ocean and might never make it back. She heard about Karl's girlfriend but she was not real to her, and Ruby felt she was barely real to Karl. Ruby relished being away not just from her family but from her friends as well—thoughts of Tim, once she passed over the threshold into camp, barely entered her mind.

And Karl was looking good this summer too. Ruby had never noticed the depth of his eyes before, blue (rare for a Jew, yes) and mesmerizing, as if they were not attached to a face at all. His hair was dark, long and full, flopping into his face, and his body was thick on top and thin on the bottom, almost to the point where it seemed the two halves of him didn't belong together, like in one of those coloring books where you aligned the legs and torsos of different characters. He was less athletic than the other guys who made up Ruby's camp friends, and would just as soon sit with Ruby and read *A Prayer for Owen Meany* on Saturday afternoons as play basketball ("Shabbos ball," a Saturday afternoon tradition at camp). He loved jam bands, they were his true passion; he had two cases full of bootleg tapes under his bed, each spine carefully and neatly detailed with the concert's date and place, the band's name drawn in a consistent hand.

And now he was spending nights in Ruby's bed. The morning after that first time, after Karl and Noah had snuck back to their bunk, just as the sun was starting to come up, Ruby's bed felt suddenly incomplete with just her in it, and she was surprised by it, strangely unsure if it had really happened, Karl's warm, soft fleecy body curled with hers for so many hours. She lay in her bed waiting for Elisa's alarm clock to go off and for her to call out, as she did every morning, "*Boker tov yeladot, nalakoom*—Good morning, girls, get up!" the words they all hated to hear. And Ruby went over the hours in her head, Karl's arm around her waist, his legs curled into hers, the warmth of their two bodies in her bed so much warmer than hers alone. She felt the slight moisture on her forehead where he had kissed her just before he slipped out the door with Noah, and she wondered at what had happened, and treasured it, as if it were a piece of candy slowly melting in her mouth.

She didn't know what it meant, it had taken her by surprise, Karl had just been there, and then he was gone, and she had not slept even for a second while his body was next to hers. But it had happened, she was sure, because Amanda smiled at her, and raised her eyebrows, and whispered, across the space between their beds, "Karl?" And Ruby just smiled, and thought of the warmth of him, and felt a new kind of longing she hadn't felt before.

And then, two nights later, he came again, and then again, and now it was a few nights every week, always just a few hours after she got back from the agam and climbed into her bed. But still, it was always only sleep; and during the day there was never any mention of it. Karl continued to talk to Ruby of his girlfriend, who called the office and left suicidal messages, and for whom he snuck out of night activities to go to the office and use the pay phone. He joked with Ruby, and shot her private glances, and put his arm around her, and came quickly to her side if she was sitting too much with other guys; he made joking-but-not-joking comments to her about what good friends she was with the others, Ari and Ben and especially Joe, who had lost his father when he was eight years old and with whom Ruby sometimes spoke on the tennis court about death, about how he chose a star that he thought of as his father and sometimes talked to it.

"We're just friends," she said to Karl. "And besides, what do you care?"

"I don't care," he said back, smiling. "You can be friends with whoever you want. But Joe? Come on. That guy is a wanker."

"Whatever."

He poked her. "You love him, don't you. You love him. You want to marry him."

"Leave me alone."

In the daytime, they were full of jokes, their affection for each other was hidden behind nudges and light punches on the shoulders. But at night their bodies behaved differently: more honest, Ruby liked to think, without the need for words.

One night, his head behind hers, his arm snaking around her waist and up along her torso to her chest, Karl whispered, "Ruby, do you want to talk about your brother? Or your dad?"

She stiffened. She didn't answer, she didn't know how. It was night; maybe he would think she was asleep. He squeezed her gently. "I just want you to know that I want to, if you ever do. When you do, I mean, I want to hear about them."

She didn't talk. She squeezed his hand so he would know she heard him. But Ruby didn't want to talk to Karl about her family. She barely even wanted to talk to Joe, on the tennis court, even when he cried about his father and showed her the star that was his dad she barely felt an impulse to talk. Even if she thought of them, which she did constantly, during the day; even if the image of Nathan rose up before her while she was with her friends sitting on the hill by the basketball court under the stars, or on the tetherball court, the ball whipping around the pole; even if she had to excuse herself from an activity to go behind the Beit Ha'am, the recreational building, and cry; even if she was bending over the water fountain attached to the building and the water was coming up in a thick arc and she was puckering her lips to receive it and she saw herself before the deaths, standing barefoot at the water fountain at Nathan and Abe's music camp, Nathan behind her in his concert whites, she pushed the images down and said nothing.

What good could talking do? Talking could do no justice to any of it. She would not let the grief set her apart; she would not let herself be marked, not here, not at camp. Camp was her oasis away from all of it—even if at night with Michael she allowed herself to feel it all, it was because she was buffered by the purity of the rest of her time there. If she started to talk to Karl, to any of her friends here, her chest might open up like a slide and her heart might glide out. If she started to talk, she might start to wonder why people weren't struck dumb by her words, why everyone's lives seemed to continue on, she might start to question the gaiety of this sacred place rather than enjoy it. Somehow not talking served to keep the deaths as powerful as they really were. Not talking kept her father and Nathan alive and intact inside her chest. She would give her body as a vessel to preserving her family.

Karl had asked her to talk, and she wanted to weep for his body against hers; she did not want to bring death into this softness, she didn't want to bring her family here, and she wished he hadn't asked. She didn't want him to be careful with her, she didn't want him to be putting his arms around her because she was sad, because she was different; she wanted his arms around her because she was Ruby, not because her brother and her dad were dead.

Only Michael had ever heard her talk about them. Not her mother, not Aaron, barely Jill or Tim, only Michael. Maybe it was because he was older, maybe it was because he was attractive, maybe it was because talking to him was removed from every other element of camp. Talking to Michael was understood, sanctioned by her counselors and the higher-ups, a treatment that no one asked her about and no one else received, which made Ruby feel special and just a little bit rewarded. Talking to Michael made her feel powerful and interesting and who she really was. Talking to Michael was the only way she allowed herself to be marked.

When Karl arrived at their bunk after Ruby came in from being with Michael at the agam, it was a trade of one kind of intimacy for another. She loved both of these men and was acutely aware, even in the span of one night, of the ending of one thing and the beginning of the other.

When it was time, Amanda and Ruby tiptoed out of the bunk, easing the door open just enough for them to slip through. The door creaked, and Ruby kept her eyes on Elisa's face as Amanda snuck through and held it for her—Elisa's face was calm and slack, turned to the wall, where ALEXA GOLD 1993 was written in white paint from the summer before—and then they were outside and tiptoeing down the porch, holding hands, watching their feet so they didn't trip. They moved quickly down the hill, blanketed in brown pine needles, across the sand path that headed deeper into the girls' section and into the main area of camp. The air was cool and thick with moisture, a blanket of fog hanging over the silent camp, so many sleeping people in a one-mile radius and the two of them, wide awake and heading for the warm bodies of boys, traversing the dewy ground.

They entered the boys' bunk through the back door, easing it open just as they did their own, and it gave off the same sighing creak. They crept in, on their toes, into the back room of the bunk, which was full of clothing stuffed into two rows of wooden cubbies. There, lying across the top of the cubbies, was the plaid flannel shirt that Ari wore last night, there, Joe's favorite sweatshirt, hanging on the nail by the door, and there, one of Jeff Weisman's shoes.

Against the far wall there was a beat-up brown couch and a coffee table, littered with the remains of a chips and salsa party—an empty salsa jar practically licked clean and the crumpled-up Tostitos bag next to it, a few crumbs scattered around. These were the remains of a good time had by these boys, their boys, present here while Ruby and Amanda were not. Even the trash gave off their presence; Ruby could see them on the couch stuffing the chips into their mouths.

Ruby often sat on this couch with the boys, in the afternoons, before or after dinner, their bodies sunk so far into the old fabric that they were almost sitting on the ground, leaning into each other, any excuse to touch. There were always chips and salsa, and if there weren't actually chips there was talk of chips, there were complaints about chips, there were yells into the main room about chips. Being in the boys' bunk, for Ruby and her friends, was always a thrill—they felt as if they belonged and yet simultaneously were breaking a rule. These were their boys—they knew the smells of their deodorants, they knew that Ari couldn't sleep without his fan, they knew that Joe was such a sound sleeper that the rest of the boys invented a game called Train, in which they shone flashlights in his eyes and paraded him around the bunk on their shoulders in the middle of the night. They loved the smell of this bunk, its slight tinge of boy body odor, because these were *their* boys, and no one else in camp could say the same.

Ruby and Amanda snuck past the cubbies, through the ripped tapestry over the doorframe, and into the main room. Noah and Karl's bed, made up of their two twin beds pushed together, was just inside the door on the left side, turned so that it faced the door. The rest of the beds were perpendicular to them and stretched out across the floor before Ruby and Amanda, each one filled with a familiar sleeping body.

Amanda pulled back the sheet and got in next to Noah, who slept on the outside. He grunted with surprise and then said "Mmm."

Ruby stood by the bed for a second before getting in, looking across the bunk. She was captivated; the moonlight filled the room with a dim glow. There was something so poetic about standing here, awake, in a room full of sleeping, prostrate boys, that Ruby felt her heart flutter. All the boys were asleep; she could hear a few anonymous snores, and she saw Ben Dratch, at the far end of the room, turn his body to the door. What was in their minds? What colors, what scenes did they see in those beds with their eyes closed? These boys, so rowdy in the daytime, so peaceful now. She saw them in their beds at home, all their various bedrooms were in the bunk with her, their baseball mitts and their stereos and their parents, hovering, tucking them in, shutting their doors—they were babies, suddenly, little baby boys.

She saw Joey Sperman with one leg out of his sheet and for a second, she thought of Nathan. Her mind started to go to the hospital, for a split second she saw him on that bed after they had removed his breathing tube . . . and then she pulled herself quickly back. She blinked and came back to the bunk. *No.* She willed herself not to think of Nathan, his helpless body, not to give in to the emotion that rose up to grip her chest. *You are fine.*

She had been given the gift of standing here, she thought, witness to this moment of peace in this place. She wished the moment would extend, she wished she could burn this moment into her body like a tattoo.

She turned to the bed and went around to the end so she could climb into Karl's side. At the weight of her, he stirred and moved over to let her in. She eased in as if onto a raft in water, stretching out, taking her glasses off and putting them in the cubby above their heads. Karl said "Hey," his voice drugged with sleep, and then mumbled, "I didn't know you were coming." He had a pair of underwear on his head; he did not explain. His hair peeked out in dark tufts beneath the elastic.

"I know," she whispered back. He put his arm around her; she faced out, toward Amanda and Noah, who lay still, and Karl pulled her close to him. He was almost asleep. She felt warm and welcome. In her ear he said, "Just so you know, I'm not wearing anything."

She turned her head slightly back to him. "You have underwear on your head."

"Yeah," he said. "That's it."

He squeezed her. That was all. He held her tight and slept.

She lay in his bed, wide awake, flushed with this new knowledge. She looked up at the wood ceiling, covered with names, at the rafters where towels and bathing suits were draped, at the tapestry hanging over the door to the back room. Karl was naked and holding her. He didn't move, so she wouldn't. He was asleep. This was the closest she'd ever been to a naked man. She lay still and tried to sleep—there were just a few hours until they'd have to sneak out again—hoping he couldn't feel the beating of her heart.

————

A few nights later, at the agam, Ruby told Michael about the photographs she took of her father not long before his death. "I don't know why I did it," she cried. "I really don't. Where did that instinct come from? Why did I want to document that?"

Michael had his hand on her back; it was just resting there, not moving.

"I took pictures of him," she said, "and now when I look at them I don't understand, they are so awful, I don't understand why I wanted to."

She thought of the pictures one by one: their hands, resting together on the sheets of his bed, her father's long, curved and graceful, paper-thin, and so soft, softer than anything she had ever touched before or since, her hand beneath his a fuller color, rounder and more plump, holding his hand gently, as if it were an eggshell; he in his wheelchair, up on the landing outside the hall of rooms, where they had wheeled him and sat with him on plastic-cushioned chairs, where he looked so small and unlike himself, and yet his eyes were imploring her—Were they imploring her to stop? Were they imploring her not to photograph him like this?—to do what she couldn't know, because by that time he couldn't speak. Were they just looking at her straight, as if to say, *Go ahead, this is me?* She thought of the V-neck white T-shirt he wore every day, of the gray and curling chest hair poking out of the top, of the bones where his neck met his chest, the way his neck stretched up from them like the neck of a bird.

She sniffled and wiped her eyes. "It's so weird," she said, "because even as I'm completely baffled by it, I'm still somehow glad I did it. I'm glad I documented him like that. But why? Why would I want that?"

Michael's hand moved, just slightly, left and right and then back. "I don't know," he said after a time. "Because you're you. Because you loved your father. Because you wanted to never forget how fucking horrible it was."

She swallowed and nodded. She looked up at the sky. "Like I could ever forget," she said. "Like I really need those pictures to remind me."

He leaned forward. His face was close to hers. "Of course," he said. "But that was your attempt at stopping time, you know? It was the closest you could get to stopping time."

She nodded. She thought of her mother when she had asked if she could bring the camera in when she came to see Dad; she thought of her, sitting across from Ruby as she pointed the camera at her father in his wheelchair, of the look on her face when she whispered, "I think that's enough, Ruby," and reached over to touch her father's arm where it rested on the chair.

She thought of the way the bones in her father's hand felt, so close to the surface, as she held it, on the bed, with her left hand, and took the picture with her right, the camera hovering over their linked hands. How strange it felt, to be looking through the lens of the camera at their two hands, to be holding her father's paper-thin hand and maneuvering the heavy camera at the same time.

A few weeks before her father left the house for the last time, in November of her sophomore year, just a few months after she returned from camp, they took a walk together, down and back up the hill of their street. This was the hill that Ruby's father had chastised her for not being able to climb on a bicycle the year before, when he went through a bike-riding phase: she remembered how, on their way back home, she got off a third of the way up and walked, her father turning back to her as he rode ahead, saying, "Come on, you chicken, you can do it, come on!" and standing up on his pedals, disappearing over the bend at the top, waiting for her in the driveway with an out-of-breath grin as she walked in, saying "Chicken" again and patting her on the back. That last day, however, they walked down the hill carefully, Ruby slowing her strides to keep pace with him.

They didn't speak for most of the walk. Ruby spotted a woodpecker with a red crown in one of the trees by the road and stopped her father to point it out; they stood for a minute and peered through the leaves at it, and her father nodded, and said "Nice," before they kept walking. The street was narrow and overgrown with trees, their lost leaves in piles along the sides; when they heard cars coming they stopped and ducked under the trees, and Ruby took her father's arm. She felt protective, in those moments, and had to resist throwing her arms out and stepping in front of him. At least for this walk, while she was with him, she would keep him safe.

They reached the base of the hill, where Ruby's childhood friend Beth Callin and her quadruplet siblings had lived, and turned around to begin the walk back up. "Ruby," her father said and took her arm. "When I'm gone, I want you to continue with your Jewish education. Keep going to camp, go to Israel. It is very important."

"Dad, you're not going anywhere." She squeezed his elbow with her hand.

"We'll see," he said. "But when I do."

"Okay," she said. "I will."

She wanted to ask him why; she wanted to ask him what he

thought of when he thought of Judaism, whether he thought of God when he thought of the tumor in his brain. Her brain lit up with questions as they walked slowly up the street: she wanted to ask how it felt to know the tumor was there, if he could feel it, and if it made him think of God. She wanted to ask what he thought of her, if he thought she was good, if she made him proud, if he thought she was his friend. She wanted to ask what he remembered about his life, right now, what he missed, what he had never told her, what she should know that she didn't already. What it was like to be him, her father, in the life he'd built, how it felt to love her mother, to drive in his car, to lie down with his memories, to live in America, to be on this street next to her, holding her arm, a tumor in his brain.

She thought of all the questions—her head was flooded with them—and didn't know what to ask. How could they begin, how could they begin now? She remembered when they had walked together out of Terezin, and she had felt a similar instinct to ask a question: if she couldn't do it then, how could she now?

She tried, she made the tiniest gesture to try, her voice came out weak and strained but she could feel herself trying, straining to push through the questions, to find one. "Dad—" she began.

"You are my Kaddish, you know, you and your brothers," he interrupted her. "You have to teach them. You have to carry on the tradition."

"Dad," she said, nearly whispering. She wanted to stop him, just as she wanted him never to stop. Was he happy with his life? Was he afraid to die? Did he think he would?

A car came by and she pulled him to the side. They stopped. He was looking at the ground, but he held on to her arm. "You are good kids," he said. "No matter what happens, I know that."

"You're a good dad," she said. He looked at her and gave her a coy little smile. She smiled back.

They kept on walking, and held each other's arms all the way back to the house.

Now, here she was at camp, as her father had asked, and yet she rarely said Kaddish for him. Was there a way to be his Kaddish without saying Kaddish?

Michael was speaking. "After my dad died," he said, "I didn't come out of my room for five days." He moved his foot in the dirt in front of the dock, his toes raised above the lips of his sandals, so the cork went into the dirt but his toes remained clean. "My mother brought me food and left it for me. She had all kinds of people coming up into my room to try and get me to speak but I wouldn't."

The pattern he was making in the dirt was vaguely triangular. Ruby was transfixed by his foot. "I remember having this conscious feeling," he said, "that if I didn't move and didn't speak, you know, then time wouldn't move. Then it wouldn't be true."

Ruby nodded, watching the foot.

"I really haven't thought about that until now. Weird. I remember it though, now. I remember just lying in my bed, just lying there. No thoughts, you know? Just trying to be so still that time would stop. Trying to take myself out of the world, to pause the world."

Ruby nodded again and looked at his face. For a second she thought of Nathan, of the way Aaron had held her, crying into her hair, when they heard he was dead. "But it didn't work," she said.

Michael exhaled quickly and shook his head. "No," he said, "it didn't." His lips pursed into the tight downward-turning line that they sometimes formed when he talked about his father, and that she had learned sometimes signaled the coming of tears.

It was raining that Friday night, so instead of having services in the amphitheater they had them in the Ben Tzvi. The mechitsa, a long curtain pulled across the room separating the men on the far side from the women close to the door, was set up. They entered the room, wearing raincoats over their best clothes, their hair curling up from the rain. They shook out their umbrellas at the door and then leaned them along the wall just inside, a long and glistening formation of colors in varying angles.

There was always a certain warmth to the Ben Tzvi when they had Shabbat services there; it was a dry refuge for them all, from the world outside wet and unwelcoming, clouds darkening what would ordinarily be a bright time of day. Normally, in the outdoor amphitheater, they sat on benches that slanted dramatically down toward the platform at the base of them, and sometimes only their toes could touch the ground, and the rabbi lifted his voice to project it all the way to the back. Praying outdoors felt forbidden, pine needles beneath their feet, and the Ben Tzvi always seemed more intimate to Ruby. Perhaps it was because everyone was on level ground, perhaps because if they were in there it meant it was raining outside.

The praying never became as intense on the women's side: the women stood, and sat, and muttered the prayers. There were a few women who sang loud, the rabbi's wife for one was conscientious, but the energy from the other side of the divider was always more palpable to Ruby, a strong, unified force that invited participation even as it dwarfed it. This was not to say that the women didn't participate, and there were moments when the energy of the entire room seemed to congeal, when the women lifted their voices and closed their eyes and were just plain part of it, and in those moments it was as if there was no mechitsa, they were all just people in a room, singing.

Near the end of the first part of the service—the Kabbalat Shabbat, receiving of Shabbat, in which the congregants greet the day of rest—they sang "L'cha Dodi." This was Ruby's favorite part of the service, and in the Ben Tzvi it took on a new intensity. The verses carried them feverishly to the chorus, and then they were all singing—

"*Ai yai yai l'cha dodi. Ai yai yai likrat kalah*"—and Ruby didn't know what the words meant but they were familiar and so she sang them out. She sang them, and everyone was singing them—"*Ai yai yai l'cha dodi. Ai yai yai likrat kalah*"—and it was as if a crack in the service had opened up and the whole congregation paused there. "*Ai yai yai l'cha dodi. Ai yai yai likrat kalah. Ai yai yai l'cha dodi. Ai yai yai likrat kalah*"—they were greeting the Shabbat as if she were a bride, and across the mechitsa the men started to move, at the front of the benches a bunch of them joined hands and started to turn, they were turning and singing and stamping their feet.

Ruby watched them, these passionate men praying, and in the group of dancing men she found Michael Fischer. He was holding hands with the rabbi on one side and Noah on the other, and he was dancing, he was shaking his head, his eyes were closed, and his face was pleading, his face was a channel for the words. She could see on his face what he was feeling; she could see on his face that he was connecting, that he was sending his words straight to God; she could see on his face that he believed. His eyes were closed and his eyebrows were furrowed and there was passion, manifested right there before her in the form of Michael's moving body communicating with Shabbat, Michael's dark and concentrating face receiving Shabbat into his soul.

She watched him and felt the words stop on her own lips. Her body surged with love. She felt proud of him, she thought of them sitting together at the agam, she thought of two nights ago, when Michael had sobbed for the first time, his shoulders rocking, and she wished she could give him this image of himself to tuck away. He was beautiful, moving like this, she thought she had never seen anything like this passionate man at this moment, communicating so fully with God. It was as if the rest of the room dropped away and it was just Michael, dancing with Shabbat, and Ruby to witness it.

Then, suddenly, it was as if a window had shut. She was watching someone she had come to know expressing himself, communicating, being free, but she felt how blocked she was from it, how much she did not belong. The sadness came on quick; it rang in her heart like an alarm. Whereas one second before she had felt close enough to Michael to touch him, suddenly she felt so far away she could barely recognize him across the curtain in that dancing ring of men. The distance between them grew wider, the feet between their bodies grew and grew, the mechitsa became thick and impassable. Who was this passionate man?

She thought of her father, in their synagogue at home, of watching him from her seat next to him as he sang out, the way he would look straight ahead, always participating and present. She used to feel so small, next to him, so curious to understand what he experienced; but there was never any room for her in her father's communication, even when she held his hand or held on to his tallis it was as if she were grasping the edge of a cliff.

Across the mechitsa, the men danced. *"Ai yai yai l'cha dodi. Ai yai yai likrat kalah."* They were winding down, getting ready to move on to the next part of the service. The sound returned, and Ruby was back on the women's side of the room, in between Jen and Amanda, who were also singing and watching the men. Ruby blinked and looked down over her siddur at her duck boots. It was raining outside; she thought of this fact, hoping to bring herself back. *You are fine, you are fine.* She swallowed, pushing the sadness down into her stomach, and tried to keep her eyes off Michael for the rest of the service.

After services, the campers milled around outside the Chadar waiting for the kitchen staff to open the doors and let them in. The rain had let up, but water still ran off the eaves of the dining hall and all the trees were dripping. Ruby stood with Amanda and Jen by the flagpole. Karl and Ari joined them, their faces flushed, kissing each girl on the cheek with a "Good Shabbos." The girls loved the Shabbat greetings after services, when the boys brought their freshly clean faces next to theirs, smelling of Brut (Ruby's favorite) or Polo Sport (popular this summer); Ruby and her friends breathed in the smell of the boys right up close as they leaned in for the kiss, the "Good Shabbos" said in low tones just by their ears. So many boys, the boys whom they loved, the boys who belonged to them.

Ruby was relieved to see Karl tonight. He said "Hey" to her as he came up, put a hand on her waist, and kissed her left cheek. He had his raincoat on over his saggy blue cotton sweater.

She surrendered to his eyes, which were light and happy. "Hey," she said and smiled back as big as she could. She felt shy, shaken from the service, and she knew he could tell. He looked at her. "You okay?"

She nodded.

All at once she wanted desperately to be away from there; she wanted to be kissing Karl in his raincoat up against a building, any building, far from here, his hand climbing up under her dress, the rain covering them, the rain slick against their mouths. She wanted Karl's eyes not to be full of concern but full of desire, hooded and ravenous.

But he was standing before her with worried eyebrows. "I'm fine," she said, a bit sharper than she wanted to. "Really."

"Okay," he said and turned to Amanda and Jen. Jen and Karl used to go out, last summer. He kissed them. Ruby felt a surge of tears. Just then the doors opened and it was time to go in.

After dinner, everyone stood around waiting for the counselors to call them to their bunks. Ruby stood with Karl and Jen and Ari; Karl was telling them a story about a friend from home who asked a guy to buy him a six-pack of beer but the guy turned out to be a cop. Suddenly Michael was there, materializing out of the darkness somewhere beyond the picnic table.

"Hey, guys," he said. "Good Shabbos."

They greeted him, and then Karl said, "Hey, Mike, check this out," and launched into the story about his friend, and Michael smiled and said, "Well, let that be a lesson to all of us." Karl laughed. "Oh, I guess that story's too *juvenile* for you, right," he said, and Ruby laughed too.

Everyone started to walk to the bunks, slowly people were saying good night, and Michael was next to her. She was nearly weak in the knees; now all she wanted was to be alone with him, for the chaos of camp to disappear and for it to be just the two of them, surrounded by the wet and dripping trees. Michael said, "Do you want to talk tonight?" and she nodded, yes.

They walked away from the Chadar and down the hill toward the playing fields. There was too much commotion by the waterfront bunks; instead, they made their way to the bleachers on the far side of the first field.

"You know," said Michael as they walked, "Karl and I had a little talk about you last night."

Ruby's heart leapt, but she kept her eyes on the ground. "Oh yeah?"

"Yeah. I mean, you guys sort of have a thing, right?"

"I don't know. . . . He has a girlfriend."

"Yeah, but come on. This is camp."

She smiled.

"Well," said Michael, "I could tell you guys had something going on, and I was with him last night, so I asked him about it. I hope that's okay."

"What did he say?"

"He said he was confused. He said he was scared. He said he was pretty sure that if he took it any further than it had already gone, he would fuck it up, and he didn't want to do that. He said, 'Every time I get involved with a girl I fuck it up. And I don't want to do that with Ruby.'"

The thought of Michael and Karl together in the darkness, probably in Karl's bunk, sitting on his bed, where she had lain, talking about her in hushed tones, thrilled Ruby. She had to fight the impulse to not quite believe it. Her two most important boys in camp, discussing her, caring about her simultaneously on a bed.

She tried to act nonchalant. Michael said, "What do you think about it?"

She thought for a second and then said, "I don't know." She thought of Karl, his deep blue eyes and skinny legs, the way he ran, his limbs flailing. She thought of the feel of him curled around her, his breath on her neck, and she knew that she loved this, that she would have this around the clock if she could. But what did that desire mean? Did she want to be his girlfriend? How would she want it to proceed from here? She didn't know. She wanted things to move forward, she wanted to be loved, she wanted to love, but she was also powerless, she felt, so completely powerless to effect any change at all.

She shrugged. "I really don't know."

They reached the bleachers, which made flat, tinny sounds as they sat down on the second row. "Well," Michael said, "you guys will figure it out."

She looked at him, in his white button-down with the sleeves rolled up. She pushed the words out of her mouth with a conscious effort. "You know it's really you and me that should be together."

He looked at her, surprised for a second, and then laughed. "You think so, huh?" He shook his head and looked ahead of them, into the darkness. "If you were just a few years older, it would certainly be different."

"Oh, come on," she said, smiling now. "I'm not that much younger than you."

"How old are you? Fifteen?"

"Sixteen."

"So, five years. That's kind of a lot right now."

She realized as he said this that he was the same age Nathan had been. It was the first time she had thought of it. The image of Nathan rose up, his body against the stark white of the bed they laid him on to die. She sighed. "I guess," she conceded.

They sat in silence for a couple of minutes. A slight breeze was blowing. Ruby took off her raincoat and pulled it down tight over her knees. "Can I ask you a question?" she said.

"Of course." His answer was quick, as if he was expecting it.

"Tonight during services I was watching you, and I had this moment where I could see how deeply you were connecting. It was *visible*, you know? And it made me feel sad somehow."

"Why?"

"I think because I felt I couldn't connect like that. It made me feel like you knew something I didn't."

He considered this. "So what's the question?"

She thought about it, looking over the field. She could hear the water running off the gutters of the building behind them. "I guess the question is," she said finally, "how can you be so connected during services? Do you really believe in it?"

She waited for Michael's answer as if the words he said next might transform him into something other than the man who sat next to her. He thought for a time, then shook his head and said, in a tone that sounded slightly exasperated, "I don't know, Ruby. I really don't."

He put both of his hands in his lap. "I just feel something when I sing those prayers, I have no idea what it is. But I let whatever it is that

I feel take the rest of me over. Afterwards, my rational brain comes back and I don't know what the hell I believe. But in those moments I'm not thinking about it."

She thought of Nathan playing his cello, his body wrapped around it, his eyes closed. She blinked and looked out, across the field, to the trees beyond. "I don't know why I can't do that," Ruby said. "I just can't seem to feel that, to let go like that, and I want to."

Michael leaned forward, his elbows on his knees. "I don't know," he said, "maybe you're trying too hard. Or maybe that's just not the way for you." He raised his left pant leg to scratch his ankle. "I know you pretty well by now, though, and I can say for sure that you are not without that, that 'connection,' as you call it. It's just, maybe praying isn't the way for you." He pulled his pant leg down, smoothing it to his shoe, and then sat back and looked at her.

Ruby stared into the trees. They were facing the field on which she and Michael had first spoken, that first night of camp by the bonfire. Now the camp was silent, save for a few shouts that came from a bunk behind them: boys.

"I guess," she said. "Sometimes I think that. But other times I'm just not sure." She looked at him. "Also, I just don't know where else to look."

He reached out and put his hand on her forearm. His hand wrapped around her arm, gently, the tips of his fingers on the underside, where her skin was pale and soft. She could feel his fingers slowly moving; the sensation of him touching her like that brought a new surge of feeling to her chest. She willed herself not to look away. All of the feeling in all of her cells rushed to the surface of her skin.

He was looking at her intently. "You will. Give yourself time. I know it."

He moved his hand along the length of her arm; the touch was gentle and strong. She could not help herself—she closed her eyes and felt it, she shrank her whole body into the skin of her arm, feeling his fingertips move on her slowly. She was paralyzed. She would never speak again, she would never move, if he would never take his hand away.

————

The night her father went to the hospital for the last time, in November, a few weeks after their walk down their street, Ruby woke to her mother at the door to her room. "Ruby," she said, her voice raised and strained, like she couldn't choose between a yell and a whisper.

"Hmm?" Ruby came awake, confused at first and then immediately alert.

"Your father's fallen," her mother said. "He can't get up. He's confused; he's not making sense. I'm going downstairs to call the doctor. Just keep an ear out, okay, for him? I'll be right back."

"What?" Ruby sat up.

"Just keep an *ear* out, okay?" Her mother was already on her way down the stairs. "I'll be right *back*!"

Keep an ear out? What did that even mean? Ruby sat up in her bed and listened. She could hear her father in the other room, muttering, in a language she recognized as Czech. She imagined him, in his striped flannel pajamas, trying to stand, his feet scrambling against the rug, his hand clutching at the bedspread. Should she go in there and try to help? Should she call out to him? Her mother had not told her to; she was frightened at what she might find.

Ruby remembered the story her parents had told her of the time her father had gotten stuck in the French language. He had been on vacation with her mother, early in their marriage—Abraham was a little boy, and she was in the first months of pregnancy with Aaron—and they had gone to Israel to see his mother, and then to France to see her mother's old friends from her year abroad. In Israel he had been speaking Hebrew, and Czech and German with his mother and her husband, who spoke both—and then in France he had been speaking French, which he knew from when he'd lived there with his first wife before he came to America. They were tired from traveling, and when they got in the cab to go to the airport he was stressed—he always got anxious when he was about to fly—and there was a lot of traffic, they were sitting on the highway, inching along. Her mother asked him something—maybe what time it was—and he answered her in French. Thinking he was just playing, she answered him back in French, to which he hissed, in French, "Speak *English*."

He was trapped in French. On the plane, he kept having to ask her mother in French for simple English words; it was as if he was learning the language all over again. It took him days to regain his language.

Ruby had always loved this story, in part because it spoke to the complexity of her father—who knew so many languages that he grew confused, whose very identity was a mix of so many foreign elements, though usually it was easy for her to forget it—and also because it broke the world open just a little bit, telling her that things could happen that she would never have dreamed up herself, that strange things, things no one would believe, could really happen in the world. In that story, her father was vulnerable and unique, and he was frightened as she never knew him to be. She always loved stories about her parents that took place before she was born: she loved the way her parents seemed eerie and unfamiliar in these stories, the way they flickered in her mind like the old home movies her father showed once on the wall of the living room. Her mother as a girl, in a four-room apartment with her Irish Catholic parents, wearing school uniforms and eating pork; her father, speaking other languages, learning to fix tractors and carry weapons to defend a country—Israel—that was not her own. Her parents, her father particularly, were unknowable in these stories.

But at the moment, he was on the floor of his bedroom, and he was muttering in Czech. Was he trapped again? What was happening in his brain to make him speak like that? Her father, the complicated man, the man who defied the rules of the world, was helpless on the floor of his bedroom, unable to stand.

They took him to the hospital. The streets all the way there were deserted.

At the hospital, they were ushered into a wide area beyond the admitting desk. There was a line of empty beds across the floor, with a series of curtains hanging from rods by big silver rings next to the beds. At the back of the room, where they stood, was a long counter with a sink and a series of cabinets. The nurse told them to wait, someone would be with them in just a minute; she disappeared.

Her father was leaning on her mother; the three of them stood against the counter. All the way to the hospital, Ruby's father had been muttering in Czech; now he was still. Her mother had her arm around his back; he had his head on her shoulder. Ruby could see that he was leaning heavily. Her mother was standing with her arm braced against the counter. "Where is everyone?" she said, looking around. "This is ridiculous. What are we supposed to do?"

Ruby moved away from the counter to the main hallway; she saw no one. She turned back to her mother. She was silenced by the situation before her; she was a marionette puppet in a hospital play set. Her father had his eyes closed against her mother's shoulder. Her mother was holding up her father. She could feel her tongue in her mouth: it was at least four times too big.

"Ruby?" said her mother. Her eyes were big and looked about to burst, as if all the energy of her body was held there. "Can you stay here with him? I need to go find someone. We need help!" She said this last bit loudly, looking toward the empty hallway, and then looked down at her husband. "Josef? Can you stand?" she said to the bald spot at the top of his head and tried to extricate herself from him. Ruby came forward, and her father pulled himself back from her mother as if he were drugged. Ruby thought this was what her father would be like if he was ever drunk, if he ever took drugs—his head lolling, his knees buckling. This was exactly the kind of loss of control that he couldn't stand, that he wanted always, at all costs, to avoid.

"Hold him, Ruby," said her mother, her hand still on him, as if her father were a doll. Ruby put her hand where her mother's was, she saw her mother's hand lift, and then her mother was gone.

Ruby slipped her arm around her father's back, where her mother's had been a few moments before. "It's okay, Dad," she heard herself say softly, "it's okay." For a minute her father stood, his knees locked, leaning heavily on her right side, but she felt his weight on her increasing and she wasn't strong enough to hold him up this way.

It was awkward. She could feel him leaning on her, he was getting heavier. She tried to move, to switch positions, but she couldn't find the right way to stand. Should she use the counter for support? Could she get him over to one of the beds without him falling?

She used her shoulder and left arm to hunch his arm up and around her shoulder. "Come on Dad," she said. "It's okay." She tried to see behind her to the hallway, but she knew there was no one there. Was he embarrassed to be leaning on her like this? She knew normally he would be and felt vaguely embarrassed for the both of them.

She turned toward her father then and put both of her arms around him; it was the only way. His arms went up and around the back of her and hung down; his head rested on her shoulder. He was still in his flannel pajamas: the feel of him as she put her arms around him was familiar, soft, and warm. There was a hint of sweat on his back. She closed her eyes and pretended she was just hugging him—she was just saying good night, hugging him before he went to bed. She breathed in and felt her father's body against her: it remained. She had never held him for this long. She was surprised by the shock of his body against hers, the way it was holdable and soft, the way it needed hers. This was a position her father would never have permitted, this was a position she never could have imagined, this was a position not to be believed. The shock of it ran through her with force as she held him. Her father was in need, and she was there for him.

His breath was against her neck. She could feel his breath, rhythmic and steady, against her neck as she held him. The breath was the clue that he was okay, she thought; she concentrated on his breath on her neck and knew that he was still alive, he was still in that body, which she held, her father's body that was pressed against her now for support. She held him tight; she found her hands at his back and clasped them together. Her father needed her, she could not let him fall. She felt love for him surge in her, she had hardly ever realized how much she loved him, she would hold him forever, she would never let him go. What was there to be embarrassed about, here? This was a father needing his child, this was an act of love, this was what people who loved each other did for each other. His strong body was pressed against hers in need. There was nothing but this, in the end: nothing but need, love, bodies, and support.

"It's okay," she said. "You're okay. I've got you."

Was he scared? Did he feel grateful that she was there? Did he love her? Was he proud?

Her father was silent.

1995

Her Room Was a Fortress

I t was the end of March, Ruby's senior year of high school, when Abe finally went back to the hospital. He had been living at home since just before her father died, almost two years ago, deteriorating, becoming part of the complicated landscape of the inside of her house.

Ruby's mother had been mentioning the possibility of the hospital more and more frequently in recent months, saying things like "I know, I'm trying," and sighing and shaking her head. "Listen, I'm working on it," she said to Ruby one morning before school a few weeks before his admittance, sitting down with her at the kitchen table. "I'm trying. The situation has been out of control for far too long, I know." She felt terribly guilty, she said, for letting it go on so long, but she was trying, and it was not simple. Abe was over nineteen, and so she was no longer his official guardian. The laws dictated that he could not be hospitalized unless he was a danger, or if he signed himself in. She had to make herself his guardian, she said, a complicated and tedious legal process. "The laws are appalling, Ruby, and it takes such energy to tackle them. I've just been in a fog." Ruby could see the tears shining in her eyes. "I can't believe the fog I've been in."

Ruby didn't know Abe was actually going until the day he was gone: a Tuesday. That afternoon, she got a ride home from school with Tim. They were talking about imagining themselves in frontier times. Ruby was laughing.

In the culture of Featherton, by the time she reached her senior year, her friends' cars had become extensions of each of them, havens of safety that Ruby could enter. Her friends' cars were tiny satellites from her world at school, protected pods of what felt like reality. At home, she could not look, touch, participate; at school she was a student like all the others. Her school community was where she felt she belonged, not so much to the general privileged population of Featherton but to the nucleus of her friends within it: religion-free, ironic and smart, jaded, artistic, carved into the larger population of money-eyed, baseball-cap-wearing "hockey sticks," as Tim had nicknamed the typical students at their school. By their senior year, her friends' personalities had conformed to their niches—positions in the clubs and activities, student government, their chosen artistic pursuits. Every morning the parking lot in back of the arts building filled with their cars.

A few of her friends—Tim; Jill; Jill's boyfriend, Tom; and Paul, who was arguably the biggest hippie in the group, with long, straight hair pulled into a ponytail and an almost constant patchouli smell about him—were in the upper class of car freedom, a level she was not granted. They had cars that were completely theirs, that their parents never used, that they were in charge of gassing up and maintaining. Tim drove a Saab; Jill drove a white Volvo sedan that roared when she started it. There was a mirror on the glove compartment door of her car that they had snorted Ritalin off of on more than one occasion, once before a dance at school the year before.

"I'm serious!" Tim said now, as they drew close to Ruby's street. There was a bumper sticker on his dashboard that said *Live Die or*

Free, and a robot with wheels on its feet that rolled back and forth. "Haven't you ever imagined yourself, if you were alive back then?"

"No," Ruby said through her laughter. "No, I definitely haven't."

"Well I have. Sometimes I really think about it. Seriously. Think about it! We'd have to get around in a horse and buggy, it would take forever to get anywhere. And what would we do at night? Seriously, what would we do?"

Ruby thought about it. "Read, I guess."

"Yeah, but what would there even be to read?"

Ruby looked out the windshield as they turned onto her street and imagined herself in a log cabin with a fire in the fireplace. She tried to read the spines of the books on the crude shelf on the wall. She was wearing a bonnet tied beneath her chin and a long dress.

"The Bible?" she said.

She was serious. She looked at Tim, who looked back at her, considering this. They broke out in laughter. "The Bible!" Tim spit, laughing.

"Seriously! We'd read the Bible!" Ruby tried to recover. "No, seriously. Wouldn't we?"

They were about to turn in to her driveway when she saw the flashing lights through the trees. Their laughter died as they pulled in. The driveway was lined with police cars, three of them, one with its blue lights silently revolving.

"Shit," said Tim.

Ruby was silent. How many times had she come home to similar scenes? Each time, when she came home to police cars or ambulances, it was just like this; she didn't know something was wrong, and then she did. Police cars: something had happened while she wasn't there. Flash: something is different.

She knew each time, immediately, whom the cars were for. The time it had made her stomach sink the deepest was for Nathan, when she and Jill came home from the Red Sox game to a line of cars in the driveway and she knew it was Nathan.

Nathan. Now that he was gone, she couldn't be affected by anything.

Abe must have done something, she thought vaguely; what had he done? Whatever it was, it was nothing. Nathan was gone, there were police cars in her driveway; this was just the kind of thing that happened at her house.

Tim stopped the car and they sat in it. Ruby looked at the cars in the driveway, the one with its blue lights circling around and around. She couldn't see any policemen.

"Do you want me to go in with you?" Tim said.

"No." She looked out at the house, steeling herself for whatever she would find. "No, it's okay. Thanks."

She picked up her backpack and opened the door. This was just what happened. "I'll call you," she said.

"Okay. I hope everything's okay," Tim said, his head ducking toward her as she climbed out of her seat and shut the door. He sat and watched her as she made her way to the front of the house.

There was a policeman in her kitchen. "Hello," he said to her as she came in. He had a mustache and was standing in the middle of the room. It was as if he had been standing there all day, waiting for her to come home. Wally was sitting on the floor next to him, gazing at him lovingly, as if he were an old family friend.

"Hello."

She walked through the kitchen to the front hall. Her mother was standing at the window with two more policemen, looking out at the woods.

"Mom?" Ruby said from the doorway.

"Oh, Ruby." Her mother turned around. She came toward her and enveloped her in a tight hug. "I'm sorry, honey."

Ruby pulled back. "For what?" she said. "What's going on?"

Her mother looked very tired, Ruby thought, tired and soft, mal-
leable, as if she could be molded into a different shape. She stood in
front of Ruby and looked at her blankly for a second, as if she didn't
understand what Ruby had asked.

"It's Abe," she said finally. "He's run away."

She pointed toward the policemen, who were still standing at the
window, as if Ruby and her mother weren't there. "He's somewhere
out there."

Ruby wasn't sure she wanted to know more. She took a step
toward the staircase, toward the beckoning safety at the top of the
stairs.

"He's still smart as a whip, your brother," her mother said. "No
flies on him. The policemen came to take him to the hospital a few
hours ago. I was hoping he'd go easily, I was hoping it would all be
over by the time you got home. But of course that was too much to
ask."

Ruby took another step.

"He was upstairs, and there was a policeman on the stairs so he
couldn't leave, but he got one look at him and took off down the back
staircase and out the door."

One more step.

"No flies on him," her mother said again. Another step. "Anyway, they're out there looking for him now."

"Okay," Ruby said. "I guess I'll be in my room." She headed
up the stairs, gaining speed. She left her mother with the men by the
window.

———

Her room was a fortress. There was barely any house without her
room. It had been a slow retreat from the rest of the house over the
last few years, so slow she barely realized how complete it was. Ruby

traveled from her room to the bathroom and back; from her room to the kitchen and back; from her room to the television and back. Always back, back to her room.

In her room, she kept her doors closed and her stereo on low. The phone next to her bed was her lifeline; she talked late into the night, to Tim, to Jill, to Amanda from camp. Talking, talking, talking, about teenage things, about people in school and who said what and who kissed whom and about television shows that sometimes she hadn't seen because she had been in her room. Outside her room, the world was unknown, bizarre things were happening, illness was afoot, the house was occupied by sadness and madness and death. Inside her room, she was a senior in high school.

Ruby was sequestered in her room and Abe was out there, in the rest of the house; this was how she lived. She had given him the rest of the house; she had ceded the territory. It was easier this way. She was minimizing the contact, and therefore minimizing the stress. Her ears were satellite dishes; she was tuned to every odd sound she heard. Abe prowled the house and she was a mouse, hiding from a hawk, frozen upright in an open field.

It seemed to her that her mother was never home, though this was not true. Her mother had worked in Boston until Nathan got sick, and after that had given up her job. But even when her mother was home, Ruby felt she was the only one listening. After a sleepless night, Abe going up and down the stairs, glasses clinking in the kitchen, the door to the backyard opening and closing, opening and closing, music coming from Abe's room, Ruby would go into the kitchen before school and say to her mother: "Did you hear him last night?" and it seemed to Ruby that her mother's answer was always no. As if Ruby was making it up, as if Ruby was exaggerating, as if it was No Big Deal, what was happening inside her brother's brain. Perhaps it was the cruel positioning of her bedroom in the middle of the house, while her mother's and Abe's rooms were all the way to opposite sides, a centrality—the detail was not lost on her—that she had loved as a young girl, cradled as she was in the heart of the house. She would take the dog into her room with her and invite her up onto her bed, thinking the two of them allies, the dog the only one that really understood. Eventually Wally would want out, scratching at the wood of the door, and then Ruby would be alone.

Somewhere inside Ruby knew that it wasn't true, that her mother *did* notice; she was constantly reminding herself that she was exaggerating, that her mother dealt with Abe much more than Ruby ever did. This was part of the contradiction she lived with, trying to be respectful, trying to remind herself of the gravity of the situation, the reality of her brother's illness, that it was no one's fault, and to balance that rational reality with the anger that overtook her. No one was more innocent in this than Abe, she reminded herself, no one had it harder than he did. What right did she have to be angry at him? She couldn't be angry at him; it wasn't his fault.

But every time she approached his bedroom door, always slightly cracked, the sound of unintelligible music from his old boom box spilling out into the hallway, music full of screams and shouts and guitars so grating they were no longer instruments, every time she knocked to tell him to turn it down and Abe didn't answer her, Ruby seethed with rage. She didn't want to push the door open, she didn't want to see her brother laid out on his bed with a blanket over his head. No more, not again, she didn't want to set foot in his room, full of his non-logic, the sound of his terrible non-music, she didn't even want to glimpse it, she wanted to be far, far away. She knocked louder; she would not enter, it was the line she drew for herself, the line beyond which she would not go.

"Abe!" she called, softly at first, and then louder and louder, "Abe! Abe!" as rage filled her chest.

"Yeah!" he finally answered. Did she imagine the edge to his voice?

"Can you turn it down?" Her voice was loud, but she was not yelling. She was almost yelling, she wanted to be yelling, she wished she could yell, but she never did.

"Okay!" he yelled back. She listened for a change in volume and heard none, and this was as far as she went. She retreated to her room and shut her door and climbed into her bed; she tried to ignore the sounds, pillow over her head, and if she couldn't, she padded to her mother's room and asked her to intervene. Last resort, using her mother, but at least she was made to know that Ruby was bothered. That all the while she wanted no part of any of this, she only wanted to sleep, sleep, like a normal teenager who had school in the morning.

Now, Ruby stood in her room and looked out the window at the driveway lined with police cars. The absurdity of this situation was extreme; she felt as if she were one of those Russian dolls, painted with flowers on the outside, with a whole series of other versions of her vying for placement inside. What could she do? She was trapped in this room. Her skin was crawling with this moment and countless moments like it before.

Months ago, in October, Abe had had beer delivered to the house. Ruby was in her room, Abe was in the house. It was late afternoon, Ruby had just gotten home from school. Her mother was not at home.

The doorbell rang; Ruby went to her window to see who it was. In the driveway was a truck with the word BUDWEISER written across the side in red letters.

She heard Abe bound down the stairs. She heard the door open. She heard Abe: "Yeah!" his voice loud and enthusiastic, strangely detached. "Right here!"

She couldn't see the beer man while Abe was talking. Then she saw him—Budweiser hat, Budweiser shirt—cross from the door to the back of his truck. He lifted the back, bending his knees and thrusting, and then he ascended into the truck. A ramp came down, and the man followed pushing a dolly loaded with . . . was that four cases of beer? More? Ruby couldn't tell.

She was astounded by what she was witnessing. A beer truck had arrived to give Abraham a personal delivery? How was it possible that he had orchestrated something like this? Did beer trucks always make house calls? She heard Abe—"Thanks! See ya!"—and she heard the door shut. She didn't dare open her door; she wanted it to be as if she had not seen this. What would Abe do with the beer? How would he hide it? How fast would he drink it? She didn't want to know the answer to any of these questions. She could see Abe in her mind's eye, right then, and the image was enough. She saw him beneath the weight of a case, making his way up the stairs, his eyes wide and fixed straight ahead, set on his goal, excited to get to the bottles inside the box. He headed down the hallway to his room, set the case on the floor by his bed, and quickly turned to go downstairs for the next case. She heard the sound of the bottles; he did not attempt to be quiet. She wondered if he even knew she was in the house, if he had processed this. Probably not. Amazing how singular he could still be, how determined. His mind could focus on one thing: being wiped out. He couldn't do anything else, he could barely even watch TV, really, except for static—but he could do that.

She sat on her bed and listened to Abe moving up and down the stairs. When the movement stopped, there was silence, and this was where her imagination really took over. He was opening the first beer, maybe he was on to the second. The relief was flooding him, he was focused on the relief, his head was thrown back and his Adam's apple was moving like a light switch, up and down, up and down. She saw it; it was happening. Down the hall from where she sat, her brother was exerting his only control.

. . .

Her contact with Abe's drinking over the years had been minimal, though Ruby remembered the morning in seventh grade—the year that Nathan, who was then a senior, drove her to school every day—when she and Nathan came out of the house and got in the car only to discover that Abe had thrown up in it the night before. There was vomit in the handle on the inside of the driver's-side door—this was how they first discovered it, when Nathan put his fingers into the puddle as he reached to pull the door closed.

"Oh, my God." Nathan looked at his fingers, and only then did it become apparent, there was vomit on the dashboard, streaks of liquid on the radio, a pool of it in the tray underneath the parking brake between their seats, and a puddle of it at Nathan's feet. They sat in the car for a few moments, dumbfounded, and then the smell hit them: alcohol, tinged with the sweet smell of digestion.

"Oh my God! Gross!" Ruby squealed. She opened her door and leapt out. Nathan was already outside, vigorously shaking his hand. "Sick!"

They ran inside, where their parents were sitting at the kitchen table. Both of their heads rose from the sections of the paper they were reading as Nathan ran to the sink. Nathan did not usually run. "Um," he said, vigorously scrubbing his hands, "it seems someone has vomited in the Dugan."

The Dugan was Nathan's nickname for the car, full name The Blue Dugan. It was a Dodge, which was the only detail that could possibly suggest the genesis of the nickname. This was how Nathan's mind worked; he thought words were inherently funny and effortlessly found the humor in them all. He would repeat words—"hot dog," for example, which he favored for a while, elongating the syllables so they sounded like *Hahhht dahhhg*.

Ruby's parents were alert. Her father got up from the table. He looked resigned and yet calm as he lifted the keys to the car their mother drove from the hook by the door and handed them to Nathan. "Here," he said. "Take the Previa. You're going to be late for school."

Nathan took the keys tentatively. "But what about Mom?"

"We'll figure it out," their father said. "Just go."

And so Nathan and Ruby went to school in the Previa, and by the time they got home in the evening the Dugan was clean, and it was as if nothing had ever happened. No one spoke of it again.

This was the way incidents related to Abraham tended to go, back then, as far as Ruby could tell—her parents handled them quickly and without comment. As much as they could, which was not entirely, they sheltered their other children from the reality of Abe's situation. But it was impossible to shelter them entirely, and after her father was gone, when Abe moved back home, there could be far less shelter for Ruby.

So at this point, really, what could shock her? She was barely even cognizant, at this point, of her house or her family. She was living in a constant state of floating, as if she were a plume of milkweed on a draft of air. Was she even in her body? Was that even her, on her bed there, staring up at the tapestry pinned above it, tracing the blue paisleys with her eyes? Were those her eyes?

She did not know what had died and what was alive. She was a teenager, and there were dark glasses that her soul must wear in order for it to survive inside her growing body. This would be true—these glasses would be necessary—even if she didn't have to live in this house, where her room was a fortress, outside of which the house was as lawless as a city alleyway. The house, home to her family, where her family had grown and laughed and loved and fought, the only house she had ever known, had, in the past two years of sickness and death, become dangerous. Rooms were occupied by her brother and his madness, by her mother and her sadness, or by memories, images that filled Ruby's eyes and mind and had the power to bring her to her knees. She adopted a style of living in her home that was akin to passing a rough city block: walk fast, don't look at that, don't touch that, keep moving, don't think about that. Always forward, forward, never pause.

She came home from school some days to find Abe on the couch in the TV room with a blanket over his head; his feet were crossed, his sneakers were on, and the television was playing loud static, grating the air. Move through the room, don't look, don't try to stop it, try not to hear.

She was going up to her room one day when her mother reached out to her from the couch in front of the TV. "Ruby, come here, sit with me," she said, her arm stretched out from underneath her striped terry-cloth robe. Ruby paused and looked back.

"Ruby," her mother said, reaching out. It was the gesture a baby makes to its mother when it wants to be picked up. Pick me up, her mother was saying. "Come on," she said, "I'm watching *Law & Order*. Come watch with me."

Ruby looked at her mother, reaching toward her in her robe; she looked at the empty space beside her mother on the couch. The empty space was dwarfing her mother, she thought, her mother was shrinking and shrinking, and still she was reaching out to Ruby, she was desperate for Ruby to take her hand as the empty space grew. "Why?" she heard her mother say. "What are you up to up there?" But it was as if her voice was coming through a tunnel, rising in pitch as it shrank farther away. Where was her mother? Surely that wasn't her on the couch, there, that shriveled, desperate creature in a terry-cloth robe, reaching out.

"Maybe in a little bit," Ruby mumbled and forced her feet to lift. She climbed the stairs and left her mother alone on the couch.

———

Ruby had told Tim about Abe during her sophomore year, late one night after a party at their friend Jen's house, sitting with plastic cups of beer by Jen's drained and empty pool. Now, Tim and Jill were still the only people she had told. She tried not to speak of Abe, but when she did it was to them. Her feelings for Tim remained hidden, though they were growing more potent and tender the more time went by. The weirder things grew at home, the more Tim was present on the other end of the phone, the more she yearned for him to be closer to her. She was still not talking about her grief about Nathan or her father with anyone; twice over the year she had cried on the phone with Tim, late at night, without saying much at all, but it was only Michael, at camp, who had ever heard her true confusion, the magnitude of her disbelief, her anger about her family's losses. She did not know why this was, except for the simple feeling that there were not words for what she felt. Her mouth was like a great wall, she imagined, beyond which certain things would not or could not pass. Her body clamped around her grief and pushed it far down, down, to where it lived beyond words, beyond the dignity that words would afford it. She was so angry at her grief that she would not allow it to surface.

When Aaron came home, he and her mother would remember something about Nathan or her father and laugh, and Ruby would look down and remain silent. They betrayed the dead by laughing, she felt; how could they ever laugh about Nathan or her father ever again? They'd invite her to spend time with them, to watch a movie with them, to go to dinner, and she would opt out, preferring always to be with her friends, who did not ask her to share, or in her room alone. Her family didn't seem to understand how awful it all was; even they didn't seem to share the real pain with her.

Ruby couldn't help but think of her father and Nathan, of course, but she only did so alone. She lay in her bed and she thought of them; the loss of them choked her and she gasped for air. It was simply too much, too much, too much to share. And the addition of Abe, like a jungle animal in the house, was just another reason for her to keep her doors shut.

Her mother worried about her; her mother tried to reach her, but Ruby could not be reached. She hardly spoke to her mother about anything at all. And her mother tried. She asked Ruby if she wanted to "talk to someone," someone other than her family, someone professional, she tried to get Ruby to spend more time with her, or even to talk to her about the things that didn't matter—her schoolwork, anything. But Ruby's feelings were too tangled; the very sight of her mother was a reminder of all the things that she wanted to ignore.

One night in December while Aaron was home visiting, Ruby came home from Jill's house and was climbing the stairs to her room when her mother called out to her from her bed. Aaron was in his room with the door closed; her mother's door, of course, was open.

"Ruby," she said, "come here a second."

Ruby went to the doorway and stood just inside. Her mother was beneath her puffy feather comforter, her body diagonal in the bed, her top half leaning over onto Ruby's father's side. Her arm and her book resting on top made a depression in the puffiness.

"How are you?" she said, smiling gently.

"Okay . . ."

"We missed you tonight."

Ruby looked at the floor. She felt bad that she hadn't stayed home with Aaron that night—he was visiting only for a few nights—but she and Jill had had plans to go to the movies.

"It's okay," her mother said, "you don't have to feel guilty, I just wanted to tell you. We missed you."

Ruby didn't reply.

"You know, Rube"—her mother grew serious—"you act like you don't have a family, but you do."

Ruby looked up at her. "I know," she said, immediately defensive.

Her mother traced a flower on her comforter with her fingers. "Sometimes I'm not really sure you do. And I don't really know how to show you that you do."

Ruby said nothing. She felt much, but said nothing. There were tears rising behind her eyes, tears filling her body. She stood in the doorway and didn't move.

"But we're here, Ruby," said her mother. "We are your family, and we're here, and we're not going away. I just want you to remember that. We may not be the same as we once were, but we're still your family."

"I know," said Ruby.

But it was too much. Even that very word, *family,* was too much for Ruby. It was a word that had been cut in half, a word that meant "destroyed," a word that brought with it all of her questions about belief, about love, about right and wrong.

———

Ruby walked down the hall toward Abe's room, looking out the back window to see the policemen in the backyard. They were searching for him in the woods. The eerie silence in the house now made her feel as if she was visiting a museum of her missing brother.

The room that she stood in used to be the family's guest room. Now, in the new format of the house, with no guests, no father to use the office next door, and no reason, really, to venture down here, except to interact with Abe, it had become a second room for him. She looked up at the frame on the wall that used to hold his TV—a gift to Abe from their father, given when Abe was still living in the halfway house and the only TV was his roommate's. Abe had set up the TV on one of those hospital-room contraptions that clung to the corner of the ceiling like a spider. He had bought the contraption in one of his late-night Home Shopping Network sessions; the HSN was the only channel he could watch, pacing back and forth in front of the TV downstairs while Ruby and her mother were asleep, sometimes waking them when he'd clap at the screen.

In this room, Ruby felt unsettled, as if she were perched on the edge of a trembling diving board over an ocean. Time and again, when her mother was downstairs in front of the other TV, or when Abe wasn't home, she convinced herself: *It's fine, there's a TV in there, why not watch it, there's nothing to be afraid of, it's not even really his room.* She wanted to watch TV—*Seinfeld, The Simpsons, Beverly Hills 90210*—stupid television that would remove her from the house for a half an hour, TV that would make her laugh as if she were somewhere else. She wanted to watch TV like a seventeen-year-old, like her other friends. So sometimes she told herself she was entitled, and she ventured down the hall to the hospital TV. She sat on the bed with her knees pulled to her chest and her arms around them. She tried as much as possible to be in the room without being in it. Her eyes were here, her brain was here, but her body was not. She did not belong there; she did not like being in there; she was not there.

She was on edge. One time, after she had been in the room, Abe left the TV on for forty-eight hours straight set to static fuzz. He told her he was "cleaning the teenage vibes" out of the machine. "Well, you watched my TV," he said as an explanation when she asked him why he left it on when he wasn't in the room, swaying forward and back in front of her on the balls of his feet. He knew she had been there because when he came home he felt the TV and it was warm— a tactic their father had used when they were little to see if they had been sneaking unauthorized television. "It was warm," Abe said, rocking, swaying. "It takes a while to set that straight."

Ruby did not want to interact with Abe in front of his TV; she also didn't want to cede the TV, or pretend that it was not there. She watched it, she hated watching it; she hated being in that room, she was in that room. If she heard someone coming she turned it off and tried to make it back to her bedroom without being seen. Sometimes she would dart to the door of her room only to find that no one was coming. Sometimes she would dart three times in the course of a television show.

One day this past January she'd come into the room to find the TV gone. The hospital-room contraption hung from the ceiling, but its black arms were empty, it had lost its heart, its raison d'être. She stood for a minute in the doorway looking at the empty thing, a gadget that made no sense at all without what it was meant to hold.

She didn't want to ask Abe what he had done with the television. She told her mother the TV was gone, and a few days later her mother explained: Abe had removed the television late one night—climbed up and unscrewed it, Ruby imagined, balanced on the bed, teetering on the mattress, holding on to one of the black plastic arms for support—and walked with it in his arms (cradled like a gigantic child, its corners jutting into his skin) down their road a quarter mile to a stretch of wooded land with a path meandering through it, where he tossed the thing into the trees.

"It needed to go," Abe said to their mother's exclamations of the value of the machine, how it was "perfectly good," how one shouldn't ever be so wasteful, one should be so lucky to be given things in this life. "It needed to go. It was tired, and there was too much of Dad in it, and it didn't want to be here anymore."

Back in her room, Ruby stood in front of her desk and looked out onto the driveway. The afternoon was still bright, and there were rectangles of light on the lawn. On the left, the blue lights were still revolving on the last car in the driveway. What a waste of energy, Ruby thought, though there was something hypnotic to the circling blue.

Directly below her window was a motorcycle, and standing next to it, a policeman who must have just arrived. He stood by his bike and from his right pocket drew out a package of green Chiclets. Ruby stood above him and watched in disbelief as he slid the tray of rectangular gum out of the cardboard sheath and punched two white pieces out of their cellophane prisons into his palm. One of them fell out of his hand onto the pavement; he bent to pick it up, then popped both of them into his mouth with one swift gesture. Then he just stood there, looking around and chewing.

It was as if he had all the time in the world, as if he were standing on a balcony over a Venice canal watching the gondolas roll by. Her brother was missing and lost somewhere in the woods behind her house, out of his mind, paranoid, psychotic, and this guy was chewing Chiclets in front of her bedroom window. She felt all of her muscles contract. She thought she might be sick; a bitterness swirled in her, a sour taste came to her mouth. She had to get out of the house.

She grabbed her backpack and ran down the stairs. Her mother and the two policemen were in the front hallway, silent and still as statues. Her mother turned as she came down the stairs. "Ruby?"

"I've just gotta go," Ruby managed. "I'll . . . I'll be back later."

She hustled out the driveway, past the police cars, and onto the road. The faster she walked the more urgency she felt. It was as if at any moment now the house behind her would explode. As if it were a ticking bomb like the ones in all the James Bond movies—the movies her family used to gather on the couch on Friday nights to watch— the big digital numbers ticking slowly down to zero, then the pause between the timer reaching zero and the explosion.

She walked down the road toward where it dead-ended on a two-lane highway. She would walk to Stop & Shop, she thought, she would call Tim when she got there and he would pick her up. She was trying to contain herself, to keep the pieces of herself inside. It would be okay, she was not trapped, she was in control. She was walking away, away. Her brother was crazy and somewhere in the woods, pursued by men in uniform. Leave it behind, behind, farther behind.

She was almost to the highway when she sensed a slow-moving presence along her left side. A police car was rolling along with her, and the passenger-side window rolled down. A policeman with sunglasses looked out. He sat next to the driver, who was almost completely obscured by shadow. "Ma'am, I'm sorry. We're looking for Abraham Bronstein."

Ruby stopped walking. What was he asking her to do? "He's my brother," she said.

"I'm sorry, ma'am, but we're going to need to see an ID."

What?

"What?" She stepped closer to the car.

"We're looking for Abraham Bronstein," he said again, looking out at her. Could that be alcohol that she smelled, wafting up from him? The policeman extended his arm.

"I *know*," she said, "he's my *brother*."

She was out of her body. She had leapt out of the top of her body, slipped out through her scalp somehow. She was lost, she didn't know where she was, but she was no longer in her body. Now there was no telling what could happen. Now nothing, absolutely nothing could make sense anymore.

"I'm sorry, ma'am." The policeman held his arm out the car window. There was a tattoo on the inside of it: an anchor. Somewhere inside, Ruby laughed at this tattoo. Of course it was an anchor, of course.

She pulled her backpack around and found her wallet. She saw her arm making the motion as if she was seeing it from miles away.

Her heart was pounding. She tasted bitterness in her mouth again. Where was she, really? How was it that there was a place such as this street on the earth, this pavement and these trees, that there were things such as cars and policemen and wallets and rules?

She shook her head as she pulled her license out of its plastic sheath, and saw that her hand was shaking.

"Abraham is a *boy's name*," she said, handing her license to the officer. "He's my *brother*."

Was she on *Candid Camera*, had her life officially reached the point where the cameraman would jump out and reveal himself? *For Christ's sake*, she thought, looking around, *reveal yourself!* Maybe she, somehow, was the cameraman, maybe in some twisted way she was creating all of this.

But no; this was real. It was all real. The policeman looked at her license and showed it to his partner, whose face she couldn't see, and then he handed it back. "Sorry," he said. "We just had to make sure." He rolled up the window.

She walked away, her legs wobbly and her face flushed, and it occurred to Ruby that she had come closer in that moment of total absurdity to experiencing what it was to be in Abe's shoes than she ever had before. As her heartbeat slowed, and her feet carried her down the highway toward the supermarket (the police car turning around behind her and heading back toward her house), the reality of this, a policeman asking her to prove she was not Abraham, the idea that she *could be* him, just the idea of it filled her with fear and with shame. She was suddenly aware of the immense privilege it was to be walking away from her house, from where her brother was tearing through the woods and scraping his face and arms and no doubt being handcuffed and dragged into a van. She could walk away; he could not. She was ashamed of the relief she felt with every step farther away. All else was a whirl in her mind and in her body. Feelings that she didn't have the capacity to disentangle, not now, not now, lest she be destroyed, lest she disintegrate, lest she lose hold of reality: her legs, carrying her away from her home, one step after another on the crumbling sidewalk, away, away, at least just for now.

At the supermarket, she called Tim. His was a voice from another world, taking her through the phone wire to a different planet. She could hear it in his voice. Normalcy: the world where he was.

"Tim," she said, trying to control her own voice, "will you come pick me up? Please? I'm at Stop & Shop."

He took her back to his house, where they sat in his room, Tim in his desk chair and Ruby on the floor with her back against the bed. She told him what she knew about what had happened, about the policeman with the Chiclets, and about the one in the car who smelled like alcohol and asked for her ID. There was something sacred in this unloading, Tim sitting across from her, listening, as the light grew dim in the room. He seemed peaceful, he was just listening, she could tell how closely he was listening and she appreciated this. The words came in a torrent, a boulder rolling faster and faster downhill.

Finally there was silence. The room was nearly dark. Tim shook his head. "I really just can't believe your life sometimes."

She sniffled. "I know," she said. "I can't believe it either."

"And the way you speak about it," he said. "I don't know. I've thought it before—the way you speak, the way you describe it. You sound like you're in a play or something."

She smiled. This made her feel oddly good. "Well of course I do! It's fucking ridiculous! Of course it would sound like a play—it certainly doesn't sound *real*." She shook her head. "It's too much."

He switched on the light on his desk. A warm yellow halo flickered on and surrounded him. "It definitely is," he said.

"I guess the only way my brain can process it is to focus on all the details," she said. "I mean, if it hadn't actually happened to me, I wouldn't believe it."

Tim raised his eyebrows, nodding, and leaned forward. "It's unbelievable."

They sat in his room for an hour more before he drove her home. He played her the latest song he'd written on his guitar, which he assured her would be a lot better with the bass and drum parts ("Just imagine there are other people playing with me, okay?" he said), and she lay down on the floor and watched him hunched over his guitar. Being with him calmed her; she felt present in the room with him, and she knew this was good. She wished he would play on forever, she wished the two of them would never have to leave this room, not ever, she wished she could stay here on this carpet and never have to look at anything else. She wished Tim would touch her, once and for all, and tell her he loved her and make her forget everything but his body. At the same time she felt this, as he played for her, she was aware of how far from him she felt, of how much more there was to her reality that she couldn't explain, that she couldn't translate for him. Tim would never know how it was, really, to be her. For him, the story she had told him was just that, a story. It had felt like a play to him, she had been a character from a play sitting there in his room with tears staining her cheeks, an actress who could cry at will. And as much as she felt like the actress he saw, as much distance as she always had from what was happening to her family, as much as it all swirled in her mind to a place where she genuinely couldn't believe it was real—at the end of the day, it had happened, and it was hers. How could she get back to Tim, ever, from where she was?

By the time he dropped her off, the police cars were gone, and so was Abe. He would be in the hospital for a month, and from there would move to a halfway house, and from there to a long series of hard-to-get apartments all over Massachusetts offered to people with disabilities. There were other stints in the hospital after that, but there were to be no more stints of living at home.

———————

Months later, in July—after Ruby and her friends had graduated, after they knew where they were going to college, after they went to grad parties and hugged classmates they'd never spoken to before and stayed up all night together on lawns lighting fireworks and swaying with their arms around each other holding plastic cups full of cheap beer—Ruby went to visit Tim at his grandparents' beach house on Cape Cod. He was there for the month, painting the porch and the basement for them; his parents were paying him to do it. Ruby had offered her services for the weekend. She would be there alone, one night, and the following night a bunch of their friends were driving down.

She sat in the driveway when she first arrived, looking at the house. Tim's car, his bumper replaced after he'd been rear-ended a few months ago, was sitting next to hers. There was something to the anticipatory moment, she ruminated, before the person you were visiting knew you had arrived. The opportunity you were afforded to anticipate, to stand outside the house and appraise it, judging, expecting, before you went inside, a moment just before an experience began. It was the closest you could come, she thought, to witnessing what other people's lives were like when you were not there. The house stood silent, and inside it someone waited, someone was going about his or her life.

She got out of the car and entered the house, stepping through a bright entranceway into the living room. "Hello?" she called. "Tim?" There was no answer.

From the living room she moved into the kitchen. The counters were clean, but the coffeemaker had half a pot of coffee in it. Over the sink was a long window that looked out onto trees. "Hello?" she called again.

The screen door off the living room opened and Tim stepped inside. "Hey! I thought I heard something." He pulled the door shut behind him and came into the kitchen. He was wearing shorts and a worn-out green T-shirt and had a drink in his hand. His right arm was streaked with paint. He was barefoot and smiling wide.

"How was your drive?" He put his glass down on the counter and came to her. "Hey," he said as he hugged her. His body was against hers. She hugged him back.

That night, they drank whiskey from Tim's grandparents' liquor cabinet and walked into town for ice cream. They had painted that afternoon, and Ruby had on her paint-streaked overalls. There was paint caked into her hair where it was pulled back into an elastic band.

They were laughing and comfortable; she felt good—just good, a way she rarely felt. Maybe it was the alcohol, maybe it was the sandy road and the beach below the house, the Cape Cod trees and the cool air, but there was no awkwardness between them.

On the way back, Tim pulled her behind his neighbors' house, where a swimming pool glimmered, lit by dim lights below the water. "Come on," he said, as he led her toward it, "they're not home. They're at their son's wedding."

Ruby stopped at the lawn just inside the gate. She was hesitant; she hadn't seen this coming, she hated swimming, and what, was she just going to take off her clothes? At the side of the pool, Tim turned back to her. His body was a silhouette against the glowing water, and she thought it was beautiful.

"Come on!" He pulled off his shirt and let it fall on the grass, then undid his pants and stepped out of them. His chest was pale, his stomach flat, his legs a little bowed. Wearing only his boxer shorts, he hurried to get into the pool; she could tell he didn't want her to see him. He climbed quickly down the stairs into the water and ducked under. When he surfaced, he tossed his head back and the water sprayed out of his hair. "Oh yeah!" he yelled.

For some reason, as she walked slowly toward the pool, as Tim ducked under again and popped up, yelling, "Come on! You've got to come in here!" she thought of the afternoon when she had finally told him about Nathan's coma. It was a day not long after the junior prom, over a year ago now, and she had pulled him from their homeroom after school with determination that it was time, she couldn't wait any longer, she had to tell him. They had walked around campus, and she had told him, and they had stopped outside the science building and leaned against the wall. Tim had been angry. He shook his head, at first, when she told him, and said "No," just like that, just "no," and then he had looked at her with his eyebrows furrowed. "Are you serious? Are you serious?" he had asked her, and her only response had been a weak nod with her eyes shut.

She'd seen the angry creases on his forehead then, creases that were so rarely there, as he had stooped to pick up rocks from the courtyard where they were standing and threw them, hard, yelling out to the playing fields, "It's not fair!" and "What the fuck!" A vein had stood out on his neck as he whipped the rocks and yelled, his voice rising higher and higher. She had stood motionless beside him and watched. "I know," she'd said flatly, as he raged. "I know." She had felt grateful to him, even in that moment, for expressing that anger, even the tiniest percentage of the anger that she felt but couldn't express.

Now, standing beside the pool in her overalls, she felt a similar difference between them—Tim enjoying the water, and Ruby standing at the edge and watching. She looked down through the water at the lights, the way they seemed to shoot hundreds of glowing worms moving through the blue. She was envious, in a way, of Tim's body moving in the light.

"You coming in?" he asked, his legs kicking under him. "It's really nice."

She hated the part of her that resisted. She undid the buckles of her overalls and let them fall, slipping off her Birkenstocks and approaching the steps in her T-shirt. The water was warm. As she descended the steps, her T-shirt billowed up onto the surface, pockets of dry, bubbling cotton like dough. She pushed it down as she ducked under and swam out to him. She came up next to him. It was instinct: she put her hands on his shoulders.

"Hey, careful," he said, but he was laughing.

"I hate swimming." His skin was slick under her hands; she wanted to pull him closer, she wanted to wrap her legs around him. Instead she raised herself up on her hands, pretending to push him under.

"Hey! It's not my fault you hate it!" He laughed, then ducked under and swam away. He surfaced by one of the walls and spread out his arms against the stone. She swam to him and held on to the wall next to him. She was definitely still drunk from the whiskey. The water felt great against her skin, oily and warm, and the light below them made the shapes of their legs incandescent and white, beautiful mythical creatures. Tim was close. She sank lower into the water, resting her chin on it, blowing bubbles from her lips. She turned her head to him. He was looking at her, and it was with eyes that were male. His eyes took her in; they moved over her face. She pulled up and didn't look away.

But then he blinked and went underwater again. When he came up, he was close to the stairs. "Let's get out of here," he said, moving toward his clothes.

· · ·

That was the weekend that Tim began to disappear from her life. On the way home from the pool Ruby was confused: why had he shut off so fast? Back at the house, in dry clothes, they sat out on the porch. The crickets were loud in the trees surrounding them, a chorus of continuous chirps. Tim, with a towel draped over his shoulders, asked Ruby if she'd had "intentions" in coming to visit him that night.

Ruby's hair was loose now, the ends of it slicked together in little points from the water. "Intentions?"

"Yeah, I mean, did you think something was going to happen between us? Did you want something to happen?"

It was the first time he had ever instigated a conversation about the two of them. She was surprised by this, and grateful in a way, but also confused. He was behaving as if she had asked him for something. Had she asked for this? She felt him drifting; his side of the porch was moving away, it was as if it were a raft on a river, as if his half had broken off from hers and was floating downstream.

She came up with the answer quickly. "I didn't think about it like that." Should she have?

He nodded. "Well, I wondered about it. I did. But I don't know, Ruby. I just get this feeling with you, like, I don't know." He leaned forward in his chair and looked down through the wood slats of the porch to the ground below. "Sometimes I get this feeling like if something happened between us then that would be the beginning of the rest of my life or something. I just feel like, well, I don't know. It's just too much. I'm not ready for that. We're about to go to college, it just doesn't make sense. I need to see what else is . . . I need to . . . Well."

She sat and watched him as he spoke about going to college, about being "free." He said, "Sometimes I just feel like one of us needs to break up with the other one, or something, or else we'll just go on like this."

Like what?

She listened to him, and as he spoke he grew smaller and smaller, fading into the distance, fading into the woods beyond the house. Her heart filled with the absence of him even as he sat before her still, even as his slowly drying curls were still within the reach of her hands.

The Highest Good

A aron is injured, and it is Ruby's fault. She has done harm to her brother. She has acted, and she has done harm.

She and her mother sit in the waiting room in the emergency room of the Bar Harbor hospital, which is small and populated by a series of hard wooden chairs with pink plastic seat cushions. Aaron is somewhere beyond them, in the depths of the hospital, being tended to by nurses and doctors, stitched, examined, prodded and sutured and fixed. Her mother is reading a magazine. How can she be so calm? Is she really reading it or does she just not want to talk? Ruby can't tell. Her mother has been silent ever since they brought Aaron in.

Ruby sits with her hands in her lap and stares straight ahead. There is nothing she can do. A television suspended from the wall in the corner of the waiting room plays Ricki Lake, who is interviewing people who are obsessed with celebrities. Her brother is inside because of her. What's done is done.

He's going to be okay of course, he will be fine. When they brought him in he was awake, he was making jokes, he said he always wanted to see the inside of this hospital anyway. He'd already been stitched on his head once before, didn't they remember, in college when he got in a drunken bar fight, and he'd told Mom and Dad he just slipped on ice? He laughed, and punched their mother lightly on the arm when she frowned, and said, "Oh come on Mom, let it go."

"It's okay, Ruby," he said to her on the drive to the hospital, as he held his bloody Red Sox T-shirt to the back of his head, "really. I know you didn't mean it. It's okay."

But what *did* she mean by it? The question frightens her. She was angry, she knows that; just before she laid her hands on Aaron she had been literally blind with rage. But this has never happened before, that she has given in to her anger like this, that she has done harm. How could Aaron forgive her so easily?

Aaron bled from his head, and the sight of that blood terrified her. He held the gray shirt to his head and it filled with blood, slowly, like a dye; by the time he went through the doors next to the admitting desk, the shirt was almost completely drenched. Her last healthy brother, losing blood from his head, and she was unable to do anything but wait.

Ruby saw the blood seeping from Aaron's skull into that shirt and she felt a corresponding seeping in her stomach, just under her rib cage. She felt nearly sure that the blood flowing into that T-shirt was coming from somewhere in her own guts, somewhere vital in her insides. When the skin on Aaron's head was punctured, right there on the rocks on the beach, before he came to, something started to change in Ruby. Even now that Aaron has disappeared, she can feel it: something is leaving her, something crucial, something like blood.

She sits quietly next to her mother and imagines the inside of her body as a liquid; she feels the liquid swirl and twist, there are currents inside her skin. People think she has bones—she looks like a normal human with bones and organs, but no, she thinks, she is liquid. The slightest nudge, the gentlest touch, and she will empty like a bathtub. She imagines herself emptying, all the liquid inside of her flowing out of the tiniest hole; she imagines her mother turning from her magazine to say something to her, tapping her on the shoulder, and the liquid spurting in a quick stream from her skin.

She wonders if she desires it, this draining of her insides—does she want her mother to poke her, does she want to see her insides stream out into the sterile room? Right now, she feels she wants nothing more than for her insides to flow from her. She is tired of herself, of what she carries inside her, of every old feeling that is echoing here in this room. She sits in the waiting room chair and wills her mother to poke her; she closes her eyes and wishes for it.

But she is not there for herself, and she feels a seething hatred for her own self-pity. She is there for her brother, for something that she did to him, and the remorse for this slaps her hands away from herself as if she were reaching for a forbidden cookie jar. It is a form of punishment, to sit there, keeping her hands in her lap, letting her bloated insides churn. No crying to her mother for help; no.

She stands, using her arms on the armrests to push herself up. Her body feels so heavy, it takes a great effort to move. Her mother looks up at her; her eyes are far away. She is trapped too, Ruby thinks, they are both of them trapped with what has happened, rooted in the trajectory of everything that has happened as in the path of a hurtling train.

"I just have to get some air," she says. Her mother nods. Ruby hesitates for a moment, and feels the desire to bend down, to fall onto her knees in front of her mother. She resists. She walks toward the door.

———

Ruby's mother had announced the trip to Maine in March—"I figure this must be far enough in advance for you to all put it on your calendar," she said in a leading tone to Ruby on the phone in her dorm room in Connecticut. She wanted the family to get away together, to "spend some time," and to revisit the place they used to vacation when Ruby and her brothers were kids.

Ruby suspected that her mother was planning the trip because she was in the process of selling their house. For months, she'd been in a frenzy of cleaning and throwing away, of going through every last family artifact to determine if it deserved to be moved, and she had been calling Ruby more often than usual, talking in excited tones, telling her about report cards she'd found, book reports and drawings, her father's stamp collection, an old coat of Nathan's, all the knitting from when she'd first stopped working, and of course boxes full of photographs that were so special they could hardly be described. She said it was hard, going through all the stuff, and she couldn't believe how little she'd thrown away over the years. "Pictures from when I was a teenager!" she gasped. "My high school yearbook! It's absurd!"

Ruby was torn between the desire to help her mother excavate, to dig her hands into all of her family's memories, and the wish that her mother wouldn't tell her about what she was finding at all. Ruby knew the house was too big for her mother alone, and she supposed it was inevitable that her mother would sell it and move. She could only imagine how it would be to live in that house—so large, so quiet, so full of ghosts—by herself, and when she thought of her mother there every night, climbing the creaking stairs to her bedroom, looking out the window at the top over the driveway to their street lined with ancient, reaching trees, the backyard where their dog was buried, the rooms around her empty and still, she knew that her mother's decision to move was right. Still, she didn't like to imagine it—the house was a familiar family member, how would they ever have a home without it? Her mother said (more than once, in a way that made Ruby wonder whom she was trying to comfort), "It's we who are the home, anyway, this is just a house." So though it seemed a little strange to go back to

Maine to spend time together when the vacation house they had once owned there had been sold, in a certain way her mother's impulse made sense to Ruby. She was reluctant, but she knew there was no way to avoid it.

When her mother had begun planning the trip, Abraham had been taking his medicine. He'd been taking it consistently for over a year, since his brief stint in the hospital the previous October—the longest stretch of time Ruby could remember him ever going without lapsing. Everyone, but especially their mother, had been feeling optimistic about him; even Ruby was allowing herself the tiniest glimmer of hope that his (admittedly compromised) stability might just maybe, this time, be dependable. Instead, he had stopped taking his medication a few weeks before they were to leave for Maine. With a flourish he'd declared that he was "better," he was "his own man," and he didn't need it anymore.

They had rented a house near the land they used to own; a little cottage right next to a marsh, decorated sparingly with impersonal items appropriate only, they decided, for a place where people were often passing through. None of them had been back to Maine, back to the land they used to own, since it was sold after Ruby's father died.

Ruby was twenty now, and every day she woke up in the world and it was the same. That is, every day she woke up and history hadn't changed, the trees still looked like trees, people were still hearing the radio and checking the weather and eating the same breakfast foods, the graveyards still had the same dead people and all the countries had the same names, people were still angry about the same things and killing each other and loving each other and killing each other again. The newspaper still arrived on the doorstep, filled with the same news; people still had cars, and espresso makers, and were still getting married and divorced and having babies and teaching their babies to read.

She felt a vague surprise, some days, at the fact of this, the way the world persisted and persisted and persisted, leading backward into time in a long, straight line. She was living her life, fine, the days were passing, and then all of a sudden one day she'd be in the college library and the fact, the presence, the unarguable nature of the books lining the shelves suddenly overwhelmed her—for the history they spoke to, the number of lives holding pens and living in the same world and using language to communicate, each one of those lives a person whose thoughts were always all they could hear in their heads. She sat in the cafeteria at school and looked around, amazed at the waves of people who came, loaded their trays, ate, disappeared, and then appeared again, life constantly flowing, moment after moment after moment without end.

Was it that she couldn't believe that she was still there, that she was in the same world with everyone else, that she was just one of the deep ocean of people who had lived and died in the same reality before her? Or was she actually surprised that the world itself didn't disappear or change, no matter what terrible things took place inside its sphere? Would it make more sense to her if she were to wake up in the morning in a desolate landscape, if she were to wake as the sole human in a world teeming only with cicadas and covered with dirt? Would it make more sense if she were to wake to a world populated by talking trees, to a world without history, if she were to wake every day in a different body, with a different mind? Often, she thought it would. Was it really true that she was a part of all of this? That her life was real and passing, that her body was as vulnerable as everyone else's, her thoughts no more lonely or strange or desperate than those of others before her?

After high school graduation, after the weekend at Tim's house on Cape Cod, as the strings of her known community began to

unravel and she moved forward to college, Ruby became convinced
that her pain was visible. She wore it like some kind of radioactive
suit. She left home, she lived with a roommate, and she went to frat
parties and took classes and got fine grades and had friends and slept
until noon. Freshman year passed into sophomore year passed into
junior year, and she was living her life, yes, living, but all the while
she moved through it as if she was inching along its walls, doing
everything just right enough so no one would see her.

Those years, she conjured the whole world as Nathan's body, the
earth as the home that was her brother. Nathan was everywhere; the
whole world was Nathan. The trees, the air, the sneakers on her feet,
her friends' voices on her answering machine: all of this was Nathan.
Her desk, piled with papers, her bed, holding her body as she slept,
the moon from her dorm room window.

Where was he? The only answer was that he was everywhere.
There was nowhere he was not. His grave, yes, he was there, but not
more than anywhere else. The grave was superfluous, the grave was
redundant. When Nathan died, he became the world, and she lived
inside of him. The thought comforted her. Nathan had always been
her protector, and when she needed him, she tried to believe he was
there.

This was the way she soothed herself, flimsy as the notion was, as
the years passed. She imagined Nathan and her father with their arms
forever locked, forming a shelter for her to live inside. She was accustomed to the swells, the rises, the dips of the world, their bodies; she
was accustomed to looking out at the world from inside her father,
her brother. It was safe in there. The thick nights of summer, her bed
like a bathtub full of hot water; the chill wind of winter, shockingly
cold, knives into her throat when she breathed in; she tried in hard
times to cultivate these as elements of the landscape of the bodies
of the men she had lost, and the belief that she was moving through
them, that she was pausing in pockets of them, that their bodies were

one and they were cradling her, calmed her. Every aspect of the world was an aspect of them and, by extension, every movement of hers a sort of homage.

The problem was that the world her brother and her father made for her, the protected haven she lived inside, had room only for one. Not her family, not her friends, no more men, no one could ever know what it felt like inside; no boy could ever reach her, for she half-believed that if a boy were to touch her he would put his hands right through her. She ducked men's interest with a lump in her throat and spent her time with boys who were unavailable, whom she could pine after in secret. There were already too many missing men, she could not stand any more.

She didn't speak of what she had been through, she hardly ever said the words; she carried her history like a bomb she didn't know how to properly store. When someone asked how many siblings she had, she'd say "two," the word slicing at her. She wanted so much for her story not to mark her that she hid it inside her skin—where, of course, it could not dissipate. She was doing just enough so that no one could say she wasn't living, just enough so that she couldn't say it to herself. But inside, she was closed for business. She was tightly wrapped in the bodies of men she had loved.

It was a security, of course, that was no such thing. Though it was a comfort at first, as she grew older it became a heavier and heavier burden: the cocoon of her loss growing more and more like a cage.

————

She sits on a bench in front of the hospital. She feels a little better, outside. The ground in front of her teems with ants; she watches them scurry about, dodging among the bricks of the sidewalk, running toward each other, running into each other, running away.

Just then an ambulance pulls up, lights flashing, and stops in the cul-de-sac before the hospital doors. Two EMTs, one male and one female, drop down from the cab of the ambulance and hurry around to the back. They open the doors and the woman climbs inside. From her vantage point, Ruby can't see the inside of the ambulance, but she sees a gurney slide slowly out of it, sprouting a pair of silver legs with wheels on the bottom. The ambulance is giving birth, she thinks. The EMT standing on the ground at the back delivers the ambulance's baby, he stands back to receive it, helping the gurney to sprout those silver legs.

Ruby feels uncomfortable around ambulances and tries to avoid the urgent, lit ones: no matter her temptation to peer inside to see the emergency, when they pass her she goes stiff and averts her eyes, feeling an uncomfortable steeliness at the reminder that terrible things are happening to people at all times; that though her personal experiences with ambulances might be over for now, they are out there, coming for others.

The doors to the ambulance stand open, just for a moment, the ambulance has offered up its cargo and now stands empty and silent and exposed, its duty performed, waiting for its next turn. Then the female EMT returns and shuts the back doors with two quick bangs. She climbs into the cab, starts the ambulance, and drives away.

Ruby is alone again. She wonders about the man who just went inside, who he is and what is wrong with him, whether anyone knows he is here. She looks down at her hands and sees the ants still teeming around in front of her and finds she must fight the urge to use her sandals to kill them all. Suddenly she is angry; she puts her hands under her thighs and sits on them, feeling the desire to run, just to *run*. What the hell has happened? How is it that she is here, outside a hospital, watching ambulances deliver sick bodies? She wants to get the hell away, she wants to run and run, but she knows no matter where she runs to she will still be herself, and this makes her the angriest of all. Why does she always, always, always have to be herself?

She hears Aaron's voice from earlier today—*It's okay, It's okay*—she hears it over and over like a pulse, though she feels ashamed and guilty for what she has already done, though she feels confused and though she wants nothing more than to let it go, *just let it go*. She squirms, she tenses all the muscles in her legs as tight as she can, she grits her teeth and tries to flex all of her muscles at once to push the feeling out. *Goddammit*, she thinks, *no more*.

The day of Nathan's funeral, after they had lowered him into his grave—after they had settled the pine box that held him onto the soil at the bottom of the pit and removed the ropes, the men from the cemetery had stepped back and away from the site, leaving the grave to Nathan and the people who loved him. These men, dressed in casual, dirt-strewn clothes, blue work shirts and Dickies, with their sleeves rolled to just below their elbows, their faces carved with wrinkles, stepped back, and everyone gathered around the pit that held Nathan, Nathan in that pine box, dead, naked Nathan in that box at the bottom. The rabbi stood at the head of the grave in his yarmulke and recited the psalm of David— *"Yea, though I walk through the valley of death, I will fear no evil"*—which always made Ruby feel so conflicted (*The Lord giveth and the Lord taketh away?* That's supposed to be good enough?), and the mourners' Kaddish, which Ruby forced herself to recite, always, because she knew her father thought it was important, because she could never forget being in synagogue with him (every time it was recited he would nudge her and gesture to the bimah, saying "You better practice"), and because she remembered his words "You're my Kaddish, you and your brothers." It made her angry to praise God at a time like this. What the hell was she praising him for when Nathan was about to be buried by the dirt that was piled over there at the other end of the grave?

Ruby stood with her family, Aaron on one side and her mother and Abe on the other, and she kept her eyes on the ground at her feet, just before the hole. Nathan's grave was just in front of her father's, all the way back in the cemetery, removed from the other graves and sheltered by two tall pine trees. Her father's grave didn't have a stone, because Jews wait a year for this, but there was a little tin plaque with her father's name on it just beyond where the rabbi stood. Ruby couldn't bring herself to raise her head, she couldn't bring herself to risk meeting anyone's eyes, she couldn't take in the crowd, which stretched behind her to the road. When the rabbi was done, he invited everyone to use the shovels provided. It was a Jewish tradition, he said, the greatest mitzvah you could do for the person who had passed on was to contribute the earth he would be buried with. The first shovelful was to be lifted with the head of the shovel turned upside down, so as to manifest the difference between this shoveling and the shoveling done by an ordinary worker for an ordinary task. He invited Nathan's family ("The Family," he called them) to go first, and Ruby's mother gestured for Abe and Aaron to go before her, and Ruby watched Aaron move forward to the pile of dirt and lift the shovel, digging it, upside down, into the dirt, pulling out a handful balanced on the back of it. His eyes were red and the back of his suit was rumpled. He looked quickly to their mother, he looked to Abe, and then to Ruby, the bit of dirt balanced on the shovel, and then he looked down into the grave and, with a quick forward thrust, threw the dirt into the pit.

Ruby braced herself for the sound. She remembered this from the last time: the sound, the sound. As the dirt fell toward Nathan she braced herself, and closed her eyes. *Flump.* There it was, that sound, that hollow sound, dirt hitting wood, dirt sealing another person she loved into the earth. Nathan! Could it really be? The sound left no room for doubt. She opened her eyes. Aaron was crying, and shoveling normally now, throwing one, two more shovelfuls into the grave. *Flump, Flump.* Every time the sound came Ruby felt a knife in her throat, she imagined Nathan down there in that box, frightened by the sound, she imagined that the dirt was burying him alive. What if he was alive in there? What if they were killing him with this dirt? She wanted to cry out, she wanted to reach for the shovels and fling them into the trees, she wanted to jump into the pit and free her brother from his pine-box prison, she wanted to throw the dirt at the rabbi, in the rabbi's face, in everyone's face, she wanted everyone there to choke on the dirt, to feel the dirt in their eyes and their mouths. How could they accept this so easily? How could they throw dirt on Nathan when maybe he was alive?

They were throwing the dirt, and Nathan was dead, and Ruby did nothing. Abe reached for the shovel and threw one heap of dirt with the shovel the right way up, a slight smile on his face. *Flump,* the dirt hit the coffin. Then it was Ruby's turn, and she performed the process through a screen of tears, just wanting to get away from the grave, doing what she had to do, what she knew she had to do, but what she hated doing with every piece of her. She did not want to throw dirt onto her dead brother. Mitzvah? What did that even mean? Her body made the motion; that was all she would do; she threw the dirt and the dirt hit the coffin and she stepped back from the mound.

After her mother came Nathan's friends, young man after young man in suit after suit, young, young men throwing shovelful after shovelful, asking for more shovels, heaving the dirt into the pit. There was Rob, who'd spoken at the ceremony, his face twisted and stained, gasping for air, leading the pack and throwing a shovelful and then turning away. The coffin was covered now, the sound was dirt hitting dirt, only one corner of the pine box was still exposed, and the young men struck the pile of dirt with the shovels and heaved, they used their strong young bodies to heave and throw and bury. There was no order, just a group of young bodies heaving in suits, heaving, heaving, grunting, scraping the shovels against the ground. Ruby stood back with her mother, who clasped her shoulder, and she saw that this was something Nathan's friends were doing for Nathan, she saw how much anguish and love there was at the mouth of her brother's grave, but it was too much for her and she could not watch. She stood back, she waited for it to end.

And then they were moving away, and there was a line of people leading from the grave out to the road, people on either side of the path leading out, people lined up one after the other, waiting for Ruby and her family to pass through. Ruby's mother had moved away from her, Ruby hadn't noticed when, but there she was ahead of her, hugging Nathan's friends, hugging them and nodding and crying, and as Ruby moved, one foot in front of the other, as Ruby's feet carried her toward the opening of the line of bodies, the mouth at the beginning of the path that she was to enter, she saw Rob, Nathan's best friend, his arms around her mother, his mouth open in the wide O of a wail.

Ruby's mother's back was to Ruby, so Ruby saw only Rob's face, his head over her mother's shoulder. His eyes were closed and he hung on her shoulders, the rest of his body almost completely slack, and she could hear his wail—*no, no, no*—and she knew that if he let her go it would be real, it would be over, Nathan would be buried. She watched Rob for a brief moment that felt like minutes, and his wail carried up and over all the other mourners and out over the line of people, past the waiting limousine, all these people waiting for Ruby and her remaining family. His wail was loud and clear; Rob was releasing his grief, releasing his disbelief, releasing his anger into the warm June air and clinging to her mother, clinging, not letting go, and Ruby saw this and felt it shoot straight down her body, and she loved Rob then. She was grateful to Rob, for she saw in the vision of him clinging to her mother a fraction of what she felt; Rob was expressing what she could not, she could not, she could not. She watched Rob. She let Rob express the fraction and she kept the rest. She looked away and moved toward the mouth of bodies.

Her eyes on the pavement, she moved down the line, she entered the mouth and moved slowly through it to the cemetery gates. She saw shoes, pair after pair of shoes and ankles, pumps and leather loafers with creases across the toes, she saw pavement cracks and grit and gravel and feet tucked into shoes, so many healthy feet in shoes. She could not raise her head, she could not face any eyes. As she grew closer to the end of the line, she recognized the shoes that belonged to her friends—there were Jill's shoes, there Jen's, there Tim's. She passed through her friends' shoes, she felt her friends watching her pass through them, but she kept her eyes on the ground. She could not acknowledge them, she could not acknowledge knowing anyone here, acknowledging anyone or any part of this would in some way be accepting it, and she did not accept it. Behind her, a line of people tucked into shoes, Jewish graves on a warm June day, Nathan's friends, college students in suits and ties stained with dirt and tears, her brothers, her mother in her black suit, Nathan and her father head to toe.

Back in the waiting room, she finds her mother with the magazine closed on her lap, looking up at the television in the corner.

"Hi," Ruby says.

"Hi," says her mother. Her eyes look to Ruby and then back at the screen. Her shirt, the purple linen one she often wears in the summertime, is stained with two spots of Aaron's blood on the shoulder.

Ricki Lake is still on; she is now interviewing a woman who wants to look like one of the Spice Girls.

"You learning anything?" Ruby sits down next to her mother. The chair cushion makes a sighing sound as she lands in it.

"Tons," her mother says.

The woman on-screen has tears in her eyes as she talks to Ricki Lake. "It has reached the point," she says, "where I don't even want to leave the house. I feel like people will laugh at me, I just feel too ugly."

She is a healthy-looking woman, a mother, with perfect skin.

"Wow, that's sad," says Ruby.

"It's awful." Her mother shakes her head. "I can't believe this program."

She looks up at the screen. The sides of her face are drawn down, and Ruby notices little pockets of skin at her jawline that she's not sure she's seen before. Her mother is getting older; there is nothing Ruby can do. "I just can't believe what's happened to our society," her mother says. "It's completely out of control." She turns in her seat to see if there are hospital staff members around. "I wonder if we can change the channel. I don't know how long I can take this."

"I mean, that woman is beautiful," Ruby says.

Her mother nods, turning back to the TV. "It's twisted!" she says with a burst of energy. "It's completely out of proportion!" She looks down at the magazine in her lap. On the cover, a woman in a low-cut halter top sits on a stool and leans toward the camera. "And this magazine," she says. "I can't believe this magazine! I have never, ever read a magazine like this. Can you believe women read these?"

"They're everywhere," says Ruby.

"I just can't believe it."

Every once in a while Ruby's mother says things that remind Ruby of the great distance between their backgrounds and upbringing; they always surprise her, the tentacles of her mother's repressed 1950s Catholic upbringing, even though in some way she expects them. Ruby knows they are in her as well.

They are quiet for a minute. Ruby looks around; there is no one behind the desk. "Any update about Aaron?" she asks.

Her mother shakes her head. "I would think it would be quick, he probably just needs a couple stitches. They're probably just understaffed. It is the weekend."

Ruby nods. "We *are* in Maine."

"Yeah. I'm sure he'll be out soon."

Ruby's guilt returns. The weight of all that is unspoken in this waiting room descends; she can feel it pressing on her shoulders, on her hands in her lap, on her knees. The echoes, the two of them in a hospital waiting room, waiting, nurses in white shoes moving by.

She goes over the moment in her mind, again and again, she tries not to but she must. Aaron's voice, and then her shove, her arms coming out in front of her and touching him, and then the sight of him stumbling, and then the fear, sharper than she had ever felt it before, fear like a shooting pain, like an instant leaking wound, fear that she can feel as painfully now, in the waiting room next to her mother.

She knows she should speak; she should fight against the instinct that wants to shut her down, she should acknowledge this moment with her mother, who has been through what she has, who will know what she means. But why doesn't her mother try to speak? Is Ruby the only one who feels the potency of what's happened, of where they are?

"It's pretty weird, isn't it," Ruby says tentatively.

Her mother looks from the TV screen to Ruby. "What's that?" she says.

"Just . . ." Is there any limit to the things that are weird? How can she possibly choose one? Can her mother really not throw her a bone? "Being here."

Her mother looks at her seriously then and nods. "Yeah." She moves the magazine off her lap onto the table next to her and then looks down at her empty hands.

"I don't know," her mother says, and sighs. "Maybe we should never have come back here. I thought it would be fun; I thought maybe, you know, we could finally all just share the memories and have it be good. But I think maybe it was just a bad idea."

Ruby realizes as her mother speaks that she is not the only one who feels guilty. Part of her is comforted by this, she is not alone, but a more familiar part feels a protective anger rise as her mother's guilt threatens to trump her own. Is she trying to make Ruby feel worse?

"Yeah," Ruby says. "It definitely didn't seem to work today, anyway."

She looks up at the TV and for a moment feels herself rise above the two of them. She sees herself, sitting next to her mother, each of them looking up at the television and thinking her own thoughts, right now, and she sees the two of them in all the other waiting rooms they've ever sat in, her mother's skin unlined on her face, Ruby's body smaller and a little bit fatter and her hair pulled back in varying degrees of tight ponytails.

"I'm sorry, Mom," she says quickly, the words surprising her as they come out. She looks down at her lap, embarrassed, angry even as she knows her words are true.

Her mother looks at her. "I know you are," she says. She reaches over and puts her hand on Ruby's. She squeezes. "I think we all are."

"I don't even know what happened." Ruby feels a knot rising in her throat. "I just, I got so angry, I . . ."

"It's okay, Ruby," her mother says. "It was an accident. Aaron knows that. I know that. I think we were all just overwhelmed, and we all reacted, in our own ways." She pats Ruby's hands. "It was just a bad day," she says. "But we've seen worse." She gives Ruby a smile. "Right?"

Ruby tries to smile back.

"Anyway," her mother says, "it's good to get angry. Believe it or not"—she holds Ruby's hands and leans closer to her as if she's telling her a secret, lowering her voice—"it was good to see you get angry."

She sits back up, smiling at Ruby. "I could have done without the bloody injury, but . . ."

Ruby laughs. Her mother moves her hands but leaves one on Ruby's arm.

"We do need to stick together better, though," her mother continues, "the three of us. You know what they say . . . divided you fall."

Ruby nods. "I just can't believe—"

"I know," her mother says and gives her arm a final squeeze. "I know. But he's going to be okay, Ruby, don't worry." She pauses. "We all are."

The night before they left for Maine, they had dinner at home with Aaron and his new girlfriend, Sophie. Sophie is French—little, mousy, French, and not Jewish, a friend of a friend.

Aaron made sure to point out beforehand that it was way too early for "meeting the family," and that Ruby and her mother were not to take it *that way*. "It's just dinner," he said. "Okay? Don't go reading into this. It's just not every day that Ruby's home, and whatever. Not a big deal. I think you guys will like her."

They ate a simple dinner at the kitchen table, chicken breasts and rice pilaf and salad, and of course there was no reason to object to Sophie, none at all. She wore her hair back, which Ruby appreciated because of the way it suggested she was not quite comfortable with herself. She seemed smart; she seemed nervous; she kept her arms crossed while Ruby's mother served, and looked at her plate frequently when she spoke to Ruby or her mother. Aaron was very attentive to her—touching her on the shoulder when he went by, offering to refill her wine, looking at her partway through any statement he made to try to catch her eye.

Ruby tried not to size Sophie up, and yet she couldn't help it. Aaron had had needy girlfriends, women who demanded his constant attention, women who draped themselves on him like blankets while they watched TV. The only women she could remember him being attached to were women who were either pouty or fawning, who were so in love with him that they didn't care how they behaved around anyone else. It was a strange phenomenon to watch, and it made Ruby realize how little she knew or understood her older brother.

Of course, Ruby had never known any of Aaron's girlfriends very well. It was only in the past two years, since he moved back from Chicago, that Aaron had been, for the first time, a less distant and more viable star in her familial galaxy. She hadn't realized, in all those years he'd been away, how different it would be to have him nearby—how it would feel to have a brother she could see and touch on a regular basis rather than a few times a year or as a disembodied voice on the phone. There were times when it seemed distinctly bizarre to her, to see familiar family artifacts in his home (the blue checkered tablecloth she and her parents had brought back from Czechoslovakia, the painting that used to hang in the dining room over the mantelpiece) or to hear him speak of growing up in the very same house that she had. "There's nothing for me in the Midwest," he had declared soon before he moved back to Massachusetts to start business school, just as her father had declared he was ready to go back to Europe all those years before.

Ruby tried not to find things to worry about with Sophie; she tried just to eat, and not to wonder about the future of this relationship, which she had no business wondering about yet. She tried not to wonder whether Sophie would be her future sister-in-law, the mother of Aaron's babies, the mother of the babies who would hold her brother inside of them, who would hold pieces of her whole family, all of them, the first offshoots of their bloodline. She tried not to think this way, not to imagine Sophie at the beach, standing in a shallow wave holding a baby to her breast, like that photo of her own mother holding Ruby that she had stuck to her mirror upstairs.

Ruby looked to her mother to see if she was having difficulty not wondering too, but she couldn't tell. Her mother was the queen of the poker face; when it came to what she felt about other people, there was no way to crack her veneer. She was always gracious and open toward people, serving them soup and clearing their bowls with cheer—it was only after they left that you'd learn, with surprise, that she couldn't stand them.

Her mother spoke to Sophie about the year she'd spent in France after she graduated from college: how she had been all ready to start a Ph.D. program in Wisconsin, she had already shipped all her clothes out there from New York, and then one morning she woke up and saw a beautiful sunrise out her apartment window ("It was simply sublime" was how she always described it) and decided right then and there that she would go to France instead.

"I had to tell my mother to get my trunks back!" she said, shaking her head. "It was a whole ordeal. I got on the plane with only one bag and I went for a whole year."

"Wow," said Sophie. "That sounds so great."

Ruby's mother nodded, chewing. She swallowed, then said, "Oh, it was. It was really one of the great experiences of my life. I just loved France."

Hearing her mother tell this story that she had heard many times, Ruby felt a bit protective, as if her mother had opened an old diary or a cherished love letter from her father and shown it to Sophie right there at the kitchen table. Sophie was saying, "It must have just felt so free, to do that, I can't really imagine." She looked at her plate. "You must have been so brave."

Ruby's mother laughed. "It's funny," she said, "when I look back on it now I see how it was brave, but at the time it didn't even occur to me. It was just something I wanted to do, and I had saved money from teaching after college, so I knew I *could* do it, so I did. It was as simple as that. I had never even been out of the States before, but I wasn't scared at all." She shook her head, smiling. There was a tiny piece of rice at the side of her mouth that she wiped off with her napkin. "I think I would be more scared to do it *now*."

Ruby watched Sophie react to her mother's story, a story that had always inspired Ruby, had always made her proud, connected to a part of her mother that she otherwise wouldn't know. She was happy her mother was telling it, she was happy her mother felt comfortable and wanted to share. Ruby looked to Aaron, and saw that he was watching their mother with surprise. "I'm not sure I've ever heard about that," he said, swallowing his food and keeping his eyes on her.

"Really?" she said, surprised. "I'm sure I've told you about that."

"Well, I knew about France, of course, and I'm pretty sure I knew about Wisconsin too, I just don't think I ever heard about that sunrise." His eyes darted to Sophie and back to their mother. Ruby thought he seemed a little bit hurt that he had never heard this before, but he didn't want to show just how much it affected him. "That's cool, Mom," he said, sitting back. "I really never knew that."

"I'm sure I've told you that before," she said. She looked at him, then at Ruby. "You've heard about that, right?"

Ruby nodded. How could Aaron have missed this story?

"I definitely never have," said Aaron. "Wow, that's cool."

Their mother nodded. "Yeah. Anyway. It was the right decision. See, how spontaneous I used to be?" She looked to Sophie, smiling. "Aaron's always saying I'm not spontaneous." She laughed. "And it's true, I've become a lot less flexible in my old age."

"Oh, come on, Mom," said Aaron.

"No, it's okay, it's true!" She took a sip of her wine. Two dark wine wings appeared at the sides of her mouth. "I guess that's just what happens," she said, putting her glass down. "But I do have it in me, and that story proves it."

· · ·

They finished and brought their dishes to the sink; Sophie offered to help clean up but Ruby's mother wouldn't let her. They had dessert, bowls of ginger frozen yogurt, and when Aaron brought Sophie hers he let his fingers linger along her neck. Ruby watched this; she was sitting across from Sophie, she saw Sophie look up at Aaron and smile.

As Aaron smiled back, Ruby tried not to imagine how her brother was when he was intimate with women. She tried to put herself inside her brother's skin—how must it be to be him, right now, with this new woman and the two women who were not new?—but she stopped herself, she looked away and focused on her frozen yogurt, in one of the glass bowls with the tiny grooves from which she had eaten ice cream her whole life. She remembered when she was young, how she would stir her coffee ice cream in these bowls until it was soup, she would spoon the ice cream soup to her mouth with exquisite pleasure. Nothing was better for a time than coffee ice cream soup; she would never eat any ice cream in these bowls unless it was soup.

She was eating her yogurt with a little spoon—she always liked to eat ice cream with little spoons—and as she thought of ice cream soup and ate with her little spoon she saw her family at the table when they were all young: her father at the head in his crisp button-down shirt, then Ruby, Nathan next to her, then Aaron, Abe, and her mother in a plastic apron. A memory rose, and she hesitated to share it, but why not share it? She said, "Hey Aar, remember when we were little and you used to set my place with the little dishes?"

Aaron nodded, his spoon in his mouth. He took the spoon out, grinning. "Of course. I only did that a few times."

"Yeah, but they were memorable."

Aaron turned to Sophie, and Ruby realized that when she'd brought this memory up she had introduced it to the atmosphere. "When Ruby was little and it was my turn to set the table," Aaron said, "sometimes I'd set her place with all the little dishes. You know, a dessert plate, a little fork and knife, a shot glass." He chuckled.

"You used to get so mad," Aaron said to Ruby.

"Really?"

"Yeah. You didn't think it was funny at all." He took another spoonful of yogurt.

"Well, you *were* an asshole to me," Ruby said and kicked him lightly under the table. "Couldn't quite ever get over your own hilarious wit."

"It's true," he said. "What can I say? You were just such an easy target. You'd get all mad, run crying to Mom. It really only egged me on. Oh, it was so fun. Remember when I put Tabasco sauce in your Fig Newton?"

Sophie made a noise as if she were about to choke. Aaron laughed and put his hand on her back. "Oh, that was *classic*," he said.

Ruby smiled, finishing her yogurt while Aaron recounted the story. She pretended to be offended, saying, "See what I had to go through?" to Sophie when he was done. But in fact she loved this story too; it spoke to her particular place in her particular family, both of which were no longer the same.

Later that night she lay in the bed she grew up in, most of her duffel bags from school still unpacked in piles on her floor. She felt the house around her, breathing, an occasional creak on a stair or a tick from who knew where, the noises of the house "settling," as her parents used to tell her when she was scared as a kid. How familiar the noises of the house were, how familiar the air, how familiar the noises outside, the crickets, the hum of some equipment of their neighbor's turning periodically on and off. She imagined her mother and her, held close inside the rib cage of the house. What would they do without the house, when it was sold, what would her family look like without their familiar skin, their rib cage to hold them?

When she had arrived home from college, the For Sale sign posted out front had made Ruby gasp. She wasn't expecting that sign, the invitation to passersby to peer in at the Bronstein home, to size it up, to buy it—just like that!—if they wished. The sign was flagrant and seemed to Ruby a betrayal; that sign made a peep show out of their house, that sign told their house to strip and stand naked and be looked at. She wanted to clothe their house; she felt angry at her mother for removing its clothes with that sign. What could their house possibly mean to the passersby? It meant too much to Ruby, she felt, lying in her bed, to mean enough to anyone else. The life of the house, like the life of everything else, now, was undetermined.

The next morning, when they were to leave for Maine, before Aaron came over, Abe arrived at the house looking skinny and wild, stinking of body odor. He had taken the subway from his apartment, in a complex with some supported living apartments reserved for people with illnesses like his—and walked twenty minutes from the train station. Ruby was going through her bags and packing for the trip when she saw him from her window, loping up the driveway, his arms swinging wildly, chest thrust out, wearing a worn white undershirt and jeans. The sight of him drew Ruby closer to the window. As soon as he appeared, she was like a hawk, watching him, sizing up his state, trying to see in that one quick stride toward the house the whole caliber of his mind, the neurons not firing, the amount of psychotropic drugs in his bloodstream, the projection of the whole trip they were about to take together. He was walking quickly and intently, his head held high, his arms swinging; this was probably not the best sign. He also wasn't carrying any luggage, but this wasn't necessarily a sign of anything.

Ruby heard her mother talking to him in the kitchen. She could hear her exclaiming happily at his arrival, and then she could hear her voice turning to questions, the notes rising at the ends of her sentences. She heard Abe responding, but she couldn't make out what he was saying, then she heard him raise his voice. She crept out of her room to the landing at the top of the stairs and down a few steps, to where she could make out most of what was coming from the kitchen.

"Anyway," Abe was saying, "I just moved recently, and I think it is important for me to establish myself there right now."

He had moved into his apartment six months earlier.

"But Abraham, we've been planning this trip for months. You've known about it for months!"

"Yes, Mother, I have, you're right," he said. "I *have* known about it for months."

Ruby could see them; as she sat on the stairs listening she could see them as clearly as if they were standing in front of her. Her mother was by the kitchen counter, her face had an expression of amazement and frustration, and Abraham was pacing, long strides across the kitchen floor, watching his feet, moving faster than the room's space would seem to allow.

"So then why did you change your mind, why today?"

"I don't *know*, Mother, maybe I'm just a little *uncomfortable*"—he pronounced all the syllables—"with spending the whole week with my mother, that's all."

This was often Abe's excuse for backing out of things. Last year on his birthday, in July, Ruby's mother had planned a fancy dinner and had told both Aaron and Ruby to be home for it, making Aaron cancel a golf trip to Nantucket ("How many times a year do you do something for him?"). An hour before Abe was to arrive, he had called to say he wasn't coming. "A man shouldn't spend his twenty-ninth birthday with his mother," he had said. They didn't know what he had done instead, but it was most definitely done alone.

"I'm getting pretty tired of that excuse, Abe," her mother said firmly. "What does that even mean? Your sister and your brother are happy to spend the week with me."

"Well, that house was Dad's, and I'm just not sure who belongs. Dad could be a very persuasive man."

"What does that have to do with anything?" She was getting upset.

There was silence. Then, "He didn't even like me to drive his boat. It just seems highly unlikely that the boat could drive itself, you know?"

Ruby heard her mother sigh. Abe's condition had deteriorated rapidly since he had stopped taking his medicine, that much was clear. Ruby was surprised to hear how disordered he was after only a month.

"No, I don't know, Abe," said her mother. "I don't understand at all. What you're saying does not make sense. And for the record, you know the Maine house has been sold, it was sold years ago. We can't even go in there anymore." She paused. "But if you don't want to come, fine, I obviously can't make you. It's disappointing, that's all, we were all looking forward to spending some time with you."

"Well, I was looking forward to it too," Abe said.

"And you will miss out on an important family trip. I'm just sorry for you, is all."

"Well, I'm sorry too."

Ruby thought she heard her mother sigh again. Then, "Your sister's upstairs if you want to go tell her."

Ruby ducked back into her room, bracing herself for the inevitable entrance of her brother.

"Hello?" he said when he reached her door.

"Hey, Abe!" she said. She stood where she was, next to her duffel bags on the floor.

"Hey sis. How are you?" He was tentative at first, in the doorway. His hair was matted on one side, from sleeping she assumed. Around his jaw were a few patches of hair that he had missed while shaving.

"I'm good! How are you?"

"Pretty good," he said, holding his hand out flat and turning it, left, right. "Mezza mezza."

"Yeah? You excited for this trip we're taking?"

He came into the room and moved toward the desk. "No. I'm not coming."

"You're not?" She feigned shock. "Why not?"

He picked up a paperweight from the desk. It had blocks of colored shells inside of it that reminded Ruby of barnacles. He held it up to the light, then put it down quickly. Abe always seemed uncomfortable when in Ruby's room. Aaron would snoop around, picking up things, looking at the old pictures that were still taped to her walls, her left-behind CDs, whereas Abe would rarely touch anything, he never sat down, and he usually didn't stay for long.

"I don't know," he said, "it's just not the right time for me."

"Well, that's too bad. We'll miss you."

"Yeah." He turned from the window and came toward her. "But anyway," he said, "how's the professor?"

Ruby tried to stand straight and not back away from him. He was close-talking again. He was leaning in close, so close, with just the top half of his body, like he was peering at a jewelry display that was her face. But he was barely looking at her, and this, more than the close talking, was the tip-off to his decline: the way his face was oddly blank even as it looked at hers, even as it expressed words, so close, so close that she moved back, always, back, and back.

She backed away. She couldn't help it. "Who? You mean me?" she asked.

"Yeah!" He was surprised she didn't know.

"I'm not a professor."

"Well, if you keep getting more degrees, you're not far off."

"I guess that's true." She moved back again.

Abe was obsessed with Ruby's degree, even though she had not received it yet. It was because Ruby was the youngest, she knew, because he couldn't grasp the reality that she was growing beyond the age she was when he got sick, when "normal life," as she lived it, ceased for him. He never once fixated in a similar way on Aaron's college degree, probably because Aaron was already in college when he got sick. Abe just couldn't grasp how his younger sister, ten years younger, had continued to grow, and was in many ways outgrowing him.

She sat down on her bed. Sitting was the best way to avoid the close talking.

"Did you know that Mom is going to sell this house?" he asked, hovering over her.

"Yup."

"So we're all going to have to be independent after this."

"That's true."

"We're all going to have to live on our own," he said.

Abruptly, he made his way to the door.

In the waiting room, Ruby's mother is asleep with the back of her head resting against the wall. Ruby is staring straight ahead, focusing on not thinking. She must not think—not of hospitals, not of what happened, not of Aaron falling, not of her anger, not of why any of it happened. She is tired of thinking, she is tired of trying to figure things out with her mind.

Just Shoot Me is on the TV now; she tries to watch, but she can't even when she tries. There is a dull fear in the bottom of her stomach that she imagines as a straight line all the way around her torso, and she finds her mind coming back to the same forbidden places. She listens to herself breathe; she tries to count her breaths.

Then the door across the room opens and Aaron is there, coming toward them. Ruby nudges her mother; she blinks and says "Hmm?" then sees Aaron and leaps out of her chair.

Aaron has a bandage taped to the back of his head, and a patch of his hair about the size of Ruby's palm has been shaved away. He waves their mother off as she comes toward him: "I'm okay, Mom." She puts her arms around him anyway. "Good," she says.

Ruby stands. Aaron appears different to her now than he did this morning, both more familiar and more distant; someone she knows intimately and yet has never really looked at before. It is like when a person's face becomes suddenly clear to you, a face you have looked at countless times suddenly changes, and you realize that you have been seeing your own version of it all along, a rendition, and your interpretation of it was never its truth.

She is awkward; she doesn't know how to behave. She has made a mistake—maybe they all have. Maybe it is not her fault, but her mistake has ended with her brother and a bandage on his head.

Her mother stands back from Aaron and peers at him. He looks at her, then at Ruby. "See?" he says, turning his head to show them the bandage. He holds his arms out. "All fixed up. Five stitches. And I don't even have a concussion."

The three of them are in a hospital waiting room and Aaron has a bandage on his head. They stand still.

Finally Aaron says, "Can we get the hell out of here or what?"

• • •

On the way to the rental house, Ruby sits in the backseat. It is dark out now, and the road from Bar Harbor to their house is pitch-black. Their mother puts the brights on, and the lights extend in a wide triangle from the front of the car, lighting the road and the woods on either side. She flicks them off whenever a car approaches and passes on the other side.

Ruby sits in the back and remembers this drive from when she was a little girl. On the drive home from Bar Harbor at night they were often quiet, whereas the drives there in the afternoon were rowdy and loud. Nathan had invented a chant that they sang on almost every drive to Bar Harbor—one person would say "Kah" in a low voice, and the others would chant back "Bah Hahba!" in a high-pitched return, like the call of some kind of bird. Like most of Nathan's inventions, no one had any idea where this had come from, but they picked it up and it became part of the family lore; on every drive they took into Bar Harbor they repeated it, it became part of the ritual of going there for dinner, as standard as eating at Carlo Pizza and buying fudge at the candy store, as essential to the trip as turning on the car.

Her mother flicks the brights off and then back on as a car passes them. Ruby remembers riding in the car, her parents in the front, driving back to their house with her brothers asleep and snoring next to and behind her on the minivan seats, the excitement of the Bar Harbor trip still lingering as they drove away from it. She remembers when she first learned of the etiquette of turning your brights off for passing drivers, leaning over the front seat to ask her father what it was he was doing when he flicked the lights, the pleasure of learning a whole piece of adult communication in that small act of unspoken etiquette. She was never able to sleep on the way home; she used to watch the road keenly instead, looking for animals to appear in front of them, lit in the white light of their headlights. They had seen all kinds of creatures—deer, raccoons, possums, even once a moose—out on that dark road coming home and had narrowly missed hitting a few of them. Their father was calm when he came across them, slowing the car so they could get a good look at whatever was making a dash for the other side.

Now, Aaron and her mother are in the front seat. From where Ruby sits, behind Aaron, she can see a tiny piece of the white of his bandage in the space between his seat and the door. She closes her eyes and feels the car rolling over the road in the darkness; Aaron has his window open, and the air comes onto her face as she leans her head back against the seat. She is herself, now, and also feels distinctly that she is that little girl, with her whole family, rolling over this same road in the old minivan; she is that little girl next to her brothers in the car controlled by her father, with no knowledge of anything beyond peering through the windshield to see what might appear. To think that these two Rubys are the same! It does not seem possible. Does she carry the both of them inside of her at all times, the Ruby before and the Ruby after? Is it possible that that little girl still lives, only waiting to be remembered, rediscovered, reactivated, and recalled? At any moment, she thinks, if we revisit the places of our past, we can conjure our parallel selves.

Aaron and her mother are in the car with her now and they were there then; they are in the car with her in both times, they are constants and they too have younger selves, yet this is difficult for her to feel right now. The events of the day have pushed her back into herself; she feels reluctant to share her memories even though they include them all.

She remembers the old drives and the excitement of those trips, how she loved that bookstore in Bar Harbor with the back corner full of pens, how the floors creaked in there, how she always wanted to stay there longer, how there was never enough time until her parents said they had to go or they'd miss the movie. She feels the three of them in the car, each of them remembering, each of them thinking about the day, each of them probably imagining her father behind the wheel, the boys asleep in the backseat. Or who knows, maybe they are not. Maybe Aaron is thinking of his stitches, maybe he is thinking of Sophie, maybe her mother is thinking about Abraham, maybe she's thinking about the house at home, maybe she's thinking of nothing at all. Ruby doesn't know; none of them speak. And so she remembers the old drives as if they were all her own, as if there is nothing for her to share.

When they arrive, Aaron insists that they have tea, as usual, and watch some TV. "I'm not tired yet," he says, "are you guys?"

He seems cheerful, which Ruby finds hard to believe. Her mother is tired but peaceful as well, humming to herself as she lines up the teacups on the counter, dropping in the tea bags, the teapot on the stove next to her whooshing as it heats up.

Ruby feels a need to be away from her family, to think over the events of the day in the safety of a space by herself. She wants to talk to someone but doesn't feel prepared to discuss the day with her mother or Aaron. She feels a familiar instinct to escape to her room and shut the door.

Before he comes to the couch, while Ruby sits alone and her mother makes the tea, Aaron calls Sophie. Ruby can hear him, on his cell phone in his bedroom with the door open, pacing back and forth between the bed and the window as he talks. Aaron loves his cell phone; he is one of the first people he knows to have one, and he swears that Ruby too will have one someday soon. "I'm fine," Ruby hears, "Don't worry, really, I don't even have a concussion," and "Aww, that's sweet," and then, "I will, I will," in a drawn-out, almost patronizing tone. He asks Sophie about her job and retreats farther into the room, where Ruby can't hear him. She hears the creak of the bed as he sits down, and then she turns on the TV so he won't think she's listening to him.

She stares at the TV screen and vaguely processes that it shows a couple talking on a plush red couch, but she doesn't watch it. She thinks, instead, about her brother on the phone in the next room, and wonders at how different their responses are. It seems that he is genuinely ready to forget what happened, that he's already moved on. She admires his cheerfulness and thinks that he has always been like this; always been able, unlike her, to bounce right back. She wonders what it will take for her to let go of what she has done. If he has truly forgiven her, if her mother is humming in the other room, then why does she feel it will take so much for her to move on from this day?

Her brother laughs in his room, and she looks down at her body, alone in the corner of the long green couch. Her mother brings the tea to the couch with a box of fancy, dark cookies. "Where's Aaron?"

"He's talking to Sophie."

Her mother settles herself on the couch. "What are we watching?"

"Oh, I don't even know, I haven't been paying attention."

"Okay . . ." Her mother reaches for her bag of knitting at the foot of the couch.

Aaron joins them. "What are we watching?"

The three of them have tea and sit together in the living room watching *Law & Order*. The back door is open, and an army of moths flutters against the screen door.

Ruby makes herself stay put. It is the least she can do, she knows, but even as she sits there, with Aaron lengthwise so his legs are draped over hers and her mother's laps, her body itches to move away. She is trapped by the warmth of her brother's legs.

Her mother puts down her knitting and looks at her watch. "You know, I should really call Abraham. I haven't called in a couple of days. Do you think it's too late?"

It is about ten o'clock. "Are you kidding?" Ruby says, her eyes on the screen. "He stays up all night, you know that."

Abe had taken to drinking a few liters of Pepsi every day and into the night—a substitution she supposes for the mostly licked proclivity for alcohol, but one that kept him up almost all of every night.

"Yeah, he's up," Aaron says, moving his feet off their mother's lap so she can stand. "But don't tell him what happened. You know how he is about doctors, he'll get all freaked out and concoct some theory about how I'm being poisoned or something. We'll never hear the end of it."

"I know. I wasn't going to." Their mother stands up from the couch with a grunt. She goes to the kitchen to use the phone that is mounted on the wall.

"Mom," Aaron calls, "you can use my cell phone. It's after eight"—he rolls his eyes at Ruby—"so it's free."

"Oh! Okay," she says, coming back to the couch. He finds the number, pushes Send, and hands it to her. She looks confused. "Hello?" she says into the phone and then, "Oh, it's ringing."

There is a long pause. Abe hardly ever answers his phone, but when he does it's usually after at least fifteen rings.

They wait. On the TV, a commercial for a car shows two people driving along a steep mountain road, taking the curves easily. The woman in the passenger seat is wearing a turtleneck sweater and gazes contentedly out at the cliff face to her right.

Ruby tries not to think of how today's incident began with a fight about Abraham. She remembers the anger that flooded her, an immediate and powerful venom, and feels its potential in the room with them as her mother holds the phone to her ear and waits for Abe to answer. Just the possibility of Abe on the other end of the phone is a link to that anger. Abraham, innocent Abraham, alone and crazy, whom she can hear as clearly as if she were calling him herself, the "Allo!" far too loud into his end. He is like a trigger, he carries on his helpless body the burden of all they are incapable of controlling, the turns of events beyond their reach.

"Abraham!" their mother says. She gives them the thumbs-up sign. "Hi!"

She listens. "Yeah? Well, I wanted to call because it had been a few days. How are you? I didn't wake you, did I? Oh, good."

She moves with the phone toward the kitchen.

Ruby knows her mother is bolstered by the memory of Abe before he was sick, a memory Ruby barely has at all, and she knows that the sense of responsibility her mother feels toward Abe is powerful, for she is the only one who looks after him. But still Ruby is amazed by her mother's capacity for hope where he is concerned. No matter the level of her despair, no matter the number of times the same pattern plays itself out, she hears what he says and engages with him in discussions and recounts them to Ruby later with an unmistakable edge of hope in her voice.

In the kitchen, she is saying, "We went back to the old house today, it is very different. . . . No, some new people own it now. There's only one house there now. . . . No, we didn't stay long. . . . Well, Abraham, why would you say that? . . . Well I don't quite follow your logic."

Their mother's thinking was that it was good to question Abe's disordered opinions, so he could understand that his thinking didn't make normal sense. They all tried to do this when they spoke to him, to get him to explain the way he made his connections, but sometimes Ruby found herself agreeing with him to avoid hearing him go deeper.

Then, suddenly, her mother signs off. "Okay, well, we'll be back tomorrow, so I'll call when we get back, okay? Do you have enough money to last you?" Abe's disability check came in on the first of the month, and he often ran out of money before the month was up. "Okay," says their mother, coming back into the living room, "Okay, Abe, okay, good. Talk to you soon. Bye."

She presses the End button decidedly with her pointer finger, then hands the phone to Aaron.

She sighs as she sits down.

"Okay, that's done."

She shakes her head. "He was listening to the radio or something, I think, something was very loud in the background. His neighbors are going to complain again, I'm sure of it." She sighs. "If he gets kicked out, I don't know where else he can go."

"Did he sound all right?" asks Aaron.

She shrugs. "Not great. Oh, let's not talk about it. We're still on vacation, right? Let's make another cup of tea."

An hour or so later, Ruby excuses herself to go to her room. Her mother says, "Yeah, I think it's that time for me too," and Aaron says, "Okay, you bums, I'll just watch TV by myself then."

Ruby says good night to him, lingering over the couch a minute longer than is necessary, feeling there is something unfinished, something she should say. In the end she grows aware that she's been standing there awkwardly and pulls herself away.

In her room, she puts on her pajamas without brushing her teeth and lies down on her bed, breathing, trying to stay calm, looking out the window into the dark. There is a gentle breeze blowing over the marsh; the curtain at the window billows out and reaches for Ruby, just missing her head.

The summer after high school, when she and Tim were at his

grandparents' house on Cape Cod, she had driven him to the hospital in the middle of the night. It was the second night she was there, the night their friends had arrived with a trunk full of beer and a watermelon that they would fill with vodka. Tim broke a bone in his foot after falling off a chair during a particularly rousing session of dancing to Billy Joel's "Only the Good Die Young." He was hurt but played it off, and it was only after everyone had fallen asleep, and the alcohol wore off, that he woke up in blinding pain and woke Ruby, asking her to drive him to the emergency room.

While they drove along dark and silent Cape Cod streets, the trees towering out over their car, raccoons scurrying out of the road, their eyes briefly catching the light before they ducked into the long grasses on the side, Tim sat back in his seat and dreamily described an imaginary future time when she would drive him to the hospital. She listened and vaguely believed him, though of course she knew he was making it up—"We'll be in Montana, you'll be out visiting me and I'll take you hunting and there will be an accident, something will go wrong with the gun"—and she took this talk as confirmation that he loved her, despite everything he had said the night before. He could see his life, she thought, and she was in it. They got to the hospital, and she sat in the waiting room for over an hour with a warm and contented feeling: *I'm here because he needs me.*

Ruby wonders where Tim is now, whether he misses her, whether he will ever try to get her back, and whether she wants him to. What a strange thing, in retrospect, to think of Tim, someone so close to her whom she barely speaks to now, someone alive whom she has lost. If you know someone once, do you ever stop knowing him?

She is afraid for the loss of everyone she has left, of everyone she will ever love. She is aware of her fear: everyone will eventually disappear. Ruby thinks of her mother, of how often she calculates the number of years she has left, worrying over the way she is aging, the way her hearing has started to go, the way she repeats herself more often than she ever used to. What will happen when she's gone, who will take care of Abe (Abe! She cannot even think of him), who will look out for her, Ruby? The fear is consuming, it is the size of the universe, it steals even her ability to think. If there's anything certain about the future, it is that it will hold more loss. This is the one thing there is to hold on to, she thinks, with horror. She closes her eyes against the thought, trying to shake it loose.

She thinks again of Nathan's funeral, the sight of Tim's shoes against the crumbling cemetery pavement, the way those worn sneakers beneath the hems of his suit pants had looked as she passed them, how they had made her imagine his face although she had refused to look up at it. Rob, at the funeral, clinging to her mother, Nathan's coffin, her father's coffin, her father silent in his grave as they buried his youngest son, the whole group of them standing in front of her father's grave and mourning again, right there, right in front of where he lay. She remembers it, she lets it come, she keeps her eyes closed and it tightens like a vise around her heart. Nathan, his body lying untied, unfettered, gasping on his final bed, as if he might gasp so much breath into his lungs that his whole body would lift clear off the mattress. Aaron, crying into her hair when Nathan was dead, and how it felt foreign and unreal, this strange man who was her brother holding her and crying into her hair, because how could the words *he's dead* really mean anything at all when it came to Nathan? How could they mean anything? What did they mean? Even now she is unsure, she does not want to believe.

She thinks of Rob, and the way she had stood back and watched him wail, the way her mother had held him, just held him, her back to Ruby, as he wailed, the way she had watched him cling to her mother and refuse to accept Nathan's death, and had felt the smallest amount of satisfaction and pride at the sight. She thinks of Tim, the day she had told him about Nathan's brain tumor outside the science building, when he had thrown rocks and sworn, and she'd stood back and watched him and felt love surge through her, as if he was doing something she had asked him to do. Something is becoming clear to her; it is just beyond her grasp, it is a shadow in a dark room and she is coming closer but she can't quite close her fingers around it. She must take hold of her feelings, that much is clear. The life she wants to live is not one where other people express anger and pain in her stead, where her feelings are held below her skin, too powerful for her to express. Not anymore.

She thinks of Aaron, coming toward her on the rocks, the look on his face as he reached for her; Aaron, her brother whom she is only recently beginning to know, Aaron, who is not Nathan, who will never be Nathan, but who is her brother nonetheless, her last healthy brother, inarguably alive. She thinks of him falling, hitting his head on those rocks and beginning to bleed.

She had expressed herself today; that had been her, expressing herself, with those hands that did not want comfort, that did not want Aaron, that wanted anything other than what she had. This expression had come unbidden, but it had come from her, and perhaps this was why it had surprised her so.

———————

She gets out of bed.

It is the end of the night; looking out the window, she sees that the edges of the horizon are just starting to lighten. She pulls on her shorts and a tank top, moving carefully so as not to wake her mother in the next room. It is already hot; she can feel the heat waking up as the sun comes into the sky. It is only the middle of June but it has been unusually hot for days, the humidity lingering in the air like a thick curtain.

She can barely move fast enough as she tiptoes to the kitchen and pulls the car keys off the table. She scribbles a note on the back of a receipt she finds sticking out of her mother's purse and leaves it on the table: *Be right back—R.* It will be a couple of hours before either her mother or Aaron is up, she figures; she might even be back before they wake.

She winces as she turns on the car, hoping it is not too loud. She is sure she must do what she is doing on her own. She is never, ever up before her mother or Aaron; she is more like Nathan in this way, always sleeping as late as possible, later now than anyone else, but she is exhilarated to be up this early, to be taking charge of her sleepless night instead of letting it own her, tossing and turning, as she normally would.

She pulls slowly out of the driveway and onto the road, the tires crunching on the gravel. She turns right by the stop sign and points the car in the direction of the old house. She is amazed at how confident she is about the direction; she knows exactly where she is going. Yesterday, when they made the trip, they had used a map.

They had been speaking of Abraham as they made their way to the old house. Aaron said, "Well, *considering*, he doesn't really seem that bad."

Her mother, next to him in the front seat, nodded. "It's true. He seems to be holding it together better, really, than he ever has off the medicine."

Ruby, sitting behind them, felt a familiar defensiveness rise in her. "He's close-talking again," she interjected. She hated these words as soon as she said them, but this was her role when it came to Abe: the pessimist, the deliverer of the caution against hope. It bothered her that she was always the one to expect the worst. But ever since Abe had stopped taking his medicine, she had wanted to say "I told you so."

She knew the stages of his decline, they had all happened before:

first came the refusal of medicine, then the close talking, then the body odor, the crazy outfits, the slow slippage back into nonsense, and then, well, take your pick: hospitalization, maybe, if he was lucky, or how about a car accident, a disappearance, a shopping spree, a late-night phone call from a stranger with fear in his voice.

Aaron was describing the conversation he'd had on the phone with Abe the night before last. "He really didn't sound that bad to me," he said. "I felt better after I spoke to him."

"The day we left he was saying things that made no sense," Ruby said.

"It's just gotta be hard, you know?" Aaron said, as if he hadn't heard her. "I mean it *is* his body, and he's the one who has to take the damn stuff. He was up-front about it, at least," Aaron continued. "That made me feel better. He said he had just decided not to take it."

They were passing familiar landmarks—there was the old grocery store, there the Laundromat—a strange juxtaposition to the conversation they were having, so rooted in the present time. Ruby was torn between a desire to look out the window and the urge to duck her head down beneath the seat. It felt so wrong, somehow, to be passing the landmarks of happy times while they spoke of something that made her feel so hopeless.

"Look, Rube!" her mother exclaimed, craning her neck out the passenger side. "Remember the library?"

Could she really think Ruby didn't remember it? Of course she did, the dusty shelves, the way the floor creaked in the main reading area, where the picture books were, the way the librarian whispered even when there was no one else there . . . But the point was . . . What was the point? Why were they here? Her father, who had loved this place more than anyone, who had found this land and brought them here, to Maine, was dead. They didn't belong anymore. Why had they come back here at all? Because her mother was selling their house and felt guilty? Because they were moving on—her mother was moving, Aaron had a girlfriend, Ruby was in college—and had to pay some sort of homage? What did it mean, to move on, if they were all back here again trying to remember?

"I'm not sure it's better," Ruby said, forcing the words out. She was trying, she was, not to clam up as she always did; she was trying to do things differently, to participate, to express herself. "This is how it begins. He starts to feel better so he decides he doesn't need the medicine. Being up-front about it in a way is worse, I think, or more determined anyway. In any case, it doesn't change what will happen to him without it."

"I guess. I'm just not sure that medicine equals sanity, is all," said Aaron, looking back at her in the rearview mirror. They were passing a bay, the road curving up and around the sparkling sea so they were looking down over the boats moored at the shore. Aaron's hands were both on the wheel. "I mean he was on one kind of medicine that didn't work, then he was on another that didn't work—"

"Well, Aaron," her mother interrupted, "it's still the best bet he has."

Ruby was grateful for her mother, who had seen every bit and more of what she had seen. Ruby's mind raced over the years, all the medicines that had failed, all relapses. It was a brief accounting, momentary, not taking more than a second, but Aaron, she noted, was not a part of any of it. She knew it was not his fault—she couldn't blame him for being away all those years, for staying in the Midwest, where he had his own life—but she was angry: How did he know? What could he know? How dare he say anything at all? This was not what she meant, but it was what she felt. Her mother's positivity frustrated her, Aaron's infuriated her.

"It's true," Aaron said, "I know. It's just that he has to come to that realization on his own."

Their mother nodded.

Ruby said, "Well, of course. But that's what's so sad. That's the nature of the problem. His relapses don't teach him anything because when he's in them he loses the ability to be aware of them." As she said this, Ruby felt the weight of its truth. Again, again, the hopelessness, the blamelessness of her brother's sickness weighed down on her.

"Well, anyway," Aaron said, changing the subject, and Ruby was grateful. This subject was not good for them. Ruby felt superior to Aaron on the topic of Abe, in a way she never wanted to feel about anything. Talking about him was a dead end at bad feeling. Of course Aaron could be optimistic, of course he could say things like "medicine doesn't equal sanity." Aaron didn't have to live with what Ruby had lived with, Aaron didn't carry the anger bred from a quarantined adolescence, Aaron hadn't had to learn what Ruby learned the way she learned it. Ruby didn't think that medicine delivered sanity, no. But medicine delivered to Abraham the only sanity he would have, however compromised. This she knew. The force with which she knew it made her feel that she was the only one with the knowledge, though of course this was not at all true.

In the end, it didn't matter if anyone knew it but Abe. Until Abe knew it, the thought was as useless as an unswallowed pill.

She drives toward the house, passing all the landmarks they passed yesterday, bathed now in the intensifying glow of the morning's first light. The landscape is deserted; as she comes into the town she sees it as she never has before—all closed and empty, as if it were an abandoned movie set.

She remembers the way the trip had felt yesterday, the memories forced and out of place, and feels ashamed for it now. The trip had felt wrong from the start—even before they left Massachusetts she had gotten into the car dreading the very idea of revisiting the old places, dredging up the old memories just to ooh and aah over what they had lost. Her mother was selling the house, her brother had a stable new relationship—everyone in the family was moving on and they wanted to bring her with them. Were they trying to dupe her somehow, bringing her someplace she wasn't ready to be, the two of them in cahoots as she used to feel they were, making her share in the family memories in a way she was not prepared to? But now a suspicion creeps to her: of course, she had been wrong. Her mother and Aaron had no ulterior motives; they had done nothing except be themselves.

There is the supermarket, there the Causeway Club, where her family had gone to swim in the saltwater pool. She remembers the women's changing room, with its dark wooden floor and stalls with thick doors that swung open and closed like the doors to some deep, dark dungeons; the sauna, the first one she had ever experienced, where the sensation of taking a breath felt like a cool tube shooting straight down her throat to her stomach; the pool itself, where she and her brothers would practice dives off the diving board and call to their parents to watch; the sloping lawn that came all the way up to the pool, so you could step off the pavement in your bare feet directly onto the closely cropped grass; and just behind the pool, through a gate closed with a metal latch and down a short path through the grass, the ocean: boulders and rocks, then water, and a dramatic stone bridge from which you could look out over the churning causeway. She remembers how she loved that causeway, sneaking out there while the rest of her family swam, standing on that bridge holding on to the thick, twisted metal cable that served as a railing, and watching the water sucked from one side to the other, the water knotting and twisting itself as it flowed quickly over rocks, pulling with it the occasional jellyfish and helpless crab, its legs no match for the current. She could have stood there for hours, staring down.

She passes the golf course and the stretch of lobster piers her brothers used to beg her parents to visit, where they'd pick a lobster out of one of three huge tanks and then, a few long minutes later, eat it off a floppy paper plate with a plastic container full of butter. She passes a stretch of woods, and then there is Gott's Store, where their father went every morning to buy the newspaper, the closest store to their house, with its sign hanging out front that still, all these years later, carries her family's favorite slogan, "Gott's got a lot, so shop at Gott's." Past Gott's, there is the lobster restaurant and the fork in the road, where she bears left, and then, just a bit farther, the little house that always had for sale the empty old school bus, painted white, which Nathan had genuinely planned, counting coins, to buy. She passes their old driveway, slowly, and thinks of how they'd turn in after their long drive, the sound of the tiny white stones crunching beneath their wheels, her brothers waking up and stretching, and her father finally declaring, "Here we are."

The memories aren't sad or provoking now; they feel only as if they are living in the air, and she is passing through them.

She aims for the school down the road where she knows she can park. Nights after going to Bar Harbor, they'd turn in the driveway and emerge from the car, and the smell coming off the ocean would be sharp and fresh in their noses, and they'd look up at the night sky and see the stars brighter than ever before. They'd pause for a minute and listen to the sound of the waves, soft and constant, before going inside; they knew where the waves were even though they could not see them, though sometimes the moon would be so bright that the whole cove in front of their house would be lit up in an otherworldly white light, and they could see the tops of the waves like shifting clouds. Then their father would open the door to the house, and they'd hear the familiar sound of the lip on the bottom of the door brushing over the carpet, and Wally, beloved Wally who died last year, would come bounding out, released from her lonely captivity, and run up to each one of them in turn for a greeting before bounding down the hill toward the ocean. And then, one by one, they'd retreat into the now glowing house, and the light would absorb them like open arms.

She is remembering it all: road trips to Bar Harbor, her father's hands on the steering wheel; the primitive video game with the two men boxing that they had in their Maine house, so old that even when it was off you could see the outlines of the men and all their poses; Maine in the wintertime, her father in his thick blue hat, cross-country ski trips and snowmen in the yard next to the house, a fire burning in the living room stove. She is at the marina, waiting for her father to pump up the inflatable dinghy that they will row out to where his fishing boat is moored; she is lying facedown on the dock, letting her head hang over as she peers at the barnacles on the underside, their tiny, clear hands reaching in and out, in and out as they grab for food. She is watching the troop of neighborhood ducks swim by, she is feeding them loaves of stale bread; she is coming in from the beach, carrying two handfuls of broken crab bodies and clamshells, her borrowed rubber boots covered in mud; she is peering over the spit bugs that are nestled in pockets of frothy foam in the tall grass by the side of the lawn that leads to the beach; she is playing Monopoly with her brothers, trying to prove to them that she can hold her own; she is eating breakfast with her parents on the closed-in porch, the radio is playing soft classical music and the tide is high. It all comes over her, so she is not remembering but experiencing, moment after moment as she moves farther down the road, past McKhekan and Hutches, and pulls into the parking lot by the school where she learned to ride her bike, her father running behind her with his hand on the banana seat.

The school where she parks is across the street from the far end of the inlet on which the old house sits. She used to love to walk from the house, down the beach to where it turned slowly into a rising strip of boulders along the water's edge, then along the boulders in back of the McKhekan and Hutches lumberyard and out to the marsh that ran under the road to the school. Now, standing in the school's parking lot, she cannot see the house, though it is close. She gets out of the car and crosses the road, so she can retrace that familiar route around the lumberyard as if she were just on her way back from the old walk.

She scrambles down the slope from the road to the beach. The early-morning sun is bright around her, the air cooler by the water. This place is not sad at all, but welcoming.

Though she does not want to, she thinks of yesterday. She remembers the way she felt after discussing Abe, isolated among the members of her family, and the way that feeling persisted as they approached the house, as they pulled into the driveway to find not their house (or even the Kanes' house next door) but a new, enormous one, still unfinished, with a giant skull-and-crossbones flag flying from its utmost peak.

Ruby felt her stomach drop. "Oh no," her mother gasped. "Wow," said Aaron, looking up through the windshield.

They got out of the car. There was an orange pickup truck parked on the far side, but no one seemed to be around. Under their feet were the same old white driveway stones; Ruby recognized the familiar crunch, and something about this detail, as she got out of the car and walked around to the front of the foreign house, was heartbreaking. What were the three of them doing here? It seemed so impossible that all that had happened was real, that the six of them had been reduced to three, that the old house was gone, and yet these stones were still here.

Aaron peered into the front window, holding on to the sill, lifted up on his toes. "It's completely different," he said.

Ruby and her mother came up next to him and looked in. The room they saw was huge and open, completely empty and white. Nothing was in it, nothing at all.

Their house and the smaller house next door, where the Kanes had lived, had vanished, as if they were dreams; the house that stood there now had no memories, it sat on this familiar land but it was unknown, an interloper. None of them had expected this.

They moved away from it quickly, down to the beach. The house was overpowering; it pushed them away.

"At least the beach is the same," said Aaron.

"The crab apple tree looks like it's still kicking," said their mother as they passed it. The tree's branches were scraggly and way-ward, as they always had been. Ruby felt torn between a sense of gratitude and bitterness for the tree's longevity. How could this tree still be here, when her father and Nathan were not?

None of them spoke after that. They moved down the lawn, over the familiar floppy lip of grass, to the old rock slope with its bank of skipping stones. With a pang Ruby recognized the stones as friends. Her feet, her adult feet, which had not stood there in so many years, stood there now, and instantly she could see her childhood self, and there were Nathan and Aaron standing next to her, flicking the stones with their wrists, letting out whoops as the stones danced over the water. The immediacy of this vision, the contrast between it and the reality of the way things were now, so lost, so irretrievable, made her knees weak.

The tide was going out, and the boulders along the edge of the beach were all exposed. They were quiet, the three of them, on the land that was no longer theirs. They walked down the skipping-stone slope to the sand, and then along the beach to where it became boul-ders, and they each climbed on top of one. They stood apart from one another and looked out over the water.

Ruby, as she stood on her boulder by her brother and her mother, felt a wave of nausea wash over her. She felt a heightened awareness: she was overhead, she could see the three of them stand-ing on the boulders not talking, and they looked tiny and beaten, so helpless, the victims of too many tragedies, grasping at memories that could not sustain them, years that were long past. They were so separate, the three of them, down there, so tiny on that beach, all with their own individual memories, their individual fears and desires and versions of loss. How could they help one another? What could they do for one another after so much pain? Was this what moving on was, moving together over this familiar beach, their younger, happy selves long gone, just moving over it and letting it go and that was all?

She didn't feel capable. She looked down and saw her younger self there too; she saw her with her bouncy curls, running over this beach after her three brothers, eager to be included, eager to explore. The difference between that girl and the woman who stood here now, alone, untouched, afraid of life, was too much for her to bear. She could not handle it, she could not bear up under it anymore. There was no help; how could there be help? It had happened, all of it, all of it: there were the three of them all alone to prove it.

She looked at her mother, standing a few feet away, and saw that she was crying. Her face was wet, the paths of a few tears on her cheeks. Aaron was farther down, a few boulders past her mother.

Ruby moved toward her, stepping over the boulders. "Mom?" she managed.

Her mother shook her head. "It's okay," she said.

Ruby felt a flash of deep anger. If she heard one more person say it was okay, it was all right, it was fine, she might die. Her mother should never again have to say that it was okay. It was not okay, it never would be okay, and Ruby couldn't stand to hear anyone say it was.

"No, Mom, it's not." She was nearing her.

Her mother nodded, wiping her tears. "It's just very sad," she said. Ruby saw her trying to push her feelings down, trying to will them away. Why should she have to do that? Why should any of them, ever, have to do that?

"To see the house like that," her mother said. "To be here . . . and . . ."

Ruby reached her and put her arm around her. "I know."

Aaron was climbing over the boulders to them, watching his feet. "Mom?" he said as he approached.

"It's okay," she said and held out her hands, resisting the attention.

"No," Ruby insisted, the anger rising in her, "it's not, Mom."

Aaron reached a boulder next to the one where Ruby was perched with her mother. All around them were rocks.

"I mean here we are," said their mother. "Here we are again, just the three of us." Her eyes filled. She pulled her head from Ruby's shoulder and closed her eyes. Tears squeezed out from beneath her lids. "It's just too much, I guess. I'm sorry. I didn't know, I didn't think . . ."

"It's okay, Mom," said Aaron. He stepped onto a lower boulder behind her and reached for her. She turned to him, leaning over the crack where the boulders met, and cried onto his chest. "It's okay," he said again, his arms around her.

"No, it's not!" cried Ruby. She stepped away from them, onto a different boulder, closer to the water. Her chest felt tight and constricted. "Stop saying it's okay when it's not okay!" She took a deep breath and tried to control her voice, but it rose again. "I'm so tired of everyone always saying it's *okay*, it's *fine*, it's *all right*, it will be *fine*, it will be *better*, it will be *okay*." Her voice twisted in a mocking tone as she spit out the words. "When are we going to acknowledge that it's *not* okay, that it's *not at all* okay, that it's completely *fucked?*"

She felt the anger surge through her whole body; it filled her every inch. She was hot, she was flushed, her body was tense with anger. So much anger, more anger rose in her than she'd ever felt, all of the anger of her life, all of it, all the anger for everything boiled over as she looked at her mother and her brother, whose eyes were fixed on her as they continued to hold each other.

"It's not okay!" Ruby screamed, and felt the tiniest bit of good in that scream, the tiniest shred of release. "We got *fucked*! We got completely *screwed*! And why? *Why?* For no reason! For no reason at all! There's no one to blame, there's no one to get angry at, and there's nothing we can do, but that doesn't make it okay, that makes it worse!"

Where would this anger go? How would it go? There was not enough she could do to get rid of this rage; she was stuck on this boulder, in this body, with this unbearable anger. Her body was a flame, consuming itself and then blazing again, insatiable. She let out a scream, her fists clenched.

"I mean, *Christ*!" She glared at Aaron. "Do you have any *idea* how hard it has been for me?" She nearly choked on this. She felt guilty speaking of herself, and she gestured to her mother, who had her face pressed against Aaron's chest. "And Mom? Christ, Mom, what you've been through . . ."

Ruby bent down on her boulder and put her knees to her chest. Aaron said, very softly, "Do you think that it hasn't been hard for me?"

Into her knees she replied, "No, Aaron, of course not." She raised her head. "Of course not. And that's my *point*! Of course not!" She stood up again. "We can't compare what it's been like for us, it's impossible, and it's useless, we can never know! It's been hard for everyone, it's been a fucking *nightmare*, okay, fine. I'm sorry that I'm pissed off about the way things were for me, I'm sorry, I know it's not your fault and it's been shitty for you too. But I'm just so *sick* of not acknowledging it! I don't know what to do, I don't know how to be angry, I don't know how to let it go, *I don't know what to do*!" She stopped, took a deep breath. She was trembling. "But it's not *okay*," she insisted, "it's just not. So stop saying it is when it's not."

Aaron let go of their mother and took a step toward Ruby, onto a lower boulder. "Come on, Rube." His voice was gentle, and he put out a hand to touch her arm. "Come on."

And then he said it again, as he reached toward her, his arm outstretched, he said it again. "It's okay."

"No!" She saw his hand coming for her and she did not want to be touched, she did not want her brother's comforting arm to smooth this over and make it all right; there was no way for this to be all right, none, ever, ever, ever, and so she put out her arms and she pushed him away. "No!" She twisted away and she pushed him, and he fell, right there on the rocks, right there.

Aaron fell between the boulders and there he lay, blood appearing on his scalp, his eyes closed and his body slack. Aaron! Her brother, down by her hands, harmed only because he'd been trying to give her love. She stood helpless on the boulder and watched her fallen brother bleed. Her anger was instantly replaced by guilt.

Her mother gasped. "Ruby!" she called out and clambered down to Aaron, putting her hands on his face, saying his name in a frantic voice.

It was only a minute or so that he was unconscious, but in that minute Ruby's head was a void of horror. What had she done? What had she done?

Then he had come to, and he had been all right; she and her mother had draped his arms around their shoulders and moved him carefully over the rocks toward the car. "I'm okay," he said, "really, I think I'm okay," and these words made Ruby cringe. When they reached the car, he took off his T-shirt, a gray Red Sox shirt he had gotten last summer outside Fenway Park, and held it to his head. The sight of his torso was familiar and made her look away.

"It's okay," he said.

But it wasn't. All day and all night since then she had been sure, there was nothing okay about any of it. Nothing about this trip, nothing about their presence here, nothing about the violence she had committed was okay. The assurance with which she felt this was a relief. How could what had happened ever be repaired?

But now, moving alone toward those very same boulders, the fresh morning sun warming her skin, Ruby imagines the three of them standing there together as they had yesterday and feels a tenderness tinged with guilt. They had been here *together*—that was the point, of course. Yes, they were separate, yes, their grief was carried alone, but there they had been, standing on this beach together. What more could they do?

Perhaps it is true that Aaron is not upset with her, that he even understands what she did. Perhaps what she did was even natural, an accident, something that had happened without intent, just as other things happen that no one intends.

She is on the boulders behind the lumberyard, not far from where she stood with her family yesterday. She breathes. She stops on a boulder and throws back her shoulders, taking the hot summer air into her lungs. The lumberyard is empty, huge piles of wood abandoned, for now, to the baking sun. She climbs over a few boulders to where they begin to curve again and she is finally in view of the house—the new, ugly monstrosity of a house, with its poison flag. She looks at it for a moment and takes a deep breath; then she turns her back to it. Like this, facing away, everything is as it once was.

She thinks of the way it felt to push her brother. If she is honest with herself, she knows that despite the horror there was in watching him fall, there was also a lightning flash of thrill in expressing herself that way. When has she ever, ever expressed herself like that? In all these years, never. Always passive and guarded and never bold. Always holding herself apart, always waiting for the world to reach her rather than reaching for the world. Always so aware that there was no one to be angry at that she never allowed herself to be angry at all. No rebellion, no irrationality, no destruction, no regrets, and so how could she expect anything to change? If she only took what fate dished out but asked nothing of it, was she really living at all?

She knows that though she has blamed all the boys she has ever wanted for not wanting her, it must be partly her fault that they did not touch her. She thinks of Tim, whom she never told how she really felt; of friends from college whom she pined after; of Karl, lying on his bed at camp and talking to her about his girlfriend. How she has allowed this to persist, how she has been complicit in this. She has turned these living boys into untouchable men, into ghosts! She has made these live, innocent people dead in their unreachableness, because this is the way she is most comfortable; because longing is where she lives, and unquenchable desire the island she understands. It is all about loss, isn't it? Loss and anger, the two of them so twisted inside her that they've turned the living world into something for her to fear.

She sits down on a boulder, realizing as she does that this might be the very boulder she stood on yesterday, from which she pushed Aaron. Looking at its surface below her, she thinks she can see a spot of blood.

She sees all the male bodies she has loved before her: Nathan's body, his round calves tucked into gym socks pulled up high, then tucked into Converse sneakers; his forearms, covered in a fur of blond hair; his chest, broad but mostly hairless, his shoulders, soft and round. She sees the many visions of his body as one entity— covered in clothes, covered in blankets, lying on the couch, lying as a lump in his bed with only his curls sticking out, playing basketball at the hoop in front of the house, playing his cello, holding it with care, his body wrapped around it and the two of them slowly rocking. Nathan's body—she feels tenderness and awe for Nathan's body, she sees it and it is tangible and present, she can just about feel its warmth.

And then she sees it on his hospital bed, she sees it on the bed where he died, gasping for breath, she sees his innocent chest thrusting off the bed looking for air, she sees him this way too.

Nathan's body; her father's body, robust and unrelenting, her father's hairy chest, her father's thick and hairy hands, her father's face, the wrinkles around his eyes like pathways, the thin hair on the top of his head, his torso in a T-shirt specked with sweat. Abe's body, pale and malnourished and yellow from cigarettes, Abe's sunken eyes, Abe's distended belly, his shuffling walk, his long and stained fingers, his face strewn with patches of missed hair. Tim's body, pear-shaped and pale, his broken foot stuffed in a bucket of ice; Michael Fischer's body, at camp, lying next to her on one of those tin docks by the agam; Karl, in his soft red fleece, holding her close, his arm around her so light and secure it was as if it were a part of her own skin. All these bodies, the bodies of the men she loves, the men she has loved, they are with her, they are inside her own body, under her own vulnerable skin.

Aaron's body, healthy and strong, crumpled between the boulders, his white ankle socks and basketball sneakers, his powerful body crumpled because of her anger, because of her strangling, too-much love.

But no, she thinks, no. It is time to forgive herself, to let herself be. She takes off her sandals and rests them on the boulder next to her. She eases herself down to the water, sits, and dips her feet in. The water is cool and refreshing; it welcomes her feet.

She peers at the water, lapping gently, and the way her feet look soft and white beneath. These are the waters that baptized me, she thinks. I have survived it all to find myself back here again. Where have I been, all these years? What ever happened to that little girl on this beach, with those three brothers ahead of her?

She hears her father's voice, as if it were in the subtle wind that cools her body she hears it: *Life is the highest good, whenever it is possible, choose life.* Finally, suddenly, she knows what he meant. It wasn't choosing a specific life, choosing her father or Nathan or Tim, holding on to them so they wouldn't disappear, taking their losses personally, so that with each one her anger was more solidly confirmed; it was the choice of life *on its own,* the choice of the world, of love for the gift of being there. It was the choice of her own life, of living it and owning it, not being so removed from her life that it was as if it was not hers. Her father, despite what he too had lost, despite his long journey, which she would never understand, had stood up and moved forward and chosen life, life, life to the point of catching flies with his hand and releasing them into the night. This was his religion—this was what he believed. And this was what he wished for her.

Life! She looks around her, the sun throwing pockets of brightness onto the water and the trees and the flowering grasses along the far shore, and she feels so lucky to be alive to see it that her chest constricts. It is all so fragile, it is all so painfully vulnerable, it is none of it permanent or guaranteed, but she is here right now to see it, to be part of this glorious mystery that is these waters, those trees, that sun, and the feeling of warmth on her skin. She doesn't know why she's here, or if she deserves it, but she is so grateful she can barely breathe.

She stands up and pulls off her tank top and her shorts and lays them next to her shoes. In her underwear, she steps into the water, which is warm and pleasant around her ankles. She moves in deeper, deeper, the water a tickling line against her stomach. These are the waters that baptized me, she thinks again. The water is the perfect temperature; she closes her eyes as she moves deeper and senses it against her, soothing and loving and welcoming. I have been baptized by greatness, I have survived, and now I am baptized again. All around me is the land I know, the land that is deep inside of me, that I carry with me as I carry so much else, as I carry my family and our story and where it has taken all of us, and how it will keep us strong. It is not a burden, to carry this: look at it. I open my eyes. The sun is sparkling against the rippling water; the trees across the inlet are tiny, pristine cones, the water against my arms is mild and cool. Right now, right this second, there is nothing to fear. I am grateful; I am myself; I accept. I am awake. I am here.

And Now

I return to my family. My mother and Aaron are sitting at the kitchen table eating breakfast and I almost cry, I am so moved to see their bodies together on those wooden chairs. I tell them where I've been, and apologize again for what I did. I tell them I promise not to apologize again.

Later, after packing the house and pulling the door shut behind us, taking a last look around a place we will likely never see again, we drive home. It is around nine, and dark, and Aaron is driving. I am in the passenger seat, and my mother is behind me.

We've been on the road for almost five hours. My mother talks about our house, and how not one person has made an offer yet, and how the other day one of the trees in the backyard fell, "just *fell*," onto the lawn. "I don't know how long I can keep it up," she says. "It's just really getting to be too much for me." I do my best not to imagine her trapped beneath a tree trunk on the front lawn.

Aaron talks about Sophie, and how he is trying not to think too much this time, he's decided he always overthinks his relationships. I laugh. "I know what that's like," I say. I look at my brother and realize how little I know him, and think maybe it is possible that we have a lot more in common than I yet recognize. That man sitting next to me is my brother, and what that means to us remains to be seen.

I ask the two of them if they remember all those years ago when I found the gun out on the mudflats in front of the house. I thought of it as I was leaving the beach this morning, and wanted to ask if they can recall it too.

Both Aaron and my mother are shocked by the memory. I can see Aaron's face change as it comes back to him, slowly, his eyes becoming wide and amazed. "Wow," he says, "I had *completely* forgotten about that!"

"I know," I say. "Me too. Can you believe that even happened?"

"Remember how angry I was at Dad?" he says. "I was so pissed. I really couldn't let it go. I remember I plotted for a good *year* or so, every time we went to Maine, about how I could get that thing back."

"Yeah," says Mom, "you acted like a real brat if I recall."

"I suppose I did." Aaron nods and smiles into the rearview mirror.

"It does seem a little symbolic now, doesn't it, that gun," my mother says thoughtfully.

Aaron and I are silent, reflecting. How strange, the way moments can feel huge while they're happening, as finding the gun did, and then turn small, only to become weighty again. How can you ever know which moments matter, if they shift in potency over time? I think of the important moments of my life as chips in a kaleidoscope, changing colors and shapes in an unceasing movement. Twenty years from now, will all of it look different, and what I remember now be gone?

We are all occupied by our own thoughts. Eventually, we play a few particularly disappointing rounds of Twenty Questions, in which my mother chooses the movie *As Good as It Gets*. I ask her if the movie is a love story, to which she answers no.

"But I asked you!" I squeal when she reveals the movie. "I asked you if it was a love story and you said no!"

"But it's so much *more* than a love story!" she replies. Mom loves

As Good as It Gets. She doesn't have much experience with Twenty Questions.

"Okay, okay," Aaron says, "it's just a game, let's move on."

"Okay, I've got one," he says. "I'm switching it up a bit. *Family* Twenty Questions, okay? I just made it up. The category is family-related foods."

"What do you mean?" I ask.

"I mean it has to be a food that we have some collective experience with."

"A food we've eaten together?"

"Yeah. Like, for example, Twizzlers could be one."

We've been eating Twizzlers constantly—on our way out of Southwest Harbor we bought a giant plastic container full of individually wrapped ones at the supermarket, and they've been living in the backseat with our mother ever since. Periodically Aaron or I will put a hand into the backseat and declare, "Twizzle," and Mom will place one in our palms. For Aaron, who is driving, she'll unwrap it.

"Are they only foods we've eaten on this trip?" Mom asks.

"No. Any time."

"Okay."

For the first round he picks *palacinky*, a Czech dish—crepes filled with nuts and sugar—that our mother used to make when we were kids. It was one of the few foods that we all considered a favorite (Dessert for dinner! Everyone was happy). Mom guesses it pretty quickly, asking, "Does it have nuts and sugar?" and Aaron slaps the wheel.

"I *loved palacinky*!" he says. "Why don't you ever make that anymore?"

"I'll make it again," she says, her voice pleased. "It's so easy!"

By now we've caught on to the game and fall into it easily. We trade off—our mother comes up with a few, then lets Aaron and me take over, choosing unique family foods and artifacts. As we play, they grow more obscure and come from further back in our past, but there is not one that we can't guess, and in far fewer than twenty questions. There is an exciting rush of discovery when we know we have a good one—when Aaron chooses Dad's old green velvety bathrobe (category: family articles of clothing), or when I choose dad's gum massager (category: family objects), which he used when he sat in the leather easy chair after dinner on Friday nights and read the paper (Aaron asks, "Is it gender neutral?" and I answer: "*Technically*, yes"); I think it's a pretty hard one, but when Aaron asks after five questions whether the object can fit in your hand and then follows up with "Does the object have a little rubber tip?" I am amazed.

"That was a good one," Aaron says, and Mom agrees, but I can't believe he got it so fast. I suppose I thought I was the only one who held the memory of our father working his gums with the golden massager so crystal clear, that I was the only one who considered that particular detail, that tiny instrument, so special. I think how recently I might have resented sharing this appreciation—resented that I was not the only one who remembered the details. Now, I wonder at the collective memory that fills the car. Aaron recalls things that I might not—he chooses fish chowder, which Mom made for us at the Maine house whenever he and the other boys caught fish; he does the fruit punch that the milkman delivered to us with our milk and ice cream at home, leaving it in the metal box by the kitchen door. The milkman! I haven't thought of him in years, and now it rushes back: the thrill of seeing his truck pull up by the kitchen window, running out to get the ice cream, gathering up the full bottles from where they snuggled within the box, loving the thick glass of them, loving pulling off their metallic tops, which would give with a gentle *pff* of breath they had been holding.

Through the windshield and the window next to me I see the sky, which is clear and filled with stars. Aaron's driving is looser now that it's late and he's been at the wheel for so long. The car periodically drifts out of the bounds of the lane and almost hits the bumper strip on the side. We are going very fast, and I am vaguely nervous, especially as Aaron gets excited about the game and gestures with one of his hands, turning back to our mother. I imagine a deer running out in front of our car, Aaron slamming on the brakes and swerving, the car speeding into the far guardrail or off the road into the ditch. Some part of me is convinced that this will happen. I am briefly overwhelmed by the fragility, the entirety of what the car holds. What would happen if this was how it all ended? How would it be to go now, while we are playing this game, so that our missing family members are here, at least in memory, in the car with us?

I think of Abraham, alone in his apartment in Westwood, the three of us hurtling back to him, and I wonder for a moment, looking out the window at the stars, Aaron's and Mom's voices swirling around me: Where is the will, ever, in what happens to us? If we cannot control what happens, if we can only live through it and keep driving as long as we can, is this ever, in the end, enough?

It is not enough; it is enough. This is the only answer. There is no control, there is no cure—for grief, for loss, for the tendrils of illness, for loving the living and the dead. We are a family, and we carry on the best we can.

"I've got one," Aaron says. He is smiling. "This might be before your time, Rube, I'm not sure. It goes way back. Family foods."

"Is it something Mom cooked?"

"Yes."

"Is it dinner-related?"

"Yes."

"Does it have noodles?" asks Mom.

Aaron laughs. "Yes!" he says, surprised.

We guess for a while, but we're stumped. It doesn't have meat, it doesn't have vegetables, but it is the main course. Finally Aaron relents: "Noodles, nuts, and sugar!"

I probably would never have thought of this meal, though as soon as he says the words it comes rushing back to me. I remember the huge ceramic bowl with the colored stripes around the middle, the hot, round penne noodles, tossed with chopped walnuts and sugar. I remember feeling vaguely confused when served this dinner, like there was something wrong with what I was eating, the warm noodles sweet and buttery although pasta was otherwise never served with anything sweet.

"Remember that?" Aaron says. "I used to love that as a kid. I thought it was totally normal, I was just like, Hey! It's noodles nuts and sugar! Now, though, I realize, it was *just* noodles, nuts, and sugar."

I laugh with him. It is hilarious to think of the six of us eating this at the dinner table, alternately loving the dish or being confused by it, but eating it because we were kids and we were being served a dinner that our mother made, understanding nothing about the world or about food, just that this dish was part of our mother's rotation.

"It had butter in it too," Mom says, a little hurt. Her defensiveness sends Aaron and me into deeper hysterics.

"Wow, that's a good one," I say. "Noodles nuts and sugar. Wow."

"Your father loved that meal," Mom says.

"Just like *palacinky*, really," I add. We laugh.

"Well, you try cooking for six people," she says, quieter.

Even as I laugh and think of noodles, nuts, and sugar; even as Aaron says it again, exaggerating the words so they make me think of Nathan, who would have turned them over in his mouth for an hour, laughing continually at the way they sound, "Noodles, nuts, and sugar"; and even as our mother finally laughs a bit too, I am aware of the car speeding through the night with its precious cargo. The moment is clear and dear to me; I am aware of all of the earlier versions of ourselves that are in the car—the three of us, our father, Nathan, Abe, and all of their younger, vibrant selves, all of our incarnations through all of the years and changes, even Abe now, as he waits for our return. If we are to go, I think, we may as well go like this. It is not enough; it is enough. The house is in the car with us, the dinner table, that ceramic bowl filled with noodles, all of our family and the three of us now, Aaron, our mother, and me, our present-moment selves, laughing and remembering, in this car headed for home.

Acknowledgments

THANK YOU to my teachers, including but not limited to Doug Fricke, Mark Slouka, Ben Marcus, Mike Curtis, Sam Lipsyte, and Nathan Englander. Thank you to Mary Gordon, mentor, inspiration, and beloved friend. Thank you to those who read the novel in earlier forms—Rains Paden, Jessamine Chan, Maggie Pouncey, Elisa Albert, Nick Yagoda, and the members of my Columbia thesis workshop. Thank you to my ever-inspiring writing group. Thank you, Karen Thompson. Thank you, Carol Rubin. Thank you to the Newton Free Library, the Vermont Studio Center, and the Millay Colony. Thank you to my agent, Ann Rittenberg, who saw it, and to the whole team at Scribner, but especially to Samantha Martin, my editor, for waiting for and then choosing my book. Sam, thank you.

Most importantly, to my mother, whose belief in me helps me to live, and whose strength is an inspiration. And to the rest of my family, without whom there would be, simply, no book. Love is not an adequate word for how grateful I am.

About the Author

Nellie Hermann is a native of Boston, Massachusetts, and a graduate of Brown University and the MFA program at Columbia University. She currently lives in Brooklyn, New York.